Also by Warren Adler

the children of the roses

the children of the roses

WARREN ADLER

SOURCEBOOKS LANDMARK™
AN IMPRINT OF SOURCEBOOKS, INC.®
NAPERVILLE, ILLINOIS

Published by Sourcebooks, Inc.
P.O. Box 4410, Naperville, Illinois 60567-4410
(630) 961-3900
FAX: (630) 961-2168
www.sourcebooks.com

Library of Congress Cataloging-in-Publication Data

Adler, Warren.
The children of the Roses / by Warren Adler.
p. cm.
Sequel to: The war of the Roses.
ISBN 1-4022-0197-4 (alk. paper)
1. Adult children of divorced parents—Fiction. 2. Brothers and sisters—
Fiction. 3. Overweight women—Fiction. 4. Married people—Fiction. 5.
Single women—Fiction. I. Title.
PS3551.D64 C47 2004
813'.54—dc22
2003020086

Printed and bound in the United States of America
BG 10 9 8 7 6 5 4 3 2 1

For Sunny

# Chapter 1

Victoria was in the checkout line at Safeway for the mid-week groceries when the cell had vibrated in the pocket of her slacks. It was there mostly for useful family communications and emergency situations.

On the line was Mr. Tatum, headmaster of Michael's school, which had her cell number on file. Her heart jumped to her throat. He was quick to reassure her.

"Michael is fine. Don't be alarmed," he said.

Then why this call, she wanted to ask, but held off.

"It's the business about the candy," Mr. Tatum explained. She sucked in a deep breath and expelled it with a sense of relief. Then disgust set in.

"That again," Victoria sighed. "So it's reached the emergency level, has it?" she said with a touch of sarcasm. As she spoke, she watched the heavyset uniformed female clerk punch in the numbers. "They're three for two twenty," she barked. "Check your ad."

"Damn," the clerk blushed, embarrassed, rereading the list of promotional prices.

"Not you, Mr. Tatum," she said into the phone. "I'm at the Safeway."

"I don't want to complicate your life, Mrs. Rose," Mr. Tatum said unctuously. "But we need you here as soon as possible."

"You can't be serious. Why?"

"We would like Mr. Rose here as well."

"That's impossible. You know he works in Manhattan. You know that, Mr. Tatum. Why the urgency?"

"It's happened again," Mr. Tatum explained.

For a brief moment, a wave of panic washed over her. Was something terrible being hidden? Surely this could not be about candy bars.

"Madeline's parents are not satisfied with Michael's previous denials, Mrs. Rose."

"Are you saying that the girl is making yet another accusation?"

"I'm afraid so."

"And the Crespos are buying it?"

"Completely, Mrs. Rose. We're sort of at an impasse."

"It's no impasse as far as my husband and I are concerned," Victoria said, feeling the heat rise in her body. Frustrated, she watched the clerk scowl at the register as if it were to blame for the error. "I've already explained this. We do not lie in our family."

"I'm sorry, Mrs. Rose," Mr. Tatum told her officiously. She sensed that Michael's accusers were witnessing his call. "We need to get to the bottom of this."

"Can't it wait until tomorrow, Mr. Tatum?"

"I wish it could."

"The Crespos," Victoria hissed, weighing her comment with sarcasm. "They're there, aren't they, Mr. Tatum?"

"Yes, they are here," Mr. Tatum said on the phone.

"And Michael?" Victoria asked. "Under no circumstances do I want him disrupted."

"At this point we hope we can resolve this without any additional trauma to the children, Mrs. Rose," Mr. Tatum said.

"Good. I do not want him present as if he were a defendant in a courtroom drama, Mr. Tatum."

"It has similarities, I'm afraid," the headmaster sighed. It was obvious he detested the confrontation.

"Give me an hour," Victoria said. "I have to carpool my daughter and her friends to ballet class."

"We'll wait," Mr. Tatum said, his voice indicating a struggle for neutrality.

Victoria snapped the cell phone closed and watched the clerk furiously punch in the last numbers. Her attention had strayed. Later she would analyze the final tape against her purchases. Vendors were always making mistakes, some in her favor, some not. Either way, it opened up opportunities to exercise her moral superiority and mathematical acumen. She had minored in accounting at NYU, rejecting going for CPA and opting for law instead. Now she was majoring in Mommy with obsessive and awesome determination.

She paid her bill by Visa, wheeled the food basket to the rear of the Ford Explorer, loaded the groceries, then headed for Emily's school, cursing the conduct of the headmaster for allowing the situation to reach this level of absurdity.

She knew the Crespos from the various meetings and events involving the school—Pendleton Hall, tuition twelve thousand a year, plus another three for incidentals. That plus another eleven thou for Emily at Episcopal. Rip-off, Victoria had concluded, making you pay over and above taxation because they let the public school system turn to *merde*. To Victoria, being suckered was a capital sin.

She quickly shrugged off the irritation. Parents preparing their children for success in the complex take-no-prisoners world ahead had no other alternative. Private schools in general, and this one in particular, provided the competitive edge. Improving the odds of attainment, in Victoria's estimation, was an essential component of good parenting.

The prospect of again confronting Helen Crespo and her big boobs and husband John with his bushy moustache and little round wire glasses made her ache with despair. He taught English at a local junior college, and she was an heiress from some pasta machine invention who did ceramics and talked a blue streak, never pausing to edit or absorb anyone else's commentary or response.

The families had also interacted at church, St. John's Episcopal, which they had joined when Michael was four, providing the obligatory spiritual component that both she and Josh had rarely been exposed to in their childhood.

Victoria had thought their initial confrontation had resolved the issue. They had met in an empty classroom after the school day with Mr. Tatum sitting behind the teacher's desk. Apparently the headmaster did not want to expose the children to the threatening environment of his office.

Michael, with all of his eleven-year-old indignation, had denied the accusation in the presence of both Crespos and their nerdy little Madeline who lisped, ogling them through goggles far too big for her pinched little face. Mr. Tatum had watched the proceedings with an expression of tolerant understanding. He was a tall, handsome man in his fifties with the tweedy, comforting look of a wise teacher. He was the respected King Solomon figure of Pendleton Hall, and he had laid down rigid standards of conduct and academic achievement. Parents and students deferred to him. His word was law.

"Did you see him take the Milky Way?" Victoria had asked the little girl, adopting her version of a sweet, non-threatening tone. The three parents who were present had been provided with adult chairs while the children sat at their regular child-size desks.

"Thee him?" Madeline replied, raising her voice, averting her goggled face from that of her interrogator. "How could I? He wath too thneaky." She looked reassuringly toward her parents.

"Then how do you know he took it?" Victoria asked, with lawyerly innocence, noting that the child's lisp reacted negatively to excitement.

Madeline raised her little face and scrunched up her nose in an unpleasant gesture as if there was a foul odor in the room.

"He thaw me eating it in the wunch room and he thaid sharing food ith an act of wuvv and friendthip."

Aunt Evie's puffed and rosy face had jumped into Victoria's mind. *Food is love* was her sister-in-law's mantra, and her bloated face and body was its logo. Madeline's assertion made her heart sink. Could it be true then? No way, she decided. In their household, telling lies was worse than the ten plagues visited upon the Egyptians in the Old Testament.

"That doesn't make him the thief, dear," Victoria said still sweetly.

"I altho thaw him eating it."

"A Milky Way? Michael?"

"Yeth. Twyth."

"Twyth," Victoria said. It was inadvertent. She had not meant to blatantly mock the child's lisp.

"Victoria!" Helen Crespo rebuked.

"That was insensitive," John Crespo sneered.

"I'm sorry. Really, I hadn't meant..." She was getting off the track. She offered the child a painful smile. "How did you know it was your Milky Way, Madeline dear?" Victoria asked.

"Becauth it wooked wike mine."

"All Milky Ways look alike," Victoria said, rediscovering her old prosecutorial skills.

"It wath mine."

"But it could have been given to him by someone else who might have gotten it out of a vending machine," Victoria countered.

"We do not have candy vending machines in the building," Mr. Tatum interjected.

"I never stole her Milky Way," Michael had protested, blue eyes blazing, lips pursed, his little body ramrod straight, adding his own clinching comment. "My mom doesn't even let us eat candy in our house."

Echoes of Aunt Evie again, but in a more positive mode. Her sister-in-law's gluttony and its obvious physical results had prompted an increase of her rejection of fatty foods and all other edibles containing high amounts of sugar and sodium. Before any food entered her kitchen, Victoria fanatically pored over nutritional tables, rejecting any foods that did not meet her strict dietary standards.

"How does Madeline get this candy?" Victoria asked, making no attempt to mask her disapproval.

"It's a treat," Helen Crespo said defensively. "We put it in her backpack."

Victoria shook her head with obvious disgust. A glance of disapproval from Mr. Tatum gave her pause.

"My son does not lie," Victoria reiterated.

"Neither does my daughter," John Crespo said.

"Perhaps," Mr. Tatum said, making a cathedral with his fingers and peeking through the steeple, "we should allow this incident to pass without resolution. These things have a tendency to escalate. As you know, the standard at Pendleton is truth and tolerance. It could very well be that each child is looking at the incident from different perspectives, both of which are correct in their own minds. Call it the Rashomon effect. Let us hope that a similar incident does not reoccur."

Which meant it was a standoff. That evening she had gone over the circumstances with Josh, who with fatherly solemnity had confronted Michael yet again.

"She's lying, Dad," Michael said, offering not a hint of guilt in expression or gesture. "I did not steal her candy. Besides, I know candy isn't good for you." He looked toward his mother. "Right, Mom?"

Victoria nodded and smiled.

"I don't mean to belabor the point, son, but this means a great deal to all of us."

"I know that, Dad."

"Truth no matter what the consequences," Josh had intoned.

"Don't you believe me, Dad?" Michael said, his eyes begging, swallowing hard, his upper lip beginning to tremble. "Mom does." He looked toward Victoria, who opened her arms and embraced him, rubbing his back.

"You know I do, darling," Victoria said.

"Mikey wouldn't lie," Emily suddenly squealed. She had been watching the proceedings from the foot of the stairs and was visibly upset by any questions concerning her brother's fidelity. "Nobody lies in our family."

At nine, Emily lived in a world of complete belief in the goodness of all people. She particularly adored, doted upon, believed in, and supported her brother in all things. Happily for their parents, it was a two-way street. Both Victoria and Josh had nurtured this idea of sibling solidarity in their children and were delighted that their wish had become a reality.

Emily and Mickey were born, according to plan, one year apart, and Victoria, an only child, had yearned for such an alliance. Josh, having experienced the strength and comfort of the sibling bond, had eagerly supported the idea. There was an irony in that, Victoria knew, since she was not exactly keen on the zealous solidarity of Josh's relationship with his sister Evie, although she understood why they had clung together so tenaciously over the years. Considering what had happened to their parents, the Roses, she had tried valiantly but unsuccessfully to temper her judgment.

"We didn't mean to upset you, darling," Victoria said, turning to Emily, throwing her a kiss. Then she turned to her husband. "This is overkill, Josh."

"You realize, Michael, that there's nothing to be afraid of," Josh pressed, obviously ignoring her comment.

"I know that, Dad," Michael said. His eyes had grown moist and the tip of his nose reddened. Victoria and Josh exchanged knowing glances and the interrogation abruptly came to end.

"I do believe you, son," Josh said, adding, "One for all and all for one." He reached out to tousle the boy's blonde hair. Victoria put her hand over Josh's and motioned to Emily who bounded to join the embrace.

"Trust is everything in this family," Victoria said.

"I know that, Mom."

Michael looked from one parent to the other, then crossed his heart.

"I never doubted you for a minute," Josh said, kissing Michael's cheek. Then he kissed Emily on the head and Victoria on the lips.

"That ends it," Josh said. "We will not have our children harassed."

As she drove, panic had turned to indignation. The old lawyerly aggression had surfaced. Abuse that child and I'll sue your ass, she heard herself say in her mind.

Memories of earlier legal tangles surfaced, dramatic confrontations with smug lawyers from the greedy insurance companies defending their suspect turf from the equally suspect plaintiffs whose cases she had manipulated and manufactured, mostly from trumped up medical evidence and fictional scripting.

In those career days, as a single practitioner in the seedy negligence law business, she was living testimony to the case for tort reform. Once she had enjoyed the hurly-burly challenge of walking the thin wavy line between the micromargins of corruption and alleged legality. Love and marriage had demanded a higher level of moral turpitude and parenting had sealed her fate, motivating aggressive psychic reconstruction.

Hadn't Michael assured them of his innocence? The Rose family built their lives on a rigid standard of absolute honesty. It was the bedrock of their behavior. The Crespo girl was imagining things.

As she approached St. John's, the Episcopal school that went only to the second grade, she had worked up a good head of exasperation. Emily was waiting for her with her two friends at the school entrance.

"Hi Mommy," Emily said excitedly as she jumped into the back seat of the car with her two little friends. The girls chirped together like hyperactive sparrows.

"Seat belts, everyone?"

"All except Bobbie," Emily giggled.

"I hate seat belts," Bobbie said, reluctantly fastening hers. "Tattle tale."

"I'm not a tattle tale," Emily said. "Am I, Mommy?"

"No way, darling. Seat belts save lives," Victoria said, offering the homily from her ever-growing collection. She headed the car in the direction of the ballet class.

"See," Emily said.

"You have to be very careful in this world, girls," Victoria said. "Safety first."

More homilies burst from her by rote. "Never take anything for granted. Always be prepared for every eventuality. Accidents occur when you least expect them." She rattled them off without thinking, her thoughts fixed on what would soon occur at Pendleton Hall.

"I have to stop by Mikey's school," Victoria said.

"Is Michael alright, Mommy?" Emily asked, ever sensitive to her brother's fate.

"Michael's fine, sweetheart," Victoria said, skirting the issue.

"Daddy says everything is good now, isn't it Mommy?"

"Daddy is right," Victoria said, wishing her daughter would drop the subject.

"My Daddy knows everything," Emily opined, bragging slightly.

Through the rearview mirror, Victoria glanced at Bobbie's face. It was pale and unsmiling. Bobbie was the child of a nasty divorce, and the father was, according to the mother, a deadbeat dad. Victoria's heart went out to the little girl. She knew the drill and had warned Emily to desist from making too many effusive complimentary references to her own dad.

"Remember what we talked about, Emily?" Victoria reminded her, with a quick look at her daughter through the rearview mirror.

"What, Mommy?" Emily asked with a look of genuine puzzlement.

"You know."

"No I don't."

Victoria felt a growing sense of frustration.

"Never mind," she said.

"Oh," Emily said, suddenly remembering. "You mean about Daddy."

"Exactly."

"I'm sorry, Bobbie," Emily said. "I forgot."

Again, Victoria glanced at Bobbie's face through the rearview mirror. The girl's eyes were glazed and her lips tightly pursed. She felt the old hollowness in the pit of her stomach, the familiar sensation that she had grown up with. There was no cure for it.

"Now if I'm a little late, girls," Victoria said, deliberately changing the subject and, hopefully, the mood, "just wait inside the door and listen for my honk. I'll honk three times like this."

She honked the horn three times, much to the consternation of the driver in front of her who raised a middle-finger salute. She mimed a gesture of apology and the girls started to giggle.

The Crespos were waiting in the anteroom of Mr. Tatum's office, both rising in tandem when Victoria crossed the threshold. It was a gesture of impatience, not respect. They wore dour, unsmiling expressions. Helen Crespo faintly nodded acknowledgement. She wore a gray sweatered dress cinched tightly at the waist to emphasize her imposing breast work. Her husband eyed Victoria coldly through his little round glasses, reminding her weirdly of old photos of European intellectuals. He turned to Mr. Tatum's nervous gray-haired secretary.

"You can tell Mr. Tatum that Mrs. Rose has arrived," Mr. Crespo said.

Mr. Tatum ushered them to a conversational grouping consisting of two facing upholstered sofas and a large winged leather chair obviously to be occupied by him. This was, unquestionably, his domain, and he ran the school with tight-fisted authority. Although there was a board that tended to administrative and financial matters, Mr. Tatum was the sole voice of academic authority. It was he who decided what students entered the school and what infractions constituted expulsion, a not-uncommon action in a school with a waiting list that went on into infinity.

"I know this is short notice, Mrs. Rose," Mr. Tatum began apologetically. He wore a gray herringbone jacket, charcoal gray flannel pants, a striped tie over a crisp, white shirt, and tasseled loafers. He had the look, feel, and image of someone who commanded respect. His expression struck her as kindly, but neutral.

"To put it mildly," Victoria said, eyeing the opposition. Staring them down had been a powerful weapon in her legal arsenal.

"It happened again yesterday, Victoria," Helen Crespo said.

"Madeline came home hysterical. We demanded this meeting and Mr. Tatum has obliged."

"Haven't we been through this? Once again I ask: did she see him do this?"

Both Crespo's exchanged glances.

"She saw him eating it?" Helen Crespo said.

"Must we go through this yet again?" Victoria sighed. "This is worse than circumstantial. It proves nothing."

"The child became hysterical in class," Mr. Tatum said. "Which raises the stakes of this issue considerably. I was immediately summoned. I called Mrs. Crespo, who was at home."

"I was at my studio, as usual in the midst of making a single stem vase, very intricate work. Mr. Tatum's call was completely unnerving. Needless to say, the work was spoiled. You see..."

"Helen called me and we took Madeline home," John Crespo interjected. "We were up all night with her. So you see this is no small matter, as far as we're concerned."

"This time we did not confront Michael," Mr. Tatum said, exchanging glances with the Crespos. "We thought it best to discuss this situation with you first. I'm sorry Mr. Rose is not present."

Two against one, Victoria thought. She looked pointedly at Mr. Crespo.

"Both my husband and I are satisfied that Michael is telling the truth. His word is good enough for us."

"Do you know what it means for a child not to be believed?" Mr. Tatum said with mild admonishment. "Not by her teachers or her fellow students. Really, Mrs. Rose, it is beginning to affect her psychologically. The child is..."

"It has to be resolved," John Crespo said pedantically, taking off his little glasses and pinching the bridge of his nose. "The child feels alienated, isolated, surrounded by hostility. Somehow we have to clear the air, Victoria."

"Michael is not a thief or a liar, John. It is the primal axiom in our household." Her gaze drifted pointedly from one Crespo to the other.

"To us, a lie is original sin. It has been drummed into our children since birth. Madeline is fantasizing."

"Once, I acknowledge, she could be fantasizing," John Crespo said, carefully refitting his glasses. "Twice could be fantasizing. This has been a repeated offense. She is certain that Michael is the thief."

"I'd be very careful with your choice of words, John," Victoria snapped, her eyes boring into those of her antagonist.

"How else would you characterize it, Victoria?"

"It is an accusation without merit, based on the hysterical comments of a child. In a court of law, John, a child's testimony is often rejected on those grounds."

She felt herself growing lawyerly now, deliberately intimidating and aggressive.

"This is not a court of law, Mrs. Rose," Mr. Tatum said, his implication clear. *I am the law* here was his unmistakable message. "We are simply looking for a solution to a dilemma. We are in kind of a double bind here. Although it might seem minor in terms of the objects at issue, it has, in fact, become a major circumstance. Both children are good students. Michael's a natural-born leader, a role model, a kind of hero to his peers. And Madeline is a lovely girl." Victoria looked toward the Crespos. "She has become even more withdrawn than before these..." Mr. Tatum coughed politely into his fist. "These allegations."

"Allegations?" Victoria snapped. "These are a couple of kids, dammit. And the issue is candy, for crying out loud. Just candy. What is going on here?"

"What's going on here, Victoria," John Crespo snapped, "could be a matter of some consequence to Pendleton Hall. We do not intend to remain silent."

"We intend to be quite vocal, Victoria," Helen Crespo chimed in.

"That would be your style, Helen...being vocal...interminably," Victoria said, regretting it instantly. Helen shot her husband a challenging stare, which he ignored.

"We're talking full-court press," Mr. Crespo said, lips pursed in anger. "Media exposure, perhaps lawsuits."

Victoria looked swiftly toward Mr. Tatum, noting a quick shrug and an eyes-to-the-ceiling gesture of frustration. Above all, Mr. Tatum feared anything that might reflect badly on the school.

"On what grounds?" Victoria asked.

"Whatever fits."

"You'll be dragging the school through the mud," Victoria shot back, noting Mr. Tatum's brief nod.

"So be it. What we want is justice for our child."

"We're talking Milky Ways here, not nuclear proliferation," Victoria said, shaking her head in outrage, fighting for control. She wished she had postponed this confrontation until Josh could be present. She felt beleaguered, blindsided, unprepared. In her legal battles, she had always been overprepared. She had calculated every possible angle. Displays of emotion were performed on cue.

"The Rose boy lied," John Crespo said, "and it has deeply affected my daughter. We demand satisfaction, Mr. Tatum."

John Crespo turned his attention to the headmaster.

"As you can see, Mrs. Rose, they feel rather strongly," Mr. Tatum shrugged. "Hence my urgency."

"What the fuck would satisfy you?" Victoria exploded. "Stand Michael in front of a firing squad before the student body? On the testimony of some pampered little maladjusted brat? I think you're both a couple of shits."

"No need to get smutty, Victoria," Helen Crespo cried in shock, sitting up stiffly, pushing out her big boobs. It was obviously her ultimate gesture of indignation.

"And don't point those missiles at me, Helen," Victoria said. From the corner of her eye she noted that the blood had drained from Mr. Tatum's face. She paused for a moment, sucking in a deep breath.

"I have a solution," she said, forcing a smile that made her mouth ache.

"Perhaps we're getting somewhere," Mr. Tatum said hopefully.

"Remove the cause," Victoria said. She could see by the glances of confusion between the Crespos that she had been too subtle. She shook her head and sucked in a deep breath. "Stop giving her those fucking Milky Ways."

"Can you believe this?" John Crespo said.

Mr. Tatum remained silent, exchanging what Victoria interpreted as a private glance of camaraderie. Helen Crespo by then had fully returned to her rocket-poised posture of indignation.

"Don't dismiss the logic out of hand, John," Victoria said, finding her old prosecutorial voice. "Good nutrition notwithstanding, candy is a temptation to any child. Someone with a sweet tooth could find the temptation irresistible."

"Someone did," John Crespo said. "Your son."

"Thank you, Captain Queeg," Victoria sighed, wondering if they would get the *Caine Mutiny* reference. "Where are your comfort balls?"

"You have a filthy mouth, Victoria," Helen Crespo sneered.

"Not those balls, Helen," Victoria replied.

"I'll show you balls, Victoria," John Crespo said, raising his voice for the first time. Obviously, the reference had touched a hot button. "You asked what would satisfy us. I'll tell you what. Expulsion, that's what. Nothing short of that."

Unable to remain seated, Victoria stood up.

"Do you people really want a settlement of this issue?" In her mind, she was back in her office now across from City Hall in Manhattan in full ball-busting mode. "That's not a settlement. That's a demand. You want court. I'll give you court up the gazoo. I am a lawyer admitted to the bar in the state of New York. For my child, I will fight to the death."

Victoria could see by the sodden expressions on the face of the Crespos that her strident attitude of intimidation had found its mark. It surprised her to discover how easily her old aggressive posture had erupted after so long in hibernation.

"We're not used to this kind of treatment, Victoria, we..." Helen

Crespo began. Victoria could tell the woman was winding up for a stream-of-consciousness assault. She looked at her watch.

"I'm sorry. I have to leave, please forgive me."

With that, she nodded her good-byes, then turned on her heels and walked swiftly out of the office, a ploy often used in her practice to humiliate potential litigants and give them time to reflect.

Back in her car, heading back to the ballet school, she felt energized to the point of explosion. She needed to vent and dialed Josh's cell phone. She couldn't get through. For some reason lately he had either neglected to charge the battery or had forgotten to turn it on. Frustrated, she opted against leaving a message through his office voice mail. She was too hyper at the moment for the nightmare of press one, press two, and press three routines. Instead, with a mixture of hope, dread, and anxiety, she called her mother in Ft. Lauderdale.

"As long as you truly believe he's telling the truth," her mother said after Victoria had reiterated the events. Her mother's voice held its usual combination of cynicism and arrogance. Time and her own life's experiences had, Victoria wanted to believe, eroded her mother's influence on her. Knowing her mother's advice was tainted with bitterness over her own failed marriage, she was, as always, wary but combative.

It had been a lifelong struggle for Victoria to find the right balance between tolerance, guilt, and understanding. It was hard not to respect her mother's strength and independence and the awesome sacrifices she had made on her behalf. Victoria considered their relationship terribly complicated, even maddening, but miraculously enduring.

Victoria was often critical of her mother's vocal outbursts on the subject of the male gender. Their clashes were heated, angry, and often abrasive, but they never reached the point of total separation. Their relationship, Victoria had concluded, had been forged on the pitted anvil of single parenting and the resultant condition of fierce and often obsessive mutual need. Who else was there to turn to in crisis and trauma? Who else could listen with such profound concern?

"Of course he's telling the truth. A mother knows."

"Who can argue with that?"

"You seem to be questioning it, Mother."

"He's still a *he*, Victoria."

"Not that old drumbeat, Mom. Not now, please. This is about your grandson."

"Was Josh with you?"

"No. He was working."

"Never there when you need them, are they?"

"Mother, please. Not today."

Victoria's mother had been a nurse and moved with her daughter to numerous cities working for various hospitals, always leaving because of some altercation with the hospital administrator or a doctor who had somehow treated her unfairly. The result was that Victoria had never known any permanence at all, chasing around the country from apartment to apartment and school to school.

When Victoria was two, her father had left their house. Her mother insisted it was desertion, which seemed logical since he had literally disappeared. Eventually, she was granted a divorce on those grounds. In further protest, she had taken back her maiden name, Stewart, and had applied it to Victoria as well.

Aside from removing her husband's name, she had taken steps to eliminate any lingering reminder of his presence. There were no photographs of him, no possessions, no memorabilia, except her own words and gestures of derision and contempt.

As Victoria grew older and more knowledgeable about sexual relationships between men and women, her mother embellished the story with additional revelations. Apparently Victoria's mother had caught her husband in *flagrante delecti* with a neighbor, the big bang of betrayal that had triggered in her a blind antagonism for the male sex. In her mother's view, all men were satyrs, adulterers, predators and marauders, disloyal liars and incorrigible villains.

At some point, her mother had also turned the idea of fathering into a biology lesson. The male has a single function in the chain of life, she had preached. Take the elephant, her prime example. He performs his function then is banished from the herd. We females take care of our own. This explained why Victoria had more stuffed elephants than other children, more elephant books, more Dumbo stories.

From overhearing telephone conversations as a child, Victoria had learned that her father had run away from Belfast as a teenager, escaping some sort of trouble, the implication being, as she learned later, that he was never loyal to anyone, not even his birthright.

While in her teens, her aroused curiosity motivated her to surreptitiously apply to the King County Bureau of records, where she learned that her father's name was Thomas Edward Holmes. In an effort to discover even more about him, she would rummage through her mother's drawers looking for clues. For some reason, Mrs. Stewart had kept her marriage license or had forgotten to destroy it. Victoria found it hidden away in a bottom drawer. Her father had signed his name merely as T.E. Holmes.

Victoria's remarkable memory for numbers caught the discrepancy immediately. She had the date of her birth and her mother's marriage date, which was merely four months before. This meant her mother was five months pregnant when they had married. As the years passed, the fact grew in importance, offering yet another clue to her mother's obsessive anger.

She had also absorbed the notion that somehow she was at least partially to blame for her father's desertion, as if her conception and arrival had raised the stakes of responsibility that he had not the character to tolerate.

Yet who could fault a working mother who had struggled and sacrificed to raise a fatherless daughter? It was bad enough to have an absent father. Her mother had escalated the condition to a disease of gender. It was the foundation of her martyrdom.

When Victoria was twenty and an undergraduate senior at NYU, she received a postcard from a man identifying himself as her father.

I am Thomas Edward Holmes, your natural father, the postcard began. It was sent through the college administration office.

He wrote that he was terminally ill and wanted to see her, giving an address in Boston. Without telling her mother, who would have exploded in anger and forbidden her to do so, she went up to visit him. It was the address of a boarding house in a seedy part of South Boston. The landlord told her that he been taken to Boston Holy Mercy hospital. She found him in a ward smelling of decay and filled with sick and indigent men in various states of disintegration.

"You came," he croaked, his first words when he saw her. "I took a chance. It wasn't easy finding you."

His eyes were sunken and glazed, although she imagined they had lit up slightly when he saw her. Studying his wasted and gaunt face, she was startled to see the familiar shape of her own mouth and the equally familiar almond contours of her eyes. The obvious genetic kinship shocked her. There's him in me, she realized, noting, for the first time in her life, that her mother's demonization of her father had carried with it a curse upon her.

"You said you wanted to see me," Victoria told him, pulling a chair beside the bed. It was obvious that the end was near.

"Victoria. It was me that named you for Gramma Holmes, my father's mother. Loved the royals, she did. We were Orangemen, you see." Victoria caught the faintest hint of memory, the old brogue speech rhythms. She hadn't heard his voice since she was two years old.

"Drove me away, your mother did. You were the light of my life." He swallowed hard and grimaced in pain. "Look at you. So beautiful." He coughed weakly and stared at her for a long time without speaking.

"She said you deserted us," Victoria said, feeling a compulsion to further plumb the truth of her mother's rage.

"She gave me no choice. Swept me away like yesterday's rubbish," he shrugged. "I did love her once. Too much, perhaps."

"Did you really?" Victoria asked, perhaps seizing the opportunity to hurt him. "I saw your marriage license. I was a bit of an early bird."

"She never loved me, you see. Never wanted to marry. But there was no choice for her in those days."

Hearing this sad, wasted man talk of love appalled her. She didn't believe a word of it, but she couldn't bring herself to dispute him.

"She became a hard, bitter woman. I was no match for her."

She wanted to nod agreement, but desisted. Too much had intervened to make him an ally now.

"She said you broke the marriage bond."

"Some people can make hell happen on this earth. Couldn't be worse on the other side." With difficulty, he sucked in a deep breath and expelled it. "It was from her I ran, daughter. Not from you."

Unsaid rebuttals crowded into her mind. But you could have stayed close. You could have visited me. You could have made yourself available. Hugged me. Comforted me. You ran from that as well. You made us struggle and suffer. You could have provided a presence, been a dad. Why didn't you challenge her total possession of me? Defend yourself?

Such questions had long been planted in her mind, like tendrils and shoots growing at random, twisting and turning in the fertile soil, nourished by fatherly deprivation and motherly rage and denial.

Instead she rebuked him silently: I am your daughter. You are my long-absent father. How dare you summon me out of the blue to give you solace on your deathbed. Where were you when I cried out for your touch in the night? No, I will not forgive you. Never.

He seemed to be studying her face, perhaps reading her thoughts.

"I'm sorry, daughter. Truly sorry."

He began to cough and turned his head away. She waited until he recovered from his coughing fit. Taking a tissue from a box beside the bed, he blew his nose and wiped his eyes.

"Looks like your mom did a damned fine job without me," he said when he had recovered, forcing a thin smile.

"She tried…" Victoria had struggled to emit the word that hung unsaid in the air. Amazingly, it came out right. "Dad."

"Dad," he repeated, his sound a wispy gargle. Tears again streamed down his whiskered and wasted cheeks. Finally, he was able to speak again.

"I had a lousy life, Victoria. No good came of me. But you were never out of my thoughts. From the looks of you, I did what was best. You were a good girl to come see your old dad." He paused again and studied her. "Your mother know you've come?"

She shook her head. It was a secret to be kept forever. Her mother would never have forgiven her for consorting with the enemy, and she couldn't bear the thought of that maternal bond broken. However weird, it was the only parental bond she had, and she clung to it tenaciously.

She saw her father's Adam's apple rise and fall as he struggled to speak again. Then he looked at her, squinting, searching her face, reading her mind.

"You're right, Victoria. I don't deserve it."

It was a moment, she would remember later, when even the most oblique mutter of forgiveness, however insincere, was called for. Yet, despite the ease with which it could have been given, she could not bring herself to offer it. She had come hoping this visit might represent some kind of closure. It didn't. This last painful snapshot of her father rose periodically in her mind, especially when she interacted with her mother.

Like now.

"I'm hanging up, Mother," Victoria sighed. "I'm getting too old for elephant stories."

"You can't deny the natural order."

"I'm not an elephant, Mother."

There was the long expected pause.

"Keep me posted, Victoria. I hope everything works out the way you want it to. But remember…"

"Please, Mother."

"You can't outwit destiny."

"What's that supposed to mean?"

"Never mind. No matter what, I love you."

"Sure you do."

Victoria flipped the cell phone shut, furious that she had reached out for succor in what was, as always, the wrong direction.

Once again, she tried Josh's cell number. Once again it failed to connect. This time she called his office directly.

"We are terribly sorry, but all lines are busy," a voice said. "But stay on the line. Your call means a great deal to us."

"Fuck you," she cried, breaking the connection as she arrived at the ballet school.

Chapter 2

"Sorry, Victoria," Josh had told her when she mentioned her earlier call. "I keep forgetting to charge the damned thing."

It was after eleven when he had gotten home, drained to near exhaustion from the day's events and the additional burden of heavy-duty guilt.

"Chill out first, Josh," she said, inspecting his face and frowning. "We've got a bit of a problem."

His pulse thumped in his throat, his anxiety level rising. Had she discovered his transgression?

"Sounds ominous."

"The case of the purloined candy has escalated," she sighed.

"That again?" His relief was palpable. It was an issue of importance, but not the potential train wreck that never left his thoughts.

"I'm afraid so."

"You could have hit my office voice mail."

"I was in no mood," she said. "Besides, I decided to cool off. I was only venting. I called my mother instead." She shook her head. "Bad idea."

"I'm sorry, darling," he said, deliberately avoiding proximity for fear that her nose would pick up the moist sexual scent of his afternoon. "Humungous day. Big pressure. Pour me a scotch, and we'll sort it out after I wash away the dust of battle." He rushed off to the shower.

It wasn't only the guilt of his affair with Angela Bocci that was nagging at him. His sister Eve's latest boyfriend had left the comfort of her ample flesh and she was about to sell yet another among the last few remaining pieces of their parents' antiques, her only recourse for financial survival.

It had turned out to be a bitter irony. Their parents had fought over their possessions in a furious contest with many valuable antiques destroyed in the combat. As children, they had been indoctrinated into believing that the pursuit and acquisition of material things was a paramount necessity and a sure sign of success. The memory of their parents' futile battle over possessions had finally disabused them of such ideas.

Eve had insisted he meet her in the coffee shop across the street from his office where their most recent conferences were usually held.

There she was sitting at a table in the rear, four jelly doughnuts on a plate in front of her, one half eaten, drinking a mug of coffee. He looked at the doughnuts and shook his head.

"Don't say it, Evie," Josh said.

"We'll leave it unsaid then, Josh love. If he had meant harm, God wouldn't have given us taste buds and all those other pleasures of the senses. Why can't people understand?"

She was at least a hundred pounds overweight and counting, a mass of soft, breathing flesh. Numerous shrinks had theorized that ingesting food was her way of preserving their mother's love. Food and its preparation had been their mother's passion, which provided the logic for every shrink's diagnosis. Evie had completely agreed with their findings, embellishing it further.

"Food does trigger fond memories, and yes, food is pleasure. Food is love. Mom knew."

Their parents' trauma had left her impaired in this way, although Evie saw it differently. Even their maternal grandparents who had raised them were her allies in the idea, further indulging her, encouraging their dead daughter's passion in their granddaughter. The difference, of course, was that Barbara Rose, Evie and Josh's mother, loved the preparation of food more than the consumption of it.

"Food is her coping mechanism," they argued. "Look how sweet and loving she has turned out."

"And dangerously fat," Josh had countered. But the health argument had little effect on Evie or their grandparents.

"She has a healthy soul and that's what counts," they pointed out.

Who could argue? Although she was older than he by four years, Josh had taken over the caretaker role when their parents had died, and he loved her with protective zeal. His children loved her as well, despite Victoria's obvious disapproval. For the past couple of years, fearing Evie's influence, she had severely limited their exposure to her. To keep the peace, despite the strong emotional bond he had with his sister, Josh had acquiesced, but under protest.

"Why can't you be more tolerant?" Josh had begged her.

"Because it's her religion, Josh. Don't you see? She has given food mystical powers. Food protects. Food is godly. She is a living icon for food. Her view is beyond nutrition, beyond health, just more and more, all kinds, the more fat-laden the better. It is a seduction for the children. She proselytizes."

And, indeed, she did.

"Has the obsession with thinness made the world a better place?" Evie would argue. "Are we less violent and hateful to each other because we have taken the fat content out of food? Has the denial of pleasure from food made humanity better or worse?"

No one was sweeter, more caring, more loving to others than Evie. Never once, in the years after their parents' "accident," had Evie ever been known to utter a harsh and unkind word. She was like a big, beautiful, cherubic porcelain doll, with cerulean blue eyes and lovely blonde hair and a smile that reminded everyone of a bright and happy "Have a good day" face. To look at her made one feel cheerful.

But her capacity for loving had its dark side as well. Despite her girth, she attracted men and her sexual appetite was apparently on a par with her love of food. Men seemed to revel in her flesh and she in theirs, but the relationships were never lasting and never resulted in matrimony.

"Too much of a good thing," seemed to be the common complaint when Josh had probed.

"Your sister is an angel," one of her boyfriends once told him. "But after a while you feel trapped in a fleshpot of goodness and pleasure. Living with her is like being in heaven. Constant paradise can get pretty boring."

Despite these endings, Evie accepted them with good humor, generously offering those of her ex-lovers who were economically disadvantaged a golden parachute, which had considerably reduced her own financial situation.

Unfortunately, Evie had never developed any marketable skills. Knowing this, Josh had turned over almost his entire inheritance to her. Ironically, their parents' remaining antique collection had grown in value, and even the home in Washington, which they had willfully destroyed, had been more than adequately insured. But generosity and profligacy had seriously depleted what was once a comfortable nest egg. Evie's future was now a worrisome concern.

There were remnants of this nest egg in her rent-controlled Westside apartment, some excellent pieces of antique furniture, a collection of their mother's prized copper pots as well as her extensive library of recipes, most of which Evie had replicated, devoured, and prepared for countless others.

Victoria and Josh's earlier visits to Evie's home had always included rich gourmet delicacies in the form of cassolettes, *pâtés*, gallantines, and helpings of exotic breads, fine expensive wines, and mega-caloried desserts. Evie was particularly proud that she had preserved their mother's old apron, on which was emblazoned the word "Hausfrau."

Since she was rarely without a live-in lover, the children had been introduced to a long series of "uncles," which eventually spawned confusion and questions requiring oblique answers. Josh, loving his sister as he did, was far more tolerant of this lifestyle, relieved that Evie had someone to share her life, fill her considerable needs, and assuage her loneliness.

Eventually, the children developed a healthy curiosity about Evie's many male friends, and Victoria and Josh's explanations became increasingly less believable. How many interchangeable uncles could there be? Besides, Victoria had also come down with a galloping case of digestive rebellion and had begun to lobby for less family exchanges.

While not happy about the growing estrangement, both Josh and Evie understood Victoria's attitude and did not make it an issue between them. This did not mean that there wasn't occasional tension between Josh and Victoria on the subject of Evie, but it never reached a level of confrontation that could not be resolved by either talk or deliberate avoidance.

Josh had never ceased to marvel about how differently their parents' terminal behavior had affected Evie and himself.

Although he had learned a great deal about food and its preparation from his mother, he took no obsessive pleasure in its ingestion. That, too, he could trace to the traumatic effects of the terrible war between his parents. Although he had not been present, he had heard from Ann, their au pair, about the *pâté* that his mother had made out of the hapless Benny, his father's adored pooch. Although Josh had long forgiven her this particular excess, it had left its scars. Pets, in every form, were barred from his household, and eating for him was more a ritual of survival than an exercise in sensual pleasure.

For Evie, the reaction to this seminal event in their lives had been completely opposite to his own. Aside from her passion for food, Evie shared her apartment with a Siamese cat named Tweedledee, sparing no expense to keep her well groomed, and, like her mistress, overnourished.

With deep regret, Josh had seen many of their parents' antiques fall to the auction hammer. Items such as the carved nineteenth-century armoire, the rent table, the leather Chesterfield, the Hepplewhite secretaire, the japanned commode, and the elaborate crystal glassware were disposed of one by one to keep Evie financially afloat.

Miraculously, the much worn Sarouk blue-and-red Persian rug had escaped the auction block, although, owing to its condition, its present value was suspect.

She had also managed to hold on to the high Chippendale bed, which had for years taken her weight with or without lovers, although Josh knew that the day would soon come when even that would go. Indeed, he half expected that that would be one of the pressing subjects of her urgent visit to the coffee shop, and he was right.

"Not the bed," Josh had exclaimed. "Oh, Evie. That too?"

"It's no tragedy, Josh. I had the use of it for nearly twenty years." She laughed, her chins vibrating. "Very good use."

"You really don't need my approval, Evie. It's yours."

"Not really, Josh," she said, pleasantly offering him a jelly dough-nut. He shook his head. Shrugging, she took one of them in her pudgy fingers, lifted it, and took a dainty but generous bite. "It's part of our heritage."

"All of it was part of our heritage, Evie."

She was right, of course. But he saw it more as that other heritage of pain and loss. It was their bond and their agony. He could never erase the memory of Evie and him standing together, arms around each other in the morning rain, looking into that grave that was swallowing their yesterdays. Despite all their parents' flaws, they knew that they had been loved beyond judgment and reservation. To lose that, Josh had discovered, was the greatest loss of all.

"I just wanted to tell you so that you wouldn't be surprised when you found it gone, and to apologize," she said. "I know how you disapproved of me selling all the other things."

"That's not what I disapproved of, Evie. It was giving so much of the proceeds to your friends."

"My boyfriends, you mean. But they gave me such pleasure. They deserved it."

He suspected then that her latest, Alfred, had either left or given notice. He calculated that Alfred, a pleasant man who sold furniture at Bloomingdale's, had been with her four years, sparing Josh the worry of her well-being.

"Alfred's gone, isn't he, Evie?"

"A lovely man." She took another bite of the jelly doughnut and gracefully removed an errant crumb from her upper lip. "Yes, he's moved to Florida. Hates the weather here."

"Why don't you join him there, Evie?"

"You know how heat affects me. I'm perfectly content where I am. I'll find another beau, Josh. No need to worry about your little Evie."

"Easier said than done," he sighed.

"Such a dear brother," Evie said, caressing Josh's arm with a pudgy hand.

"I hope you get a good price for the bed," Josh said, patting her hand. "But please, Evie, you must be more careful with your money. It doesn't last forever."

"I wish I was as good a manager as Victoria," she mused.

"A tall order, Evie. I don't know what I'd do without her." Victoria handled every detail of their finances.

"I just wanted you to know about the Chippendale bed, Josh dear," Evie said, polishing off the last of the doughnuts. He felt heartsick. Food might, by Evie's lights, be love, but it was also her assassin.

He got up and kissed her on both cheeks.

"Give my deepest love to Victoria and the children," she said.

He turned away, barely able to contain his tears.

Although he knew Victoria awaited him with bottled-up emotion, she showed sensitivity and understanding about the pressure of his job. From the beginning, they had scrupulously analyzed their roles and apportioned their labors accordingly. Every move was carefully considered with a view, always, to preserve and enhance their relationship as a married couple, then as parents. They had committed themselves to the concept of a family, a family fortress, each member interdependent on the other.

Both had acted contrary to their expectations. Josh's fear of entanglement stemmed from the awfulness of his parents' demise. For his parents—for reasons he would never understand—terror had replaced tranquility and hate had replaced love. They had turned on each other like predators over carrion, causing a bizarre mutual death scene. The weapon had been, of all things, a crystal chandelier. He could never ever look at a crystal chandelier without a chilling reaction.

Until Victoria came into his life, Josh did not think it possible that he would ever overcome his reluctance to risk marriage. He and Victoria considered it a miraculous irony that both of them were blindsided by attraction strong enough to erase their unwillingness to find a mate.

Contrary to what was now politically correct, Victoria had given up her law practice when Michael was born. By then, Victoria had eschewed morally ambivalent negligence law as a career choice and was working for a large law firm on Wall Street. Because she was giving up a lucrative salary, her resignation was met with raised eyebrows. Nevertheless, with skill and good management, she had parlayed their net worth into a secure nest egg, and Josh's excellent earnings were more than enough to support a fine suburban lifestyle. One day, they had both agreed, when the heavy early load of child nurturing was over, Victoria would return to the practice of law.

Because of the destructive nature of their parents' experiences, they had amplified the essence of their marriage vows beyond merely "love and honor" and "until death do us part," to the absolutes of honesty, openness, truth, and, above all, faithfulness. They allowed themselves to believe that such virtues, if practiced by their parents, might have avoided all subsequent horrors. Currently, most if not all of these bedrock virtues were being badly betrayed by Josh's behavior. As a result, guilt and self-loathing were eating him up alive.

Before getting into the shower, he placed his cell phone in the charger to cover his story, then inspected his shirt for any telltale stains. He had contrived a costume of white cuff-linked shirts with a kind of attached shallow priest-like collar, which he wore to work under shapeless Italian jackets.

It was, he knew, a deliberate creative director's ploy to emphasize his individuality, a kind of armor to allow him the distance and mystique of eccentricity, which, in his business, translated into the perception of talent. It was, he knew, a benign form of deception, at the heart of the advertising game he played so well.

Satisfied that he had obliterated all clues, he threw the shirt in the hamper, sniffed his jockey shorts—they were brand new and slipped on after the tryst, a deliberate caution to mute the scent of any residual body fluids. He imagined a faint sign but not enough for danger and flung it after the shirt. Only then did he step into the hot shower soaping himself raw to remove any tangible signs of Angela Bocci.

God, how I hate myself, he cried in his heart, emphasizing this heavy burden of conscience by vigorously soaping the root cause of this problem. You Lobo, he whispered, slapping his penis, hoping humor might restore his equilibrium. You made me do it.

Cleansed of all microscopic evidence, he baby powdered himself, slipped into pajamas, slippers, and robe and padded down the hall to the bedrooms of his sleeping children. He watched them for a moment from the doorway, then entered and planted kisses on their cool foreheads. The act punished him further, bringing tears to his eyes and a lump to his throat.

Taking deep breaths to stem a sudden pang of anxiety, he moved downstairs to the den where Victoria lay curled on the couch. She offered him a troubled look and handed him the glass of Glenfiddich, half of which he polished off in a single gulp, hoping the surge would chase the panic.

"You look pale, Josh."

"I'm bushed," he replied, sinking flatly into one of the easy chairs opposite the couch. The den was spacious, with exposed beams and high ceilings. It offered a calming effect with its polished cherry wood panels and floor-to-ceiling book shelves. They were filled with his prized collection of books on advertising art and her leather-bound sets by Victorian authors. Above the bookshelves in the space between the shelves and the ceiling nestled her colorful collection of Victorian straw hats.

His wife had filled every available surface with her collection of Victoriana knickknacks, inkwells, porcelain vases, angels, and cobalt blue bells that she had lovingly acquired over the years. Lined up on the mantelpiece were more of her knickknacks.

These displays were not limited to the den. Throughout the house were framed "fashion plates" of that era. When her mother came to visit on Christmas, she would often heap vocal criticism on what she called "a pack of old junk."

The *pièce de resistance* was the oil painting of Queen Victoria in her prime that hung over the fireplace. Josh had bought it for her on their honeymoon in England. In an odd way, he considered it a not-too-subtle attack on Victoria's mother, who had never been told about her daughter's visit to her estranged father.

Victoria was, after all, as her father had revealed, named after this long-reigning royal. No psychiatrist was needed to explain the obsession. It was a validation of sorts, a link to absent and unknown antecedents. In an upstairs closet, she had a collection of Victorian dresses, which she would occasionally try on in the privacy of her bedroom. Early in their marriage, such episodes had been a sexual turn-on, especially for Victoria. Josh viewed it as a harmless eccentricity.

Josh understood it perfectly and had his own less extensive but equally heartfelt nostalgic exercise. He had retained those few still-intact Staffordshire figures that had been his father's pride. Scattered among the books were what was left of his collection of Napoleons and Shakespeares, as well as a prized Neptune that had escaped the carnage.

As a sentimental gesture, he had purchased another set of boxers, figures of the eighteenth-century combatants Cribb and Molineux, that had brought his parents together for the first time at an auction in Cape Cod. They faced each other in imaginary combat, Molineux the black man, Cribb the white, in a glass box especially made to protect them.

Periodically, Victoria would devote a day or two to dusting, cleaning, and often rearranging the various objects in her collection. She never trusted the job to cleaning ladies.

The den, which was by far the house's most dramatic and dominant room, had been chosen as their designated place of family gathering, reflection, and refuge, and so far it had served its purpose handily. It was also the central point for their stereo system, which played through speakers strategically located throughout the house. They both enjoyed classical music. At the moment he could hear the strains of Chopin's polonaise.

"Maybe you're pushing too hard," Victoria sighed.

"I'm fine," he said, brushing her sincere worry aside. "Now tell me what happened at Michael's school."

Victoria had a narrative style that left no detail expunged. She described the Crespos and Mr. Tatum, mimicked their words contemptuously, and provided an analysis of her own reaction and possible scenarios for further action.

He listened patiently, watching her, marveling at her still-lovely alabaster skin, unblemished and white against her black hair, the bangs deliberately cut imperfectly, giving her a perpetually windblown look. He had always admired her chiseled nose, slightly off-center smile, and her almond-shaped eyes with their hazel irises, which burned as vivid as emeralds in the bright light.

She was tall, her posture straight as an arrow, with a lithe, efficient body, small breasts, and flat stomach, which miraculously resisted extra flesh. She had the movement, style, face, and figure of a young Jane Fonda lookalike, a comparison that she dismissed although he could tell it pleased her immensely. Knowing he had betrayed this lovely unsuspecting woman for the past six months made him ache with remorse. It was a violation of such enormity that the very thought of being discovered was enough to trigger the shakes and nausea. He was sick at heart.

Glenfiddich in hand, he listened to her narrative with a conscience so burdened that he felt as if a gargantuan weight was pressing painfully on his chest.

"He says the Crespo girl is lying."

"Then let's leave it at that."

"One would think a mother has a sixth sense about these things. I know my child and I know the atmosphere in which we have raised him. Trust is everything in this house."

He felt his stomach tighten and a backwash of liquor singed the back of his throat. He could barely nod his agreement.

"Everything," he managed to croak.

"Any doubt might destroy his trust in us."

She stroked her chin and squeezed her eyes shut.

"We must never do that."

"I will not confront him again. No more. Nor will I allow the Crespos to intimidate us. No way. Their child is obviously a border hysteric. They raised the question of expulsion, which infuriated me. Never will I let that happen. Never."

She was obviously deeply troubled by the event at the school.

"I wish I had been there with you," he said. "You shouldn't have to go through this alone."

Later, lying beside her in bed, tears seeped out of his eyes and ran down his cheeks. He could not carry the burden of Angela any longer.

Angela was one of the most talented designers on his staff. Even in her initial job interview he could see by her samples that she had a flair for design. She had showed him some of her paintings as well, and he was astonished by their skill and imagination. He hired her on the spot. At the time, his only consideration was her work. Her gender was immaterial. He had hired men and women both and nothing beyond their work had ever entered his mind. In terms of the women, sexual stirrings were as far away as Mars. Then why?

Angela was married, the mother of two young girls. She lived in a row house in Brooklyn with her husband Dominic, who was the manager of a men's clothing store in Queens. The Boccis were one of those very close-knit middle-class Italian families. While she worked, her mother cared for the kids. Nothing in her background could provide a clue to her subsequent behavior.

She was only marginally pretty in the conventional sense, with black curly hair cut short, a high arched Roman nose, cupid lips, and a thin earnest face. Her body was, despite birthing two children, hard and tight. Yet, no one would take her for possessing such an aggressive and explosive sexuality.

"To the whole world, I'm a nice Italian girl. I'm a good mother. I'm a model spouse. I go to church. I go to confession. On the outside I'm a very traditional breeder wife with a typical macho Italian husband whose brains are in his dick and who treats me like an entitlement. He is totally ignorant of my talent and my inner world. I play my part. Who would suspect?"

She had said this wiping her mouth with a tissue as he hiked up his pants in his office, feeling like he had just stuck a knife in Victoria's heart. The fact that she had been the aggressor was hardly a reason to absolve himself of all blame. He had been an ardent participant.

They had been looking over her concept for a hosiery ad, sitting together on his office couch, and she had reached out and rubbed his thigh.

"This is not smart," he had told her, removing her hand.

"What has smart got to do with it?" she had said, looking at him with large Mediterranean eyes. "I want this." Again she put her hand on his thigh.

"I'm not looking for trouble."

"Do you think I'm looking for trouble?" She giggled. "Here's what I'm looking for." She began to stroke him.

"Don't, Angela," he said, but he did not remove her hand.

"You see. We've got his attention."

"We're putting ourselves in jeopardy," he whispered. But by then he was already yielding, feeling the pleasure take hold.

"From the moment I saw you," she said. "This is what I wanted."

"I can't do this," he had protested.

"So I see."

She lifted her skirt, pulled down her panty hose, moved to her knees and inserted him, putting her knuckles in her mouth to squelch any sound. She came before him, then came again. Her body vibrated.

"Oh my God," he cried, feeling the pleasure start in his toes and rise in him like a geyser, exploding.

Even before he had calmed, he felt remorse.

"This can't go on."

"Yes it can. Don't worry so much."

It was then she made her speech again about being a good Italian girl, to which she added, "I've never done this. I swear it. Not since I've been with Dom."

He distrusted her explanation. She had been too wildly aggressive, too uninhibited and immodest.

"Neither have I."

That, he knew, was the absolute truth.

"Everybody knows you're a straight arrow around here, Josh, a real family man." She pointed to a photograph of his wife and children. "She's a knockout and the kids are gorgeous."

His reaction was to turn the picture around.

"It's only a picture, for God's sake. This has nothing to do with them. Or my family. This is about me and you, about our needs." Her eyes glazed and seemed to be consulting some inner muse. "I need to feel. I need an outlet for my passion. Up to now I've been a very good girl. All the guys see me as untouchable. Don't I keep my public aura forbidding? Nobody would dare hit on me at this place."

"Because it's too dangerous, Angela," Josh muttered.

"Not with me. I promise you." She made the sign of the cross. "Don't ask me why, but I'd like to be your whore. It's a mystery. I've been walking around here wet as hell since I first met you."

Despite what they had just done, her language shocked him.

"Why me?"

"Call it one of life's mysteries," she said.

"Dammit, Angela. This is crazy."

"Tell me about it. I never thought I'd have the guts to do this."

"Let's forget it ever happened," he told her.

"Why do that?" she pouted. "I'm not talking involvement here. I don't want to mess up our other lives. I'm talking recreation, entertainment. Wild passion. Hot sex. I promise you no complications, no angst." She crossed herself again. "I love hard, quick sex. It's what I've fantasized about. With you. Where's the harm? You loved it, too. Admit it."

It was as if a satyr lay hidden in his psyche, waiting for the moment to emerge and possess him. He found himself looking for logic in a place where it was alien. He hadn't realized he could be so vulnerable. But then such an aggressive female had never approached him.

"I'm your boss, dammit," he said. That wasn't all. Angela's work was imaginative and multi-faceted. She could design and illustrate with a gift for articulating an idea that made her a standout at meetings. She was a recognized major asset to the creative staff, and, because of her talent, he was grooming her for bigger things. The implications of their relationship were endless.

"Makes it even safer. We work together. People around here know I'm teacher's pet. Deservedly so, right? We can pick the safest time and the safest place. No fuss, no muss, no bother. I'm on the pill. I haven't been with strange men and you haven't been with strange women. That eliminates the AIDS issue and means we can ride bareback. No misplaced condoms to worry about. We're okay as long as we keep it in the right compartment. No emotional brouhahas. Just dirty sex on demand. And this I promise. Whoever wants out, goodbye. No tears or torment."

"You've sure figured it out," Josh said, genuinely stunned but starting to feel amused by her explanation. "You make it sound like an ice cream break."

"Not a bad image, Josh. Especially if you think ice cream cone. I love to lick it down to the nub."

"Jesus," Josh mumbled. She reached out for him again. Despite the recent episode, he did not fail to react.

"See. It has a mind of its own. Let it run free, Josh. This has nothing to do with home and hearth. The heart stays out of it. No references to that other world. Above all, no emotional involvement. *Capisce?*"

Emotional involvement? The idea scared the hell out of him.

"I'm not so sure it's possible to hide these things," he said, sensing that his protest had lost all steam.

"I'm not in this for trouble, Josh. I promise. Trust me."

She squeezed him there and winked and headed for the door.

"And I love that ice cream cone you're carrying," she said, pausing, turning. "Just make sure there's plenty left for me."

So far it was six months of nerve-wracking danger, a miracle of ingenuity and luck. They had done it in his parked car in the office garage, in his office, empty offices, in stairwells, bathrooms, telephone booths, even movie houses, never hotels or the apartments of single friends. No sexual activity was verboten. They left no sexual stone unturned. It was frenzied, wild, crazy. All done during the working day. Sometimes two or three times. Once four. As far as they knew, no one suspected.

The danger itself became a turn-on, heightening their pleasure. It was unrelenting madness. He had become an addict. Time and again his mind told him he wanted to break it off. But his body told him otherwise and he never succeeded in mustering the courage to call it a day. Angela had entered his sexual psyche. She was even there when he made love to Victoria, a pallid and less frequent occurrence, which, he hoped, she attributed to overwork. It took more and more effort to close the compartment door.

Lately, this other thing had emerged, the feared emotional involvement. He hungered for Angela when he was away from her. It defied his comprehension. He felt himself being sucked deeper and deeper into an emotional whirlpool. He had followed his bliss and it had taken him straight to a wild hell of ecstasy and sexual gluttony.

He was not happy until he saw Angela's face in the morning. He wrote her little unsigned notes on yellow stickums. He whispered bizarre endearments on the telephone in the office and insisted that she wear no panties. In what was certainly a fit of madness he bought her an 18-carat gold slave bracelet, which he insisted she wear only in the office or when they had sex. It was engraved with the words: "My delicious whore. J." She loved it.

Sometimes he sent her flowers or candy, always paid for in cash to avoid Victoria's detection when she went over the credit card bills. Was he falling in love? Not once did he use the word, not in his notes or on the telephone or when they were having sex. But he thought about it. He wanted to say it. Worse, he wanted to hear her say it.

Their public office conduct, they were certain, was exemplary.

"See. We can hide things," she told him.

"Not from ourselves."

"You're right. I don't."

It seemed a strange answer and he questioned it.

"What does that mean?"

"I confess my sins to my priest. A few Hail Marys and I'm unburdened. My sins are forgiven. That's why it's so nice to be a Catholic. You should try it sometime."

At this admission, his pores had opened and his entire body became moist.

"You what?" He was stunned.

"I confess. No big deal. I've done it since I was a little girl."

"You tell him everything?"

"Of course."

"He's only a man, Angela. He'll talk."

"His vows will not let him. He is constrained by them. He absorbs everyone's secret sins. That's his mission."

"You're frightening me, Angela."

"Don't be. This will chase the fear," she said, lifting her skirt.

The hardest part was keeping his home life completely separate. He felt like Dr. Jekyll and Mr. Hyde. Wasn't his life with Victoria and his children his first priority? Sometimes he was tortured with doubt. Guilt plagued him. Nevertheless, he clung to the concept that the family was sacrosanct, inviolable. It will burn out, he assured himself, but his assurances were losing steam.

How could he ever explain that, when they were together, he turned off his cell phone, making it a deliberate act of separation, as if home and family did not exist during those stolen, guilty moments of excruciating pleasure?

He dared not get out of bed or show his restlessness. Victoria would question him out of concern and he would have to compound the lie. It might also provide a hint that he might be questioning her faith in Michael's truthfulness. Considering his own tattered credibility in that department, how could he maintain such faith in his own son, despite his upbringing, despite their solemn pact of total family openness and scrupulous honesty between them?

Feeling his thoughts wander backward in memory, he let it happen, following the path to the very beginning between them, the initial engagement.

"Are you squeamish?"

These were her first words to him from behind her desk, a long polished table on which were various odd knickknacks. Later he would learn they were part of her treasured Victoriana collection. The office was small, the table taking up almost its entire width. He sat on a straight-backed wooden chair. Behind her was a large window overlooking the bustle of Manhattan. He recognized City Hall and the leaf-strewn park in front of it. It was autumn, mid-October, windy and bleak.

He had entered through double wooden doors on which were emblazoned in gold letters the names of the various tenants, an export company, a manufacturer's rep, a couple of lawyers. Hers was the last name on the list, the lowest down, Victoria Stewart, Counselor at Law. He had busted up his Honda, broken a few ribs in the process, and a casual friend, a local bartender in Greenwich Village, had recommended her.

He had come into the bar walking stiff, and it pained him to hop on the barstool. He hadn't intended any legal action. He was actually more at fault than the cab driver with whom he had collided. But the bartender was persistent and persuasive and he recommended this ball-busting female attorney. He had dismissed the idea until the next morning, when it hurt to get out of bed.

She was younger than he, tall and on the thin side, with only her eyes made up with black eyeliner. No lipstick, no anything between her alabaster skin and his gaze. She had black hair cut into casual bangs and he noted that her lips seemed pugnacious, a long bow for an upper lip and an aggressive lower lip, leaving an opening for snow white teeth to be exhibited. If you're going to be a ball-buster, he concluded, this is the way to look, cool and beautiful with a mouth poised for love or talk.

The emotional pull was apparent immediately. He knew it then, defying logic and resistance. Later he would explain it as Cupid's arrow getting him in the gut. He did not know that another arrow from the same quiver had gotten Victoria in a similar place.

He hadn't answered her immediately since the question about his squeamishness and everything else about her was so unexpected. With her spotless and crisp white blouse, her strangely cluttered desk, her thin wrists, the left wound with a distinctively masculine watch with a leather band, the right sporting a thin gold-linked bracelet, she exuded the no-nonsense aura of someone who knew exactly where the soft spots were.

The details of her office were embedded in his mind, the diplomas on the wall, New York University Bachelor of Arts, another from Brooklyn Law School, a law degree, the bric-a-brac-covered desk, the neat piles of file folders, piled edge to edge, the sure sign of an organized mind. There was barely room for two file cabinets.

Because he was distracted by intense observation, she had to repeat the question.

"Squeamish? About what?"

"I'm in negligence law. Used to call us ambulance chasers. Some still do. This is the ass-end of the law business. I take 40 percent plus expenses. That makes us partners. I'm the partner who does the work and takes the risks. I win for you. I win for myself. The deal is that I lead you through the minefield and you follow, blindly and without question. If your sense of morality is too rigid, there's the door."

"You haven't heard my story."

"On the phone you said you think you've got some busted ribs. That's good, but not enough to get the blood-sucking insurance company to open its pocketbook. It's a game, you see. We over-claim. They under-claim. We meet somewhere in the middle. It's bullshit from beginning to end. Once in a while, they have to show their muscle and they take us to court. Sometimes we get outlandish in our claims just to keep them in line. Every body part has its price. Ribs are a start, but not a clincher by themselves. We must exaggerate the pain and the hardship."

"How do we do that?"

"We have doctors who know how to make a thorough diagnosis."

She was all business, making no attempt to ingratiate or charm. Later she would admit that the arrow had entered her psyche. She would be as confused as he. It was the primal mystery. When all secrets were unlocked by time and science this one would remain.

"Do you understand what I'm saying?" she asked.

"Perfectly. You're inviting me into your scam."

He had half-expected to be asked to leave. Instead, she studied his face. Then she nodded and smiled, not broadly, but enough to engage him irrevocably. The enticement, he realized even then, was not primarily the money.

She had him sign the appropriate papers and the next thing he knew he was following her blindly through, as she put it, the minefield, being examined after hours in a Brooklyn clinic by a little brown man from India who introduced himself as Dr. Singh.

"Veddy dire," he said looking grave, speaking in singsong English. He had put finger pressure on Josh's cracked ribs. "Veddy dire."

"That bad, Doc?"

"Veddy complicated."

"Really?"

"It troubles you to breathe?"

"When I do it deeply, which is not often."

"You feel pain when you jog?"

"I don't jog."

"But you would if you did."

He shrugged.

"Would I?" he asked. He had all he could do to contain his laughter.

"My diagnosis is that all movement must be veddy difficult," the doctor said.

"Not all..." he began. The doctor cut his comment short.

"What of sexual congress?"

"Congress?" Josh chuckled. "Are we talking politics here?"

"This is no laughing matter, Mister..." the doctor said, looking at the card he had filled out. "Rose."

"All right then, the fact is that I've had no congress since the accident." And not much before, he had thought. Such congress encouraged relationships, of which he was wary.

"Veddy dire. Veddy dire. I assure you, you would have no pleasure."

He watched as the doctor wrote furiously, asking more and more questions about his difficulties with all sorts of locomotion. Finally, the doctor stopped writing.

"I will give this report to the lawyer," he said.

It was more, of course, than simply cutting corners and scamming insurance companies. It was downright fraudulent and potentially dangerous. Still, he could not reconcile the act with the person who had set it in motion. Worse, he had gone along knowingly as a participant not because of any greedy intent. It had become a means to an end, the end being Victoria Stewart.

A few days later, realizing he was hopelessly engaged emotionally, he called her.

"Have you assessed my condition?" he asked, deliberately larding his approach with lightness and humor.

"Yes, I have."

"Veddy dire. Right?"

"Veddy."

"I would like to discuss this case further, Counselor. A lengthy discussion, I'm afraid. Easily it will consume the time of drinks and dinner."

She offered a surprisingly girlish giggle and he knew she had accepted his offer.

They met at a darkly romantic Italian restaurant in the Village, which offered an ambiance that was the opposite of any professional pretension. Candles stuck in the mouths of empty Chianti bottles lit the tables softly. In that light she looked particularly radiant and he could not keep his eyes from staring into hers. Why, he wondered? Why her? He had never experienced moments like this before.

He wanted to know everything about her life, to plumb the depths of her, to turn her inside out. But rather than push it in her face, he opted for keeping the conversation initially pointed in his direction.

"What exactly does a creative director in an advertising agency do?" she had asked.

"My job is to find different ways of communicating," he said with some pride. Knack of unique expression was his special skill and considered high talent in the advertising business. "I'm a specialist in enticement. I find ways to buttonhole people through images and ideas."

"In other words, your objective is to make people buy things they might not have thought about buying."

He hadn't expected her directness. Although her looks belied the fact, especially in candlelight, her comment put things in perspective. He had probably fantasized away her hard edge.

"Okay then, let he or she who is without sin cast the first stone," he said pointedly.

"Might as well clear the air before we get too deep into this," she said laughing.

"Into what?"

"Into us."

He was stunned by her candor. But she was exactly right.

"You sure don't leave much room for subtlety," he said.

She shrugged, shook her head, and took a deep sip of the wine.

"I'm sorry, Josh. I'm always lousing up the ritual." She sipped again and they silently inspected each other.

"I was hoping we could dispense with it."

"That would imply we've already come to some agreement."

"Maybe we have and don't know it."

"Maybe," she agreed, lifting her glass. He lifted his and tapped hers. Then they drank.

"This is beyond belief," he told her. "I've been avoiding this moment forever."

"So have I."

"To tell you the truth I'm very confused by it."

"Me too."

"Are we getting too personal?"

"Yes," she sighed.

"I think I better order," he said.

She listened while he made elaborate inquiries of the authentically Italian waiter, showing his own expertise, soliciting Victoria's approval of his choices. He ordered rotelle al vitello, ossibuchi al pomodoro, and anatra all'arancia.

He looked at Victoria and winked.

"Cartwheel pasta, veal shank with tomato, and roast duck with orange sauce."

"You seem to know a lot about Italian food," she said.

"I was hoping you'd be impressed," he replied, thinking of Evie, sensing the need to provide her with a historical perspective of himself. Better sooner than later, he decided. "My mother was a great cook and a caterer."

"Was?"

Calculating her interest, he plunged forward.

"She was killed. My father as well."

She appeared stunned and for a moment offered no comment.

"You are good at it, Josh."

"Good at what?"

"Getting people's attention."

"I was hoping it would get yours. You said you wanted to clear the air," he said. "I've got a lot of smog to dissipate before you can get a clear picture of my character."

"So do I."

He was overwhelmed with this sudden compulsion to recount his family tragedy. It was, after all, the fundamental experience of his life, the quintessential reference point. There was no way of truly knowing him without knowing these circumstances.

"I was twelve," he said, watching her face. In it, he could see pity begin, which worried him. He didn't want to inspire sympathy, only knowledge. Know me, he urged silently, offering a pun to take the edge of the sentimentality. "It was the die that cast me."

She smiled and nodded. Then, after a short silence, she prodded him.

"How did it happen?"

"The chandelier fell on them."

She looked at him with an expression of disbelief. Her lips formed a nervous smile.

"You're pulling my leg. I was expecting a sob story."

"It is," he said. "The line between comedy and tragedy is a thin one."

"So which one is this?"

"Both."

"Was it an accident?"

"That was the official explanation."

"And the unofficial?"

Although he needed to tell it, he could never get to the root of it. Why had his parents turned on each other with such unmitigated ferocity? What had transformed their once-loving relationship into hate and horror? Why had it taken such a tiny spark to set it off? Had the fuse been set at the very birth of their relationship? Or before? Could such an affliction be inherited?

He had thought about it obsessively from the moment of his and Evie's discovery of their parents lying lifeless under the smashed chandelier. No explanation could ever satisfy him. And here he was seriously contemplating such a commitment to a woman he had been with less than an hour. Scared? He was petrified.

Nevertheless, he told her the story with all its subplots and meanderings as if she needed to know it with the same attention to detail that he needed to tell it. He went through it incident by incident, including what he had seen with his own eyes or heard later.

He told her from Ann's reminisces of his father running over his mother's cat, his mother feeding his father *pâté* made from his beloved dog, his father adding a powerful laxative to his mother's elaborate dinner for her fancy guests and causing immediate diuretic havoc, his mother's locking his father into his sauna in an attempt to create a human roast, his father's binging on their rare and expensive wine collection, the deliberate mutual destruction of their carefully chosen antiques, the obliteration of their elaborate Staffordshire collection, their dogged hate-inspired fight for turf within their own scrupulously decorated and proudly self-designed home. Skirmish by skirmish, battle by battle, he squeezed out the painful story of their domestic war and the Armageddon finale under the deliberately unscrewed chandelier.

It was, he told her, pure hatred run amuck as his parents destroyed their coveted possessions one by one and eventually themselves. As he told her this, he could barely keep his inner hysteria under control.

She had listened in silence, mesmerized.

"Beyond belief," she whispered when he had finished.

"There was nothing Evie or I could do to stop it," he sighed.

"What could young children do?" she said, her eyes misting.

"It's something we think about often."

"You were helpless children, innocent bystanders."

He had told her the story, knowing it was a reconstruction based on the biased and limited observation as seen through a child's eyes. What she really needed to know, he had decided, was its impact on him and how it would color any relationship established between them.

"Losing one of them would have been bad enough," she said finally, when it was obvious that he had emptied himself. "But both together. You both must have been basket cases."

"We were," he said. "My sister Evie and I. She's four years older. Fortunately, we were raised by devoted grandparents."

He told her about his sister, then paused and their eyes locked.

"Evie's got her problems," he sighed dismissively. He'd leave that story for later.

"And you?" she asked gently.

"We all carry strange baggage," Josh shrugged. "Some stranger than others. I've opened mine for inspection."

"I guess you mean it's now my turn."

"Only if you want to."

"I'm afraid there is no comic relief. It's got some pretty heavy downside." She could not stop a nervous giggle. "Although nothing compared with your tale of woe."

She told her story and he listened intently, moving his food around the plate, eating little. The part about meeting her father put a lump in his throat.

"So where do these tales of woe leave us?" he sighed.

"Who was it that said that if we forget history we're doomed to repeat it?"

"Forget? You've just seen the scars of my operation and I've seen yours."

"Well," she laughed. "Now that we've got that out of the way, let's inspect the healthy parts."

"That's a creative way to put things," he said. Their faces moved toward each other across the table, joining lips.

"This runs counter to my plans," she sighed when they parted. The touch of her lips seemed to send shock waves through his body.

"Mine, too."

"Maybe this is a dream and we'll suddenly wake up."

"It's as good a cliché as any to hide behind."

"I'm very frightened, Josh."

"So am I."

"How do you test these things for authenticity?"

"Only one method comes to mind," he answered after a long pause.

She said nothing, nodding her consent instead.

The memory of this encounter was vivid. It was, up to then, the all-time happiest moment of his life.

After dinner they had gone to his place and made frenetic love.

"Is this the real thing?" Victoria said in a moment of repose as they cooled.

"It has all the markings." He hesitated for a moment. "And we mustn't let it go away."

"No. We mustn't."

"We could gamble. Go all the way."

"I thought we just did."

"You know what I mean, Victoria."

"Are you actually proposing? Good God. Considering what we've both been through, how could we possibly trust the institution of marriage?"

"In this case maybe two wrongs will finally make a right."

"I love the way you put things, Josh."

"It may never come again, Victoria. I've had enough regrets for one short lifetime."

"Me, too."

"Then it's settled?"

"Maybe it was settled before we got to this point."

It seemed a natural progression of events, a necessary validation of what they both felt. If there were maybes then, all of them vanished in their frenzied sexual exchange.

"It sure puts the lie to our little scam," he said, as they lay entangled in his bed. She appeared suddenly alarmed.

"What lie?"

"That one about sexual congress."

"That's the best lie of all," Victoria mused. "Who can refute it? As we've just demonstrated, it requires locomotion."

"There are no best lies, Victoria." Josh told her. "Only lies."

"It's just business, Josh."

"Business is also life. You get used to it, soon you can't tell which lie goes where."

"It hasn't happened yet."

"It will. Wind it down, Victoria. Let's start fresh, clean, and open. If we don't chop down cherry trees, we don't have to make the truth an issue."

"Why so paranoid about the truth?"

"The married state demands it," he said.

"So this is a firm proposal," she giggled, searching his face to be certain.

"Never doubt me. Never. Ever."

"I won't."

He propped himself on an elbow and studied her face for a long time. He imagined he could see her thoughts tracking through her brain. Then, suddenly, she lifted her head and kissed him on the lips. They held the kiss a long time.

"There's more," he said after a long silence. He had been thinking about this ever since he had become accustomed to the inevitability of their relationship.

"More?"

"We need kids. We need to be a real family. A real family will do the trick."

"What trick?"

"We are both in need of repairs, Victoria."

"Two, then. I wouldn't want an only child. It's bad enough to be fatherless. But an only child? No way."

"Agreed," he said, holding out his hand. She took it.

It was another happy moment, and they sealed it with yet another test of authenticity. Later, it was Victoria who spoke first.

"We're very vulnerable," she said.

"Very," he agreed, knowing exactly what she meant.

"We'll never escape our conditioning, Josh. Never. Means we have to be alert when the garbage we're carrying starts to seep out of the suitcase."

"How will we know?"

"Probably by the stink."

"Whoever smells it first will tell the other that it's on its way."

"And then?"

"We'll fumigate our souls."

"There you go again, saying it in an odd way."

"By any other way, they're still the true words of Rose."

"A rose is a rose is a rose," she mumbled, making a face.

"What you see is what you get. I'd like all Roses to be like that."

"Message received," she said, patting him on the penis. "Besides, I just love the long stems."

His case was her very first resignation.

How could he have known then that he would be the first to chop down a cherry tree?

Lying there beside her, he felt his stomach heave and he pounced out of bed to go the bathroom.

"Are you okay, Josh?" Victoria mumbled when he came back.

"I'm fine," he whispered.

But he wasn't fine. There was only one way he would be fine. Tomorrow, he decided. Once and for all, he would make himself fine again.

Chapter 3

It was weirdly ironic. Here he was sitting at the very same table in the very same coffee shop where he and Evie had had their discussion only two days before. Only now he was dealing with a different kind of pain.

"The fat lady has sung, Angela," he said, noting the power of association. Still, he hoped the reference would put a lighter spin on the circumstances of this meeting. It didn't.

"I didn't hear the song," Angela said, her cheeks flushing, lips tight as she aggressively leveled her eyes at his face. "All I see is a chicken dancing around with his head cut off."

Her outburst surprised him. He had expected reluctant acquiescence, not aggression.

"We agreed, Angela. When one person wanted out, it was over."

"You think I can't tell when it's over? Yesterday it wasn't over. Remember yesterday?"

They had done it in the back seat of his car in the building garage in the middle of the day. And he had sent her one of his weird stickum notes and offered sweet nothings on the telephone. Two days ago he had sent her flowers.

"I know this is abrupt, Angela. I'm sorry. I can't hack it. It's eating me up alive. Some people are built for this kind of secret life. I'm not. You know my family is my first priority."

"Of course, I know," Angela shot back, raising her voice. A man at the next table turned around. Thankfully, it was mid-morning. The breakfast crowd had ebbed and the lunch crowd hadn't yet arrived.

"Keep your voice down please," he whispered.

She moved sideways in her seat and lifted her left leg, showing him the "slave bracelet."

"Don't tell me this no longer has meaning, Josh."

He looked down and shook his head.

"Get rid of it, Angela."

"Destroy the evidence?" she snickered.

"Angela, don't make this any harder than it is."

"You are a chicken, Josh. What the hell are you afraid of? We're coworkers. That's our cover. Hell, we haven't had the slightest bit of flack." She looked at him pointedly while he sipped his mug of coffee. She hadn't touched hers. "Does your wife suspect?"

He shook his head.

"Not a clue," he muttered.

"So where's the problem? I'll tell you where. It's in your own head."

"I'm sorry, Angela. So far we're in the clear. Let's keep it that way. I just can't take the pressure anymore."

"You worry too much."

"Of course I worry. I don't want to blow my life away."

"I'd love to blow your life away," Angela said with a wink.

"I don't have a priest to tell it to," he said. "Well, his good times are over. I suppose he knows every little detail."

"Just the broad strokes. The sin is adultery. I get forgiven."

"I hope you didn't name names."

"It doesn't matter. He's sworn to secrecy."

"So he knows who I am?"

"So what?" Angela pouted.

"And you wouldn't get absolution if you didn't tell him every little detail." He felt his gorge rise.

"Look, Josh, I'm just one of many. You sin. They forgive. It's been working for a couple of thousand years."

"He doesn't tell you to stop?"

"That's not his job."

"What does he say when you tell him about us?"

"He gives me penance. Lots of Hail Marys and Our Fathers."

This had bothered him from the moment she had told him.

"Hell, he's only a man."

"Nobody's perfect," she snapped. "If it'll make you change your mind, I'll stop going."

It was another assertion he hadn't expected. Looking at her, he saw tears in her eyes.

"Angela, I'm sorry. It's over."

She started to sniffle, took her napkin, and blew her nose.

"What is this, Angela? It had to end someday. Didn't we agree? One person wants out, it's over. You remember the rules."

"I love you, Josh," she whimpered, her eyes red, tears streaming down her cheeks. He looked around him. People were straggling in for an early lunch.

"Jesus. Don't say that, Angela."

"I love you. I'll say it anytime I want. You are my need."

A bolt of fear shot down his spine.

"Dammit, Angela. Never say that again."

"Don't worry, Josh. I won't do anything stupid."

"Let's get back to the office," he said. He stood up, picked up the check, and paid it at the cashier counter.

In the street, she stopped and looked up at him.

"No matter what, I love you, Josh."

His heart lurched and a wave of anger rolled over him.

He got back in time for a luncheon conference in the staff dining room. He had expected to be relieved. Instead, he felt depressed and slightly disoriented.

After lunch he checked his voice mail. He heard Victoria's urgent message and the food in his stomach seemed to congeal. Was this it?

Picking up the phone, he called home. No answer. He was panicked. She knows, Josh thought. Either that or something terrible had happened to her and the kids. A form of retribution. He punched in her number, closed his eyes, and took a deep breath.

"What is it, Victoria?" he cried when she answered the call. He heard voices in the background.

"I can't talk now," she said. "I'm carpooling. I've got a full house."

From that he deduced that the problem might not be about her or the kids. It had to be the one thing he feared the most.

"You said it was an emergency," he pressed.

"It is."

"Dammit, Victoria. What's the problem?"

"Just come on home. Emily is sleeping at her friend's house tonight."

He felt an accelerated pulse-beat in his throat. He began to hyperventilate.

"You can't tell me now?" he urged her.

"Just come home, Josh."

She hung up. He sat by his desk for a long time trying to catch his breath. Finally he calmed and found the will to buzz his assistant.

"Trouble at home," he said. "I'm outta here."

By the time he arrived home, he was a wreck. His shirt was soaked with perspiration. Victoria was sitting in the den, a drink on the table beside her. She rarely took a drink, a fact that only exacerbated his anxiety.

"Better pour yourself one," she said, pointing to a bottle of Glenfiddich beside her glass. "You're going to need it."

Taking her words as a command, he reached for the bottle, and taking a glass from the bar poured himself a heavy shot. The glass shook in his hand. She knows, he thought again. He felt like a man being led to a firing squad. She waited until he had taken his first deep swallow.

"Michael did steal those Milky Ways," she said. "I was putting his pants in the washing machine. I found these in his pants pocket." She put the wrappers on the coffee table.

Josh looked at the four candy wrappers, laid out in parallel lines. He felt a sudden tremor of disorientation. Was this about Milky Ways?

"Our son is a thief and a liar," she said, raising her glass, looking at him over the rim. "How do you like them apples?"

"This is the emergency?" Josh asked, dumbfounded. Then suddenly, the truth of her accusation dawned and he felt engulfed by a wave of enormous elation and relief. He upended the glass and let the liquor roll down his throat. He felt himself smiling. When he looked at her again, she appeared displeased by his reaction.

"Don't you understand, Josh? Our son has betrayed us. We believed in him. He's pulled the rug out from under us."

"Victoria," he began.

"Don't say it. I know exactly how old he is."

He had intended to reassure her, to tell her what he had said to Angela earlier, that it was not the end of the world.

"Make allowances for that," he said. He poured himself another shot.

"I wanted you here when he got home from school," she said. "I wanted both of us to be here."

"Jesus, Victoria, what are we going to do, put him in the stocks?"

He watched her eyes narrow as she blew her bangs in obvious frustration.

"You don't get it do you?"

"Of course I get it," he said. "He stole. He lied. It's awful and he must be punished. As far as I'm concerned, he's grounded. We'll pull him off athletics. No television. No movies. No online. No stereo. The works."

"That goes without saying, Josh. But that doesn't get to the heart of why he did it. How can we trust him ever again? Don't you see? It's totally against the grain of everything he's been taught. He's betrayed us. Never mind the embarrassment to me. You should have seen me in Tatum's office. I was a fireball of intimidation." She shook her head. "How the hell can I face him? And the Crespos? They want Michael expelled."

Although he felt her consternation and could imagine the scene in Mr. Tatum's office, he could not bring himself to the same pitch of outrage. The other matter on his mind triggered a higher level of tolerance. The logic of Michael's lie seemed clear. The temptation was just too much for him, and he lied to cover up his embarrassment and spare himself the punishment. It was a perfectly human reaction.

"He chopped down the cherry tree, Josh. He's supposed to admit it, come clean before he's found out by other means. If he gets off lightly, he might want to chance it again. Next time the stakes will get higher."

"I'm not saying he shouldn't be punished," Josh said meekly.

"He needs to be chastised."

"What does that mean?"

"He has to admit his guilt."

"To whom?"

"To the authorities. To Tatum, for openers."

"Won't that risk expulsion?"

"We'll have to chance it," Victoria said. "He did say that if Michael had come forward and admitted his...his indiscretion...he would have been forgiven and the incident closed."

"But why a public mea culpa?"

"You really want to send that message, Josh?"

"What message?"

"That cover-up is an appropriate choice? That keeping silent is also a lie? Fidelity, remember. Is that what you want to teach your son?"

"What I'm saying is, give him the chance to prove to us that it won't happen again."

Victoria contemplated his argument for a long time while he finished his drink.

"Your point is well taken."

He went to where she was sitting, bent over, and kissed her on the cheek. She caressed his face and nodded.

"Nobody's perfect. He's been caught with his hand in the cookie jar. A little tough love might be called for here."

Despite his duplicity, he felt satisfied with his advice. After a long moment of contemplation, she looked up at him and nodded in apparent agreement.

"Tough love?" she sighed.

"It may be our only option."

Finally, she nodded. "I'm not comfortable about it, but I do get the message." She took another sip of her drink. "You have to have the wisdom of King Solomon to be a parent these days," she muttered.

Leaving her in contemplation, he went upstairs, changed into jeans and a sweatshirt, and called his office. He was relieved to discover that any residual anxieties he had about Angela doing anything stupid had disappeared.

Michael came home soon after, running into the house with his usual air of excitement, oblivious to what had happened in his absence.

"Let's not pounce," Josh warned, dreading the coming confrontation. He had put the Milky Way wrappers into the pocket of his jeans.

"Dad," Michael said, bursting into the den. "What are you doing home?"

Instead of answering, Josh looked toward Victoria, who shrugged. It was obvious she had tendered him the role of disciplinarian. Michael's smile faded as he looked from one parent to the other.

"Something happen?" he asked. "Is Emmie okay?"

"Emmie's fine."

"Then what?" he asked, frowning.

"This happened, Michael." Josh said, showing him the Milky Way wrappers. Michael looked at them and flushed deep red. He began to tremble.

"Where do you think I found them?" Victoria asked.

Michael bowed his head and looked at his hands.

"You know where I found them, don't you, Michael?"

He kept his head bowed and nodded.

"We're very disappointed in you, son," Josh said.

"Very," Victoria seconded. "You've lied to us, Michael."

"Repeatedly," Josh said. He felt awful. "And we need some sort of explanation. This can't go unpunished. You know that. No sports.

No music. No online. No movies. No television. You're grounded, son. School and homework. That's the ballgame for you from now on. Do you understand?"

Michael nodded, but he did not lift his head and look them in the eye.

"What neither your mother or I understand is why. Why did you take the candy, and why did you lie about it?"

Michael shrugged and raised his face. It was blotchy and tearful. He wiped his tears on his sleeve.

"I'm talking to you, Michael. I want to know why."

Josh's heart went out to his son, but he said nothing, waiting for the boy's reply.

"I didn't...." Michael stammered.

"You did," Josh corrected severely.

"We do not lie in this family, Michael," Victoria said. Her eyes were moist and she turned away to wipe them with a tissue.

"It's not like you think," Michael said, sniffling. Victoria and Josh exchanged glances.

"What is it like, son?" Josh asked gently.

"She promised," Michael said.

"Who promised?"

"She."

"Madeline Crespo?" Victoria asked.

Michael nodded.

"What did she promise?" Josh asked.

They watched as Michael went through a long hesitation. His small body seemed painfully rigid.

"That she would give me Milky Ways if I..." Michael sucked in a deep breath.

"If you what, sweetheart?" Victoria said, glancing at Josh.

"If I let her copy my math test."

"And did you?"

Michael nodded, flushing red. It was clearly a breach of the school's academic honor system, Mr. Tatum's fondest bragging point.

In Mr. Tatum's world, any violation of that honor system was a crime for which no punishment was too much. Examples of expulsion for this infraction were legendary.

"You knew this was against the rules?" Victoria asked.

Michael nodded again. They could see the fear in his eyes.

Josh and Victoria exchanged troubled glances.

"So you let her copy your math test?" Josh reiterated. "And she gave you the Milky Way."

"No, she didn't," Michael snapped. "And I let her copy my answers."

"Then why didn't she fulfill her part of the bargain?" Josh asked, confused.

"She said she didn't see my paper," Michael said. "She's a liar. I showed it. And I got a hundred on the test."

"Did she?" Josh asked.

"She got two wrong," Michael said. "I can't help it if she couldn't see all my answers. I showed her my paper and I saw her looking."

"So you took the Milky Way out of her bag?" Victoria prodded.

"It was mine," Michael said, his voice rising. "Then I took it again the next day. She promised me two. She's the one that lied first."

"We're not talking sequence here, Michael. Never mind that she lied. That's her and her parents' problem. You lied and that's our problem and yours," Josh said.

"But she lied first," Michael said, obviously convinced of the justice inherent in his eleven-year-old logic system.

"And you lied because you were afraid to tell Mr. Tatum that you participated in test cheating," Josh said, as if he were coaching him through it.

"A lie is still a lie, Michael," Victoria said.

"And he was protecting the Crespo girl," Josh added, as if he had become a defense witness.

"So that's why she was so hysterical. She had to tell her parents something," Victoria said.

"Mystery solved," Josh said.

"Not quite, Josh. He still lied to us."

Michael nodded.

"It was a bad thing, Mom. Madeline made me do a bad thing."

"Madeline didn't make you lie, Michael," Victoria said gently. "You have to be responsible for your own actions. You lied to us, to Mr. Tatum, to the Crespos. Pure and simple. You can't just decide when to lie and when to tell the truth." She turned to Josh. "This is the real lesson here. Never mind the extenuating circumstances. A lie is a lie."

Her rigidity was terrifying, triggering both shame and thankfulness that he had found the courage to sever the relationship with Angela.

"Do you understand the severity of your act, young man?" Victoria asked.

Michael lowered his head again. It seemed like a gesture of contrition and Josh felt the boy's pain. He turned to Michael and tousled the boy's hair. In his mind, the incident was over.

"Feel better now that you've told us?" Josh asked.

"We can't leave it at that," Victoria snapped.

Josh turned to his son, assuming, for Victoria's benefit, a severe expression.

"You know your punishment, Michael." Michael nodded. "No privileges until we decide when it ends. Now you run up to your room and get to work," Josh said, feeling flushed with parental wisdom and command. Michael embraced both his parents and went off to his room.

When he was gone, Josh poured them both drinks and they sat down beside each other on the couch.

"Emergency over," Josh said, lifting his glass and tapping hers. He felt exhilarated, relieved, and slightly manic.

He laid his glass on the table, got up from the couch, and locked the door to the den. Returning, he gently removed her glass from her hand and placed it beside his.

He then embraced her, kissed her deeply, and maneuvered her lengthwise on the couch and began to unbutton her blouse. He kissed her nipples. She seemed pliant but not eager. He continued his effort despite her tepid acquiescence.

"I need you," he whispered.

"It's all right," she said, caressing him.

She could not have possibly interpreted his sudden elation as anything more than the brief pleasure of his orgasm. It had not been mutual. The timing was, after all, not even remotely appropriate. Her mind was obviously elsewhere, dwelling on the future of their child.

In this brief encounter no images of Angela intruded to prod his libido.

Chapter 4

Victoria rose early to prepare a healthy breakfast of Irish oatmeal and honey, topped off with fresh fruit. Emily called to say she had a wonderful time at her friend's house and the routine of the day began with no mention of yesterday's trauma. As far as Josh was concerned, not only his affair with Angela was over, but also the case of purloined Milky Ways. The very fact that it went unmentioned at the breakfast table was proof positive of its demise.

"It'll work itself out," Josh said as he kissed Victoria on the forehead.

"We'll see."

He arrived at the office in a cheerful state of mind. The condition dissipated quickly when he learned from his assistant that Angela had called in sick. It was an unexpected absence. She was working on a new concept for an important client with a close deadline.

"Was she sick? Or her kids?" Josh inquired.

"Her husband called," his assistant replied. "Said Angela was sick."

"Serious?"

"He didn't say."

He pondered the answers, then ordered his assistant to postpone the presentation for a day or two.

"Did he say whether she would be in tomorrow?"

"He made no other comment."

Josh hung up and tried to keep his mind occupied, certain that Angela's absence had nothing to do with physical illness.

At eleven his cell phone buzzed and he answered it with trepidation.

"I've got good news and bad news," Victoria said.

His heartbeat accelerated and his breath came in gasps.

"Bad news first," he managed to say.

"Mr. Tatum called. The incident is over. The Crespos have withdrawn their complaint. Bygones are bygones."

He was startled. "That's the bad news? So where is the good news."

"Same news."

"I don't get it, Victoria," he said, confused.

"It means they've accepted Michael's lies as the truth. Tell me, Josh. Who wins here?"

It was not a subject he wished to tackle at this moment. Why was she agonizing over this?

"We win," he said, finally finding his bearings. "Michael wins. You're going to drive yourself crazy over this Victoria. The important thing is that Michael has acknowledged his lies to us and given us his reasons. That took a lot of character."

"Then why am I uncomfortable?"

"Because you're not thinking clearly. He's being punished, remember? And we haven't risked his future. Providence has smiled. Accept it. The long-term weather report is cloudless and sunny."

"Is it?"

"Don't be so damned rigid, Victoria," he said with impatience.

"I'm not being rigid, Josh. This is the wrong tack."

"Stop this."

"He gets away with this, he'll repeat the performance."

"This is the wrong time to discuss this, Victoria. I've got enough on my plate as it is."

"I'm sorry to bother you."

"Put it behind you."

That was exactly the advice he had given to Angela yesterday.

"I'll try," she said.

The similarity to Angela's reaction was uncanny. All women were connected by the common bond of illogic, he told himself.

"Don't *try*, Victoria," he said with frustration. "Just do what I suggest. Put it behind you."

He waited for her response, hearing only her breathing beyond the silence. Despite his advice and worry over their son, he secretly admired her adherence to principle and wished he could muster the courage to follow her example.

He thought fleetingly of Angela and their terrible deception. Again, he cursed his weakness. He wished that, once and for all, he could stop berating himself. His reform would be militant, he vowed. Never again!

"Victoria," he said, his voice rising. "I need to tell you something."

"What?" she asked.

He sensed that he was on the verge of confession, then stepped back, clearing his throat.

"I think you're terrific," he said.

"That's a heavy burden, Josh."

"He's just a child. Cut him some slack."

"I'll try," she said abruptly, breaking the connection.

Still, he could not shake his worries over his son, nor could he dismiss a lingering anxiety over Angela that her abrupt absence had triggered. Hadn't she promised not to do anything stupid? His thoughts were disturbed by a sudden buzz on his consul.

"Mr. Bocci is here." It was the familiar voice of the receptionist.

"Who?"

For a moment, he felt disoriented.

"Angela's husband," the receptionist said.

"What does he want?" Josh asked, barely managing to get the words out.

"He wants to see you."

"I'm really very busy, Miriam, tell him no." He quickly reconsidered. "Wait." He sucked in a deep breath. "Does he look angry?"

"Not at all. Very pleasant."

Always thinking the worst, he told himself.

"I hope it's not anything serious about Angela," he mused aloud, feeling a brief twinge of panic. "Give me a couple of minutes, then send him in."

Despite the receptionist's assessment of Dominic Bocci's demeanor, he needed to calm himself. What could he possibly want?

Dominic Bocci came in bearing a broad smile and appearing benign in demeanor. Josh could detect no sign of hostility, which relieved him considerably. He was a good-looking compact man with black curly hair, a dark complexion, and a large curved nose. He was dressed in a blue blazer with gold buttons, a white shirt, red tie, grey flannel pants with razor-sharp creases, and spit-shined black shoes.

Josh got up from behind his desk and ushered his guest to a seat in the conversational grouping that he used for visitors and casual meetings. It crossed his mind briefly that he had fucked this man's wife on or near every piece of furniture in his office. A sourness invaded his chest. As he sat down on one of the upholstered chairs, Dominic Bocci shot his cuffs, carefully crossed his legs, and seemed to study Josh with more than passing interest.

"I hope Angela's okay," Josh said clearing his throat. "We depend on her a great deal here."

"She's pretty upset," Dominic said, striking a sudden ominous note that belied his expression. "But that's understandable, considering..."

"Considering?"

"Come now Mr. Rose, we both know what's going down here."

Josh's first thought was that this man was an actor playing a role in some bad movie. But that thought quickly disintegrated under the excruciating burden of another, more poisonous, idea. The reality hit him with the force of a spear through his body.

"What does that mean?" Josh asked, but his tongue could not move the words.

"I'm hoping we can settle this quick time," Bocci said. He was cool, which was doubly disturbing since Josh felt his entire body break out in an icy sweat. "Look," Dominic said. "I don't want any trouble, either. I'm here to avoid trouble. Hell, I got a family, too. I ain't gonna begin to break up mine."

He squinted and contemplated Josh's face, his lips curling in a smile that did not show his teeth.

"Frankly, I don't give a shit what happens to yours," Dominic said. The sudden burst of hostility was a clear indication that the man's conservative Ivy League clothes, general attitude, and movie gangster pose betrayed street smarts that put Josh at an immediate disadvantage.

"I...I really am at a loss..." Josh began, realizing suddenly that any pose of innocence or denial would fall on deaf ears.

"Look, I know about Angela and you. Don't think I feel good about it, but I have no intention of being physical. So rest easy on that score. I made my peace. I'm not some crazy guy with a sliced-up ego comin' here to tear your balls off."

"Just what do you think you know?" Josh said, attempting without success to find his own brave facade. Dominic gurgled a kind of chuckle, shook his head, and continued to gaze at Josh with his odd squint.

"Hey, Rose. You think you can fool this Guinea? No way. Fact is, I knew for a while. You've been boffing my wife and now it's over, right?" He chuckled. "I know you're sweatin' bullets tryin' to figure out what I have in mind. When I found out, I hung back. I figure you got to be a nut case putting yourself in such a spot. Not in today's world, buddy. No way. Them days are over. You want strange, you got to go to strangers. Am I making myself clear?"

"Explicit," Josh groaned. "I don't know about clear."

The man leaned forward on the couch and looked from side to side as if to make certain he would not be overheard. It was more of a gesture of extreme confidence than a necessary caution.

"Rose, I want you to know that this isn't personal. I'm a man of the world myself. Sure I was pissed off. Angela's a hot little number and maybe I wasn't doin' my homework. She's also ambitious and talented and a helluva good mother. You gotta weigh these things. We went to the priest and got everything straightened out between us."

That priest, Josh thought, offering silent condemnation. Defrock the bastard, he cried to himself.

"Forgive and forget, right? I ain't no angel myself." He smiled without warmth and continued to squint at Josh. "You neither."

For the first time since he had walked into his office, Josh saw a flash of anger and determination in the man's eyes that belied his attempt to maintain a calm exterior. He means business, Josh thought, his heart thumping against his chest.

"So you're asking what I'm doin' here?" Dominic said, tapping his knee. A gold bracelet slipped down his wrist and settled near the base of the thumb of his right hand. Josh kept his silence waiting with trepidation for the other shoe to drop.

"I thought about this ever since, you know, ever since I found out. Here you are, Angela's boss. Means you got power over the people who work for you, like Angela. Let's face it, you can bestow favors. You can make or break a career, kick someone up, kick someone down. Give raises. Make recommendations. To the people under you, you're one important dude. Right?"

"I think your perspective is a bit off center," Josh said.

"It ain't my perspective, I'm speaking for Angela."

Josh resisted the urge to make any further comment. He felt a giant hole being dug in front of him with Dominic about to push him into it.

"So I figure that if we file a harassment suit against you, we got you dead to rights."

"Angela couldn't contend that."

"Why not? As I said before, you're the power, man."

"But she was already on the fast track on her own. Everybody around here knew it. She's a first-class designer. She could go anywhere. No one held her back. Besides, she's a valuable colleague. I needed her. She made me look good."

"You betcha. She's one talented lady."

"And definitely not an innocent victim of harassment."

"Look, man. Would she want to file a suit? No way. I hadda talk her out of it."

Josh was dumbfounded. A lawsuit? Not Angela. Hadn't she been the aggressor? Had he failed to see the dark underside of Angela's character? Had he bothered to see her as anything but a sexual pleasure machine? Nothing in their relationship, whether as working colleagues or frenzied sexual partners, suggested such a cruel destructive motive. She had said only yesterday that she had loved him. And he, Josh, had once believed that he might be in love with her. Good God! Was this the retaliatory action of a scorned woman or had he been set up by Angela from the beginning?

"It's hard for me to believe Angela could be part of this," Josh said with faltering conviction.

Dominic shrugged and unconsciously picked imaginary lint from the sleeve of his blazer.

"I guess you just don't get it. Believe me when I say that no one, especially Angela, wants trouble. So here's what she's willing to do. I'm just the messenger here. For a couple a hundred grand we're outta here..."

Without waiting for him to continue, Josh stood up. He felt a sudden hammer blow to his head, his skin became hot with anger, and sweat broke out on his body.

"You slimy blackmailing bastard. Get the fuck out of my office or I'll have you thrown out."

Dominic shook his head, chuckled and smiled, and lifted both hands, palms up.

"Hey man, cool down. You don't want this. Next thing you know, this whole thing will be out in the open and the shit will hit the fan. Do you really want that, kiddo?"

In the pause that followed, Josh fought his anger. A sudden nausea seized him and he had to swallow hard to keep from vomiting. He felt trapped in a maze, unable to find the right path to the exit. He sucked in a couple of hard breaths, forcing his calm while his mind raced to assess his position.

Suddenly he felt the full impact of his victimization, reviewing events that led to this moment. It was Angela who had pursued him, who had seduced him with her overpowering sexuality. Hell, he wasn't made of stone. And she had shown such enthusiasm and lack of inhibition. Had he unwittingly fallen into a trap? Whatever the motive, he was in deep shit. Let's see you wiggle out of this one, Mr. Creative Director. Finally, he managed to get himself under control and sit down.

He had no illusions about the impact of a sexual harassment challenge. The company had run numerous sensitivity seminars as a cautionary measure. Nevertheless, people took chances. The agency, with many young men and women employees, was a hotbed of consensual sex. He was certain, too, that there were the usual trade-offs, sexual favors for material enhancement. It had never entered his mind that his affair with Angela was in this latter category. She was already teacher's pet.

"That's better," Dominic said when Josh had settled down again. "This is deal time, man. I know what you make. I know where you live and how. I seen your house. What's two hundred grand to you? You get to keep your job and your good lifestyle. The wife's no wiser. The boss don't know. Pay up. Walk away. It's a one-shot deal."

"What about Angela's career? She'd be finished here. How can we possibly work together after that?"

Dominic nodded his head.

"Now we're making headway, man. I don't want no sleazy under-the-table deal here. What do you think we are? What I'm lookin' for here is a private settlement. A legal piece of paper that goes right into the vault. And a check. The real thing. The paper says you sexually harassed her and the two hundred thou is your settlement chip. It also says that you can't badmouth Angela ever. You're right, man. She can't work here. You said yourself she's good. I want that paper to say that if anyone asks about her you tell the truth about her work. No paybacks. What do you think, because I'm Italian, I'm some Mafia hood? I'm talkin' legal here."

"Legal?" Josh snapped. "Besides, you'd be asking me to put my signature on a lie. I did not sexually harass her."

"Hey man, don't talk to me about lies. Here you are porkin' my wife and lying to yours. Come on now. Get real," Dominic said, still picking at the imaginary lint. "Think a minute and take a look at the other side. We could just as easy go to your bosses. You think they want the stink of a harassment lawsuit? We go to them for the settlement. What would you do if you were them?"

"Fight it. You think they're that stupid? Word gets out that they're a patsy for this kind of payoff and there'll be others standing in line. You can't keep these things hidden. They've got lawyers on the payroll for just such contingencies. It will cost you a fortune to fight them and you might just lose. And no one in the field will touch Angela with a ten-foot pole."

He was beginning to find his courage now. I will not let this happen, he told himself. He'd show this son of a bitch what he was made of. "Listen, you low-life little crud. I don't know how you got Angela to go along with this, but I got a pretty good idea. You might as well get the whole story. You should know that we fucked our brains out, every chance we got, anywhere, like rabbits in heat. Best blowjob ever. Swallows, too. Loves to take it up the ass."

Josh felt a nerve palpitate in his jaw. His breath came in gasps. Was this Josh Rose talking? His mind raced with images of their sexual frenzy. The irony was that he was spouting the truth. He watched Dominic fight to retain his cool, but the sudden flush attested to how deeply Josh's words had struck. He wasn't finished. "Poor deprived Dom. She told me she doesn't play those games with you. Says you pop too soon." He paused and watched him squirm.

Dominic rose like a shot from the couch, the veins in his temples engorged. His eyes seemed to pop out of their sockets. Josh stood his ground. Suddenly one arm stiffened in Josh's direction, forefinger poised like the barrel of a pistol. He waved the finger in Josh's face, bending his arm so that he was eyeball to eyeball. He began to speak and Josh felt a shower of saliva on his face.

"You fuck. I tried to be nice. So here's the deal. I want a certified check for two hundred thousand bucks made out to Angela Bocci, and I want your signature on this piece of paper. He pulled out an envelope from his inside jacket pocket. "Read it. Get your own lawyer if you want to." He took the paper out of the envelope and pushed it in Josh's face. "See that signature on the bottom. Angela Bocci, nota-rized and all legal. You sign it and get it notarized. Hell, they do it at the bank where you're gonna get the bread. Two hundred thousand. Not a penny less. All wrapped nice and legal. We'll even give you a copy for your records. I figure a guy like you could get a check cut…say, by eleven tomorrow. I'm gonna make it easy. I'll stop by to pick up the paper and the dough. You don't even have to see me."

Dominic straightened his blazer, which had ridden up on his shoulders, shot his cuffs, and did a little neck dance as if to ease the tension.

"Don't even think about it. Just do it."

Josh finally found his voice. When he spoke it sounded reedy and uncertain.

"What you're asking is impossible."

"Hell, you're the creative man here. Come up with a way. If you don't have it, borrow it. Call it a bridge loan. Who the fuck cares? We're not playing games here."

"Even if I found a way…" Josh began, then paused to catch his breath. "I couldn't do it that fast." He was about to tell him that his wife handles the finances, but held back.

"Don't be dumb, Rose. Do it. And read the paper. Lets you off the hook, too. It's a settlement, man. Make the deal. We're outta here."

Dominic straightened his blazer, shot his cuffs yet again, offered a version of a military salute as a good-bye gesture, and left the office. Josh stood rooted to the floor, too stunned to move.

His telephone rang. He could not summon the energy to answer it. After a while the ringing stopped, and he could hear his voice mail kick in. He managed to reach the couch and lay down. More calls came in. He didn't answer them. The calls continued. Still he did not answer them. Then, from out of the depths of his consciousness, he began to realize that the amount of calls he was getting seemed inor-dinate. He picked up the phone and tapped into his voice mail. There were more than six urgent messages from Angela. He saw it as a grain of hope and called her home.

"How could you?" he began when he heard her voice. She cut him off.

"Forgive me, Josh. Please forgive me. I had no choice."

She sounded on the verge of hysteria.

"No choice?"

"He knew. The priest told him. You know, hinted. They were buddies. But I didn't think...I swear. Dominic knew about us for weeks. Then last night I went to confession and told him it was all over. After, they made me come to this meeting and then forced me to tell them everything. I can't believe a priest could do this, even if he said it was only a hint to keep my marriage together for the sake of my children. Oh God, I don't want to lose my children."

"Why have you done this to me, Angela? He wants two hundred thousand dollars. And you signed that paper."

"They made me."

"You're trying to destroy my life."

"They made me, Josh. I'm so sorry."

"You're sorry?"

He felt as if he were talking into a tunnel, making sounds that she could not hear.

"Pay him, Josh. Pay him. I beg you."

"I don't understand, Angela," he cried, raising his voice.

"He'll take my children. You don't know him. He will."

Josh was dumbfounded. He searched his mind for some appropriate answer.

"We seem to have competing agendas, Angela," he whispered, hanging up. It seemed a stern and officious statement. He felt trapped, unable to think straight. Again he lay down on his couch. The hours slid by. He felt enervated. There were fewer telephone calls. Still he could not find the energy to answer them.

After agonizing away most of the day, he called the one person in the world that would never be judgmental, the one person who loved him without reservation.

"I'm in trouble, baby," he said.

There was a sudden gasp.

"An accident, Josh? Are the kids okay? Victoria?"

"Nothing like that, Evie. It's me."

"I'm here, darling."

"I need you, Evie."

"Come to supper. I'll make you a wonderful meal."

"Don't bother, Evie. Please."

"For my dearest most wonderful brother, why not?"

Then he called Victoria's cell phone. It didn't answer, which was strange. He called the house and left a message on the answering machine that he was having dinner at his sister's home.

Chapter 5

Mr. Tatum called and informed Victoria that the dispute was over, that the Crespos had surrendered their position. The news should have been received with joy and relief. Instead, she felt uncomfortable, the perpetrator of a deception.

The call roused her to action. She knew what she had to do. Most people would think it foolhardy. And if it resulted in bad consequences for Michael, Josh would be furious. But her instincts told her that Mr. Tatum would welcome honesty and understand her motives. He might be a bit stiff and priggish about some things, but she felt certain that he knew the psychology of students of that age and would be fully aware of the principles she was trying to instill in the rearing of her son.

She called Mr. Tatum's office for an appointment and he had quickly obliged. As she drove, she turned off her cell phone. She did not want to tell Josh what she had in mind or where she was going. She would tell him only after the fact.

When she arrived, Mr. Tatum stood up to greet her, then sat down at his desk. He moved quickly through the small talk of welcome, made his trademark finger cathedral, fixed his eyes on her face, and waited for her explanation.

"I'm sorry to disturb you today, Mr. Tatum, but there is something you must know about the..." She had decided not to mention the Milky Ways. Mention of the objects was too trivializing. Besides, the issue was truth and candor here. The confection itself, in this context, was an absurdity. Instead, she said, "the incident with the Crespos."

"I thought I made that clear. It's a thing of the past." Mr. Tatum smiled. Victoria had the sensation that she was being studied with an intensity she had not sensed before.

"Not to me," Victoria said. "I would like to call Michael in here and let him speak his piece."

"Really, Mrs. Rose, that is not necessary."

"It is to me. And please don't tell him that the matter has been closed."

"Very well," Mr. Tatum said. He pressed a button on the console on his desk and asked that Michael Rose be brought to his office. Then he swiveled back on his chair and continued to study Victoria with penetrating eye contact.

"If it means that much to you, Mrs. Rose, then I certainly would like to oblige," Mr. Tatum said. "We educators must work in tandem with parents. Nothing happens in isolation."

Michael arrived, flushed and nervous. Victoria brushed his hair back and kissed him on the cheek.

"No problem, sweetheart," Victoria said. "I just thought it would clear the air if you told Mr. Tatum what you told Dad and me last night."

"This is your mother's idea, Michael," Mr. Tatum said, offering Michael a benign smile.

Only slightly reassured, Michael recounted the story he had told his parents the night before. Mr. Tatum smiled and nodded through the confession.

"I do appreciate this, Michael. It is, indeed, a sign of courage and good character." He paused for a long time, cutting a glance at Victoria. "Unfortunately, young man, the question remains." Suddenly, Mr. Tatum's expression, which had seemed friendly and benign, turned severe. "You knew, of course, that you were violating the sacred rule of Pendleton, our honor system. Surely, you knew that. Then to compound it with lies."

Michael flushed and looked helplessly toward his mother. It was a tougher reaction than Victoria had expected. She had believed that he would be a willing partner with her in her son's chastisement. After all, the purpose of the exercise was to teach him that lies demanded penalties. She dismissed her anxiety, half expecting him to throw her a wink at any moment.

"That's why he's here, Mr. Tatum. To clear the air. To absolve himself."

"Confession is not absolution in this context, Mrs. Rose," Mr. Tatum said, his expression growing in severity. "You must realize," he said, offering a deep sigh as if his words were too painful to utter, "that this violation of our honor code alone is grounds for summary suspension. We at Pendleton have never tolerated such an infraction. Never. There have been no exceptions. None." He turned toward Michael. "As for your deliberate lies, they go even further to influence the expulsion action that I am compelled to consider."

Victoria felt her innards freeze. She studied Mr. Tatum's face looking for clues to his intention. The very word "expulsion" was a spear point that had found its mark.

Michael's lips quivered and his eyes glazed. Surely this was his way of driving the point home. Victoria's heart went out to her son. It's purely a tactic, she reasoned. Mr. Tatum was wise and experienced. Wasn't he merely carrying out her plan? After all, how could Michael possibly learn that a lie had consequences if severe punishment wasn't, at the very least, considered as a possibility?

"I can assure you, Mr. Tatum, and Michael would agree that this...infraction...the lies as well...will never, ever happen again. Isn't that so, Michael?"

Michael nodded. She noted that his legs seemed to be shaking under his pants.

"Tell Mr. Tatum," she prodded.

"Never, Mr. Tatum. I promise."

"A bit on the late side, young man." He turned to Victoria. "I'm not certain, Mrs. Rose," he said calmly, "that I can bend the rules, even in this case."

"You seem serious," Victoria blurted out, on the point of panic. How could she have so profoundly misread his reaction?

"Dead serious, Mrs. Rose," Mr. Tatum said, his words intoned through his finger cathedral.

"Surely, the fact that he has come forward..." Victoria's voice cracked and she had to clear her throat.

"That does not mitigate the circumstances," Mr. Tatum said gravely. Her heartbeat accelerated. She felt faint. She looked at her son, who stood shaking and ashen-faced in front of Mr. Tatum's desk. "Rules are rules."

"But you said if he did come forward, he would be forgiven," Victoria pleaded.

"Earlier. If I recall, I said earlier."

"My God, what have I done?"

"I'm sorry, Mrs. Rose, I'm going to have to take this matter under advisement."

Was this tough love she had pushed him into? Or a scarring life-time trauma? She could hardly believe Mr. Tatum's threats. In her scenario honesty was to be rewarded with, at the least, understanding and compassion.

"And what of the Crespo girl?" Victoria said lamely. "She tempted him to violate the rules."

"That, Mrs. Rose, is Michael's story."

"Well then, confront her."

"We've already had quite enough confrontations on the matter. I am, after all, responsible for the entire school, not the concerns of one or two students. We have a standard to be maintained."

"Are you serious, Mr. Tatum?"

"Very."

"Could you please dismiss Michael now?" she asked, swallowing hard, sensing the pleading in her voice.

"You may go, Michael," Mr. Tatum said severely.

Michael glanced toward his mother. She saw the look of helplessness in his eyes.

"Don't worry, Michael. It will be all right," she said, kissing her son's cheek. His skin felt hot and she knew he was about to cry. Tears would come, she was certain, as soon as he left the office.

"Well, he certainly should feel chastised now, Mr. Tatum," Victoria said when her son had gone. "I thank you for that, Mr. Tatum." She searched his face, hoping to see the expected smile of complicity. It never came.

"You've put me in a terrible position, Mrs. Rose," Mr. Tatum said. He got up from his chair and planted himself on the front edge of the desk, directly facing Victoria. He crossed his legs. "Expulsion is a real possibility, I'm afraid."

"I don't believe this," Victoria mumbled, completely confused.

"I'm sorry about this, Mrs. Rose. I really am."

"But surely such a confession counts for something. It was my idea. I wanted the lesson to sink in."

"I'm sure it did, Mrs. Rose," Mr. Tatum said. "May I call you Victoria?"

He uncrossed his legs and put his palms on the surface of his desk.

"Of course," Victoria replied, her mind completely dominated by her son's plight.

"You can call me Gordon," Mr. Tatum said.

"You're not serious, then?" Victoria asked hopefully, seizing on this first-name intimacy as another hopeful sign. She noted that he had opened his thighs. The movement seemed inadvertent, and she averted her gaze.

"About what?"

Victoria's eyes drifted around his office.

"Expulsion," she managed to whisper.

"There are good grounds here, Victoria. If I make this exception, the rules would be compromised."

"But this is an eleven-year-old boy. Think of the trauma...."

"Victoria, I deal with children of that age every day of my life. Believe me, I understand. But I must not flinch at making such hard decisions. I have to think first of the impact on the entire student body and the reputation of Pendleton. If that is compromised then all my work is for naught."

"Believe me, Mr. Tat...I mean, Gordon. I do understand that," she pleaded, her confidence badly shaken. "My husband was against this. He was all for not coming forward. He doesn't know I'm here. Please, Gordon, don't let a mother's good intentions go awry. My children are everything to me."

She felt him watching her as she opened her pocketbook and took out a tissue. Rarely had she ever cried. But the present circumstances were devastating. She had put her child in jeopardy. Never had she felt so totally defeated.

"Now, now," Mr. Tatum said, leaning forward and putting both hands on her shoulders, drawing her to him.

"You mustn't do this to Michael," Victoria pleaded, dabbing her eyes.

"I don't want to, Victoria. Believe me."

"Please don't then."

"You make one exception and the door is opened for others."

"I'm pleading for my son, Mr. Tatum."

"Gordon. Call me Gordon."

It was only at that moment that she was aware of what was happening. Her cheek rested against his crotch and she suddenly realized that it was lying against his erection.

"Oh my God," she cried, jumping out of the chair, breaking his grip on her shoulders.

"What is it, Victoria?" Mr. Tatum asked.

"I'm...I'm not sure."

It had to be inadvertent. But she couldn't be certain. Sometimes, she had observed in both her husband and son that erections often occurred involuntarily in men, often at inappropriate moments. It suggested something that she was not willing to comprehend at this moment. But she could not dismiss the possibility.

Her eyes drifted to his crotch, which, through his pants, still showed signs of excitement. He made no move to conceal the view.

"Let it sit overnight, Victoria. I'll make no precipitous moves on expelling Michael. I am willing to keep an open mind, Victoria. Why don't you call me in the morning? Perhaps I'm being too..." He paused. "Unbending. Nothing is cast in stone. I could be persuaded. But I would suggest, however, that the matter be kept strictly between us. There is no need for your husband or the Crespos to know anything about this."

She studied his face and nodded. She could find nothing in his benign expression to indicate any hidden motives. But his sexual exhibit and his admonition to keep the matter confidential were too suggestive to summarily dismiss.

"Believe me, this will not be an easy decision," he continued. "I have to weigh all the pros and cons. I do see your point of view, Victoria. I'm not here to hurt people. Let's both think about this. Perhaps I have been too...too parochial and single-minded." He paused for a long moment, studying her. "But I leave myself open to be persuaded." ·

Open to be persuaded? Should she interpret this as a direct request for a sexual favor? She was not totally naïve, although she had never in her life ever been confronted by such a situation. But considering the stakes, she could not put it out of her mind.

"Until tomorrow then," he said.

She nodded, rising from the chair, discovering that her knees wobbled.

He slipped off the desk and moved toward her. She tightened suddenly, expecting an embrace, but she did not make an effort to move away. He kissed her chastely on the cheek.

"I'll expect your call," he said.

"Tomorrow," she whispered, turning, starting to move toward the door.

"Victoria," he said sweetly.

She turned to face him.

"You're a very attractive woman."

They exchanged glances for a moment. She felt sick with humiliation and despair both for herself and for Michael. What had she done?

Chapter 6

Josh arrived at his sister's apartment, which was filled, as always, with the tantalizing aroma of cooking odors. It was a sharp reminder of their mother, who was forever cooking wonderful dishes for her catering business. He was immediately captured by the power of nostalgia and showed it when he embraced his sister. She returned his embrace with enthusiasm. In her arms, surrounded by her loving warmth, his body was suddenly wracked with sobs.

"What is it, Josh?" Evie asked soothingly. She, too, had a familiar aroma about her as he nestled himself in the ample and warm flesh of her body and held himself there for a considerable length of time. He felt her hands caress his hair as she offered him her sisterly comfort.

"For a moment there I thought I was back home with Mom and Dad," Josh whispered, still holding her, but at arm's length now, looking into her cherubic, dimpled face and the same blue eyes that had miraculously resurfaced in his son.

"Happens to me a lot, Josh. They're never out of my thoughts."

He nodded and brought her closer to him again. Looking up, he saw Tweedledee, the Siamese cat, sitting on an upper shelf of a bookcase watching them with vague interest.

"I'm sorry Evie. Laying this on you."

"For what, sweetheart? You're my dearest little brother."

It was an odd reversal of sorts, since, despite his being four years younger, he had always performed the role of Big Brother.

"Your little brother has a big problem," he managed to say.

"No problem is too big for a solution. And nothing makes me happier than your coming to me for solace."

She had obviously dressed for the occasion, putting on her long black velvet dress adorned with a single strand of pearls, certainly faux since she had sold their mother's jewelry years ago. The dress covered her ample body like a shroud. Yet she looked lovely, like a giant porcelain doll.

"A little drinkee?" she asked. "I made these lovely hors d'oeuvres." She pointed to a familiar table, one of the few remaining furniture antiques on which he could see a *pâté* under a sheen of gelatin. Beside it was bottle of Dry Sack, her favorite sherry. He sat down beside her on the couch as she smeared the *pâté* on a square of pumpernickel.

"You'll love this, Josh," she said. "It's *pâté en gelee.* Mom used to make it." He knew what was coming next. Food. Although his stomach rebelled at the richness of her concoctions, he made no attempt to admonish her. Love, whether it came in the form of food or anything else, was what he needed most at that moment.

"Liver *pâté*, deviled ham and cream cheese, Worcestershire sauce, and, oh yes, a few wee drops of cognac brandy, beef consommé, some of this gorgeous Dry Sack, and cover it all with gelatin. Taste it, darling. It's a gift from heaven."

It was not enough simply to serve the food. She had to embellish it with the ritual of identifying the ingredients, as if it were somehow part of a religious experience. She handed him the square of pumpernickel, heavily smeared with the concoction, and poured him a glass of the Dry Sack. Then she gave herself an equally generous portion and poured herself a drink.

"First taste, darling," she said, delicately biting into the smeared pumpernickel with her usual "ahs" and "ohs" of gustatory joy. He forced himself to take a bite and say "delicious," then took a sip of sherry and settled back on the couch.

By then, Tweedledee, as round and bloated as her mistress, had bounded from the bookcase shelf and jumped into Evie's lap. As if by rote, Evie smeared some *pâté* on a tiny piece of pumpernickel and gave it to the cat, who munched it eagerly, then settled down to nap.

"I can't believe I've done this," he began, taking a deep breath, not quite knowing where to begin. "I'm embarrassed and ashamed, Evie. And you're the only person on earth I have the courage to tell it to."

"Haven't we always been there for each other, Josh?"

"Always."

He told her about his affair with Angela, leaving out the more intimate details, but pointing out that from the beginning the affair was to be risk-free. He described how it had driven him into paroxysms of guilt and anxiety and how he had finally found the courage to break it off. Then he explained how her husband was now approaching him for money.

"It was getting crazy. From the beginning it was supposed to be pure sex. Then I was actually falling for her. It was bizarre. It had nothing to do with my family. I guess I went nuts. Can you imagine the energy it took just to dissimulate? It was like... like..."

"It was only a little interlude of pleasure," Evie said as she dipped into the *pâté* again. "You, Josh?"

"No thanks. You go ahead, Evie."

She spread more of the *pâté* on a piece of pumpernickel and downed it with gusto. Despite his fear that she was eating herself to an early demise, he chose not to lecture her and intrude on her perpetual state of good cheer and sense of well-being.

"You're a beautiful, attractive person, Josh," Evie said when she had eaten the *pâté* and washed it down with sherry. "I'm sure many women have wanted to park their shoes under your bed. When the pleasures of the flesh beckon, it is sometimes hard to turn down."

"Evie, you know I was never the type to sleep around. It just wasn't my thing. And not once since my marriage vows have I ever stepped out of line. Not until this weird episode. My wife and family are everything to me. Everything! This was madness, pure sexual obsession."

"I've been there, Josh," she sighed, leaning over to smear more *pâté* on the pumpernickel.

"The guilt of it gave me great pain. But I'm afraid I am doomed to punishment. You know how her husband found out. Her confessor told him."

"They can't do that," Evie said. "They're not supposed to tell."

"The thing is, her husband knew about it for a while. Angela said all the priest did was hint, but I'm sure the hints were broad. I was being set up. Not by Angela. I can't believe she would have thought of it. But by her husband."

She finished the hors d'oeuvre and licked her chubby fingers. "Are you sure Victoria doesn't know?" she asked.

He shook his head vehemently. "God forbid. That's the end of the world for me. And the kids, if they ever get wind of this..." his voice trailed off.

Evie smiled and shook her head. Her chins quivered.

"Now, now," she said, patting his hand again. "Maybe you should give him the money."

"That's just it. I can't. You know why? Victoria controls the money. I can't ask her."

"Is it a great deal of money?"

"It's two hundred thousand dollars."

"Oh dear God."

Josh recounted how the husband showed up in his office and gave him an ultimatum.

"He wants it by tomorrow."

Evie dipped into the *pâté* again. "You must eat, Josh. It will give you confidence."

"It's not confidence I need. It's money."

It occurred to him suddenly that the day would come when he would have to ask Victoria for help in supporting Evie. He brushed the thought quickly from his mind.

"This will require a bit of thinking, Josh," Evie said. She seemed lost in thought for a moment, then looked around the apartment. Josh followed her eyes.

The apartment was a large rent-controlled place in a building that had seen better days. But it did have a wonderful view of the Hudson. Scattered around the apartment were the odd remnants of their parents' antique collection. There were also many framed pictures of them with their parents before the "accident."

"I've been offered $50,000 for the bed, Josh. I haven't sold it yet. I think I could get more at auction. But you can have that and the rug and the other odds and ends might fetch more."

Through the sudden mist filling his eyes Josh could still see his sister's face. They had stuck together through thick and thin, worried about each other, and he had gladly, eagerly turned over his half of their inheritance to her. Bending over, he kissed her forehead.

"Dear, dear Evie."

"Maybe her husband will be reasonable?"

"No way," Josh said. "He's seen our house. He knows what I make. He wants a certified check and my signature on this ridiculous legal document." He patted his inside jacket pocket, which held the envelope. "I'm not supposed to badmouth Angela, and it says I admit to sexual harassment, a bald-faced lie. The woman seduced me. The fact is, I'd sign it and get it over with if I could come up with the money, which I can't. Hell, Evie, I don't even know where our bank accounts are. In fact, I know zero about our finances." He shook his head. "My fault there as well. I never cared to know."

"Then we'll have to figure out a way. But first dinner."

"I'm really not that hungry, Evie."

"That is the source of your consternation. An appetite for food is an appetite for life."

She gently pushed Tweedledee off her lap and then got up, took his hand, helped lift him from the couch, and led him to the dining room. She had set two places.

"Mom's dishes. And those wonderful Waterford crystal wine glasses," Josh said, observing the care she gave to setting the table.

"Wait'll you taste what I made. And the wine."

She had already opened it, and it stood on a little silver tray. He noted it was a La Tache, and it crossed his mind that she had preserved it from their father's extensive wine collection. On closer inspection, he realized that it was a '91 vintage, which put it more than a dozen years after they had died. He figured the wine cost nearly three hundred dollars, but he refused to rebuke her for her extravagance.

"Dad had '66," Evie said, seeing him inspect the label. "He had such wonderful taste." She shook her head sadly. "God, I miss him."

"So do I," he said. "Very much."

When he was seated, she went into the kitchen, which wasn't far from the small dining room.

"You just sit there, brother mine. What I have for you will make everything all right."

He studied the table settings, remembering the dishes, glasses, and napkins that their mother had loved. For some reason, they had not been caught in the crossfire of their war. Looking at them, touching them, he tried yet again to fathom what had happened between his mother and his father to create such animosity and hatred between them. Through it all they had been exceedingly loving parents. It would forever be the great riddle of their lives.

"Ta da," Evie chirped, bringing in a tureen, also recognizable from their mother's collection. She ladled out the soup into his bowl and her own. He watched how she dipped her nose close to the soup and waved her hands in an upward motion to get the full aroma.

"It's butternut squash soup, darling. Squash, of course. Lots of heavy cream, onions, cloves, parsley, and a dash of curry. It's a miracle soup, really. Come on, now. Do your duty. It will make you courageous."

They ate their soup in silence. Josh tried his best but left more than half in the soup plate while Evie polished off her own as well as what was left in the tureen.

After she had finished her soup, Evie said, "Just suppose you fessed up. Is Victoria willing to destroy the family simply because you were briefly unfaithful? Surely she would not take such drastic action? I've found that the honest truth is always the best policy."

"I couldn't agree more. That was always the basis of our relationship. That's why I feel so awful about this. I betrayed our principles. I lied. I cheated. I betrayed her. Now it's come home to roost."

"Sometimes things are irresistible, Josh. No matter how hard you try to resist. People who love you have to make allowances."

"I'm afraid Victoria has become a bit of a purist." He was tempted to tell her about the incident with Michael, but held off.

Evie got up from the table and collected the soup plates and the tureen and went back into the kitchen.

"Ta da," Evie cried again, bringing in a serving plate, then going back to the kitchen and returning with another. Then she sat down and poured the wine, pointing out the dishes she had prepared.

"That's sweet potato casserole. It has pecans in it and butter and cream, of course, and an egg and just an inchy binchy pinch of mace." She smiled and turned her attention to another dish. "English Pot Pie," she said. "It's got everything. Veal kidneys, butter, brandy, paprika, Worcestershire, Tabasco, fresh tarragon. I mean *everything*. And look how pretty it looks." She winked at him. "And don't forget to leave room for the coconut cake and my special chocolate dish. Now just dig in."

"Evie, you really shouldn't have gone to all this trouble."

"Trouble? Josh, the preparation of this food is my expression of the truest love I have for my brother. You must understand that there are consequences to thinness. Deprivation makes people..." She searched for the right word. "Arid."

He forced himself to eat and show passion for her food. In a strange way, he felt his morbidity disappear. It was soothing, too, to know that Evie was happy to have him there. He was surrounded by love and felt its power.

"You really think I should tell her?" Josh said. "Confess all?"

"When you tell people they've done the wrong thing, they often will look inside themselves and see that they, too, might, given the right circumstances, do the very same thing."

"Victoria wouldn't see it that way. For her, it would be the death knell of our marriage."

"What about the children?"

He shrugged and thought about it for a moment.

"Yes, the children," he sighed. "We've been there, Evie. We had no choice in the matter."

"What could we have done?"

They grew silent. He watched the moisture gather in his sister's eyes. It was the only subject that could ever move her to tears.

Recovering, she rose from the table and came back with a coconut cake and two long glasses filled with a dark brown substance that she identified as Chocolate Chantilly. She placed the cake plate and the glasses of chocolate on the table and proceeded through her litany about ingredients. He watched her cut the cake and move one of the Chocolate Chantilly glasses in front of him.

He dipped his spoon into the chocolate and let a gob of it melt in his mouth. It permeated through his taste buds and, despite his attitude toward food, it did give him a momentary lift.

Somehow, Tweedledee had materialized on Evie's lap. Evie ate her Chocolate Chantilly and then went to work on the Coconut Cake, sharing it with Tweedledee. Josh forced himself to finish the piece that she had cut for him.

"It was wonderful, Evie. Wonderful. Just being with you has been of great help."

They moved back to the living room and again sat on the couch. He had offered to help with the dishes, but she would have none of it.

"I have found," Evie said, her chubby hands clasped about her expansive middle as if still in thrall to the food that she had ingested, "that good people sometimes do bad things." She paused for a long moment, holding back tears.

"Like Mom and Dad," he sighed. "And now me."

They exchanged glances and she took a few deep breaths and brushed aside an errant tear with the back of one hand.

"But you're still here, Josh."

He reached out, took her hand, and kissed it.

"Dear sweet Evie," he whispered.

"And Josh. You both must not do anything that will hurt your children. We both know too much about that, don't we?"

"It may be too late," he sighed.

"Far from it," she insisted.

He was silent for a long time. Evie always saw the glass as half full.

"Thank you, Evie," he said. "For being my sister."

Later, as he drove home, mulling over various ideas for tomorrow's confrontation, he felt suddenly nauseous. He stopped the car and stepped outside to vomit. With the undigested food gone, his pessimism returned in force.

Chapter 7

Victoria called Gordon Tatum as soon as the house was empty. She hoped that he would not notice the tremor in her voice.

"Victoria," Tatum said pleasantly at the other end of the phone. "This is a surprise." Smooth as silk, with apparent utter disregard for the agony she was going through.

"Surprise? But Gordon…" How she hated to speak his first name. "You said I should call you tomorrow, meaning today, and here I am."

"I'm delighted," Gordon said.

She worked her way through a long pause in the conversation. Delighted? He's torturing me. She forced herself to get on with it.

"Have you thought about the matter we discussed yesterday?"

"A great deal, Victoria."

Again there was another long pause, this time at his end of the line.

"Did you make any decisions?" Victoria blurted.

It was, she knew, a statement of desperation. If he had made a positive decision regarding Michael, it would have foreclosed on her plan. She had not, of course, put much stock in such a miracle happening.

"I really feel we must discuss this further." There was a long pause. "Face to face."

"I was hoping you would have, you know, reconsidered…." She felt tongue-tied for a moment.

"I'm mulling it…Victoria. And I am looking forward to our further discussion."

"Yes, of course," Victoria said, forcing a sense of pleasant expectation. She tried to put a smile in her voice.

"I have an idea, Victoria. This is very fortuitous. I have some errands to do that will take me in your direction. We can talk in the car. I have to sign some papers in our lawyer's office in Tarrytown. Should last no more than fifteen minutes. And I can have you back in a couple of hours. Why not meet me at the north end of the Country Mall parking area? Say about ten? Does that suit you?"

"If it will help, Gordon. Of course, I'll be there."

"Wonderful, Victoria. I'm really looking forward to our discussion."

"So am I," Victoria said. She slammed down the phone. "Bastard," she cried aloud, hearing the echo ramble through the empty house.

Yesterday had been a nightmare for Victoria. Michael came home from school pale and depressed, his eyes swollen with crying, which greatly upset Emily. She was also involved in her own major crisis. She had been picked for the chorus for the annual Easter musical play, which might not have been a problem, except that her friend Annie was picked for a starring role. Both children needed big-time soothing, and she had saved Michael for last.

She had picked up Josh's message about having dinner at Evie's house, which stirred up some glowing embers. Evie, in Victoria's mind, was a train wreck waiting to happen and Josh could refuse her nothing. She was a stone around his neck. Nevertheless, Victoria was loath to interfere. The bond between them was too strong. At the very least, she had managed to diminish Evie's influence on the children. For that she was thankful. But anything that went on between Evie and Josh was worrisome.

Despite her attempt at tolerance and understanding, learning about this dinner through the answering machine irritated her. Then she remembered she had cut off her cell phone, which mollified her somewhat. In the end, she was thankful that he had not come home to dinner. She would have been hard-pressed to keep her silence about her own stupid decision and how it had backfired. Josh would have been justly appalled at Tatum's incredible proposition and her equally incredible reaction to it.

She looked at her sniffling daughter. "Emily, you can't think you've failed because one of your friends succeeded. Besides, she's your best friend. You should take joy in her success."

"I'm as good as she is," Emily whined.

"What would she have felt if you were picked?"

"She'd be jealous."

"Like you are."

"I'm not jealous. I'm mad."

"Because you're jealous."

"Mommy, you just don't understand."

"Yes, I do."

"No, you don't."

It had reached an impasse. Nevertheless, Victoria embraced her daughter and sent her off to her room to do her homework. Then, with trepidation, she entered Michael's room. He was lying on his bed, staring at the ceiling with swollen eyes.

"I'm sorry, Michael. I didn't think it would go that way."

"He's going to expel me. I know he will. Why should I get the blame? Madeline also broke the rules."

She sat on the edge of the bed and put her hand on her son's chest. "There's no sense in discussing the merits of the case. Whatever happens, you did the right thing. You came forward. That took great courage. I'm very proud of you."

"Mr. Tatum wasn't," he murmured.

"It will be all right. I promise you."

"No it won't. Mr. Tatum is very strict. He'll expel me. I know he will."

She brushed the hair off his forehead and searched her mind for some comforting comment. "Telling the truth never hurt anybody."

"Well, it hurt me," Michael said.

"No it did not. Trust me, Michael. I love you with all my heart and soul. I will not let Mr. Tatum expel you. No way."

"How can you stop him?"

"That's my job, Michael."

He turned his gaze away from her. She knew her credibility with him was at stake, and she was determined to protect that aspect of her parenting with everything she had.

"Just don't do anything that will make the kids laugh at me."

"Trust Mom, darling. I promise."

Michael shrugged. She watched him for a long time. Tears seeped out of the corners of his eyes. She was certain that her pain was as palpable and intense as his. She also knew that she had crossed a Rubicon. Making good on her promise was now etched in stone.

"I have one small favor to ask, Michael. Would you grant me that?" She took his hand, kissed his fingers, and looked into his eyes.

"What is it?"

She felt she was standing in quicksand and it was pulling her further into a morass.

"Just don't tell Daddy. Okay? I don't mean a forever thing. I mean just until this blows over."

It was, she knew, a violation of the family ethical code. Here she was nibbling away at her vaunted morality. Silence, she once had preached, was also a lie.

"If I get expelled it won't be a secret," he reasoned, accurately.

"You won't. As soon as we're out of the woods, you can tell Daddy all you want. He has the right to know. But not yet. Okay?"

He nodded and she held him in her arms and kissed him.

"God, I love you, Michael," she said. "Nothing bad is going to happen to my little boy."

She was doubly thankful that Josh was not around. It would have been an awful complication. She got into bed early, hoping she could sleep. After a long bout of restlessness in which her mind worked overtime, she drifted off into a dead slumber.

The next thing she knew, Josh was shaking her awake.

"I'd like to talk, Victoria. It's important."

His voice seemed to come from far away.

"I'm sleeping."

"It's important," he persisted.

"Please, Josh. Leave me alone. I need my rest. I have an important day tomorrow."

She was immediately sorry she had anointed the day with such importance. Thankfully, he did not ask for an explanation.

"I need to know about our finances, Victoria."

The idea barely penetrated.

"Not now, Josh. Not now."

"It's important."

"We'll discuss it in the morning."

"It occurred to me suddenly. If something ever happened to you, I'd have to take over. I need to know, Victoria."

"Is that what you discussed with Evie? Nothing good every comes of your time with her."

"We both know she's hopeless with money, but it got me to thinking. I don't know a damned thing about our finances."

"That was your choice."

"I'm thinking of the kids. I was wrong."

"Tonight?"

Her thoughts had returned to Tatum, the dilemma it posed, and how she had to cope with it.

"My thoughts are elsewhere, Josh. Let me sleep."

"Okay then, but tomorrow…"

"Of course, tomorrow."

She suffered silently through the night, her mind churning madly, far from their financial matters. She forced herself to confront the outer limits of her own vulnerability. She had actually gone biblical in her search for the right path to take, citing God's injunction for Abraham to sacrifice his own beloved son Isaac. If Abraham had been a mother, she had reasoned, God would have had one bitch of a crisis on his hands. Not even God could induce a mother to sacrifice her son. She would have figured a way to save him, as Victoria was doing at that moment. She was, after all, keeping her thoughts in context, dealing with the devil himself.

Finally, she slipped back into torpor. If Josh spoke again, she didn't hear it.

In the morning as she prepared breakfast, she noted that everyone looked pale and wan. Questions were answered with grunts.

"Remember what we talked about last night. Our financial situation."

"I remember."

"I want to have more responsibility about our finances, Victoria. Is that too much to ask?"

"Too much, Josh? I welcome it. You should care about such things."

"Well then, I need to know where everything is."

"For years I begged you to participate. Now you want to know immediately."

Sour faced and grumpy, the children kissed their parents and went off to catch their respective school buses.

"They both look angry," Josh remarked.

"Probably stayed up too late waiting for Daddy to come home."

"What's that supposed to mean?"

"You could have told me earlier about having dinner with your sister."

Above all, she needed some deflection, choosing the old standby, her annoyance with Evie and her relationship with her brother.

"Not that again, Victoria. She needed to talk and I had to be there."

The deflection worked. The subject of Evie had a Pavlov's dog effect. Josh always reacted to it in the same way.

"Down to the last antique, is she? You want to know how to handle money and what did you do? Throw away your inheritance on a glutton."

Why am I doing this, Victoria asked herself, knowing her answer: to keep my mind off what I have to do.

"No. No more," she said. "I apologize, Josh. I'm very edgy this morning. Forgive me."

"Could we go over it now?" Josh asked. "The finances."

"Now? This minute?"

"I want to know."

She noted that his look was determined.

"It's all in the computer," she said. "All our investments down to the last penny."

"Well then, show me."

"Not now, Josh, please. I have things to do."

"When then?"

"Tonight. How about that? I promise. Actually, I'm really happy you want to get involved. You're right. Something could happen to me. Then where will you and the children be?"

"Exactly."

"Tonight, okay?"

She kissed him on the lips and headed up the stairs. Finances were the farthest thing from her mind. She had to get dressed for the day's main event. Even the details of dress had been carefully worked out. Tatum was, after all, an older man, nearly twenty years her senior. His looks, which were distinguished, even handsome, were hardly a saving grace. She was dealing with a version of the devil and her stomach was in knots.

After showering carefully, she put on a plaid pleated skirt, high socks, loafers, a cashmere sweater, a discreet necklace, and not too much make up. She then dabbed herself with her best perfume. Her outfit was a far cry from her workaday clothes.

"You look like a kid," Josh would say on the occasions when she wore the outfit she had chosen. "Turns me on."

"It's only an illusion," she would respond. "Probably feeds your Lolita fantasy."

"Are you wearing little white panties?"

"See for yourself."

She drove to the specified parking lot, parked at the north end at five minutes to ten, and waited nervously in the car for Gordon Tatum to arrive. The north end of the lot, as she suspected, was deserted. It was meant to take the parking overload on busy days. The choice of place suggested that Tatum had either done his research well or used this area as a meeting place before. She did not delude herself into believing that she was Tatum's first victim.

Despite her nervousness, she did feel an odd thrill of sinful conspiracy. This was a totally unique experience, completely against the grain of everything she believed in. She had even worked out a mental state that might carry her through the process with the least amount of pain and humiliation. Relying on cunning and singleness of purpose, she was determined to steel herself against any outrage and indignity and transform herself into a mere spectator hanging in space, observing, listening. She saw herself now as the lioness who would fight to the death to protect her cub.

His black Cadillac suddenly pulled up beside hers. He waved and smiled, and she stepped out of her car and entered his on the passenger side. She could feel his eyes studying her as she got in.

"You look like a pretty Scottish lass," he said as he maneuvered the car through the town streets, then headed into the open road. She sat beside him demurely, legs together, hands clasped on her lap, her pocketbook on the floor between them.

"Soon the buds will be bursting, Victoria. Don't you just love spring in the country? Stirs the heart, doesn't it?"

He was, she noted, remarkably dignified and self-possessed, considering what she believed he had in mind. For a fleeting moment she wondered if she had misinterpreted his action.

"Yes it does," she replied, feigning interest. He was obviously a man used to an audience. When he spoke, he turned to face her, offering his benign smile and pleasant façade.

He chattered on about spring as the Cadillac moved through secondary roads and country lanes. As they drove deeper into the wooded areas, he would occasionally touch her arm. Then with one free hand, he reached for hers. She had wondered how he would handle his opening gambit and here was her confirmation. His touch made her skin crawl.

"The forsythia is always the first to bloom," he said, stopping the car in a clearing beyond which was a meadow. Forsythia plants framed the periphery of the meadow. "Aren't they gorgeous?" She wondered how many times he had been here with others.

"Yes, they are." No longer needing one of his hands for driving, he began to play with her hair. She offered no resistance. "Exactly where are we, Mr. Tatum?"

At some point, she knew instinctively that subtlety would fade and he would have to become aggressive and blatant. She waited, expectant and prepared.

"Mr. Tatum? Really, Victoria, I was hoping we had reached a higher level of intimacy."

"Gordon," she said, pretending to observe the scenery. "I don't believe I've ever been here before."

"One of my favorite spots, Victoria. Quite conducive, don't you think?"

"Conducive?"

"To romance, Victoria."

"Oh, that."

He chuckled and turned to face her, smiling broadly, his expression that of a kindly father figure. He still held her hand while the other caressed her cheek. She forced herself to meet his gaze.

"Seems an odd place to conduct school business."

His hand moved from her cheek to her chin, which he lifted gently.

"Unique, yes. Odd, no. We can get to know each other better in this environment. It's spring and you know what happens to a young man's fancy in that season."

"Tell me," she said.

"It also happens to mature men," he whispered.

She remained silent. She felt herself beginning to perspire.

"I love that outfit, Victoria. I am, after all, only human. It makes me forget propriety."

The hand that was caressing her chin now moved to her neck. Her body stiffened but she made no move to reject his advance. Suddenly her mother's mantra echoed in her mind. Men cannot be trusted. They are liars and cheats. Here was proof positive.

"We're here to discuss Michael's future," she said cautiously. "You said you were going to take under advisement the issue of his expulsion."

"Exactly," he said, turning his body. He began to caress her knee. The other hand finally reached her breast. A finger began to play with her nipple. Despite her disgust, she felt it harden. "You are a very exciting woman, Victoria." He reached under her skirt and began stroking her thigh.

"Have you reached your decision?" she asked suddenly, trying to ignore his touching, enduring her repulsion. She willed her body into the space above them. By now his hands were moving franticly up her thigh.

"Not quite, Victoria. Not quite."

"What will it take, Gordon?"

"A wee bit of cooperation, Victoria."

"You mean...this?" she asked, hoping she would sound slightly coquettish.

His hands were working feverishly now.

"I need to know your decision, Gordon. It's very important to me."

"I think we are heading for an understanding, Victoria," he said, his breath coming on the heels of little gasps of quickening excitement. Nor did she resist when his hand began caressing her crotch.

"You will not expel him then?"

"I'm leaning in that direction, Victoria."

He unzipped his pants and exposed himself. Her heart pounded. She tamped down a sudden wave of nausea. But she did have the presence of mind to open her pocketbook. She extracted some tissues and left it open.

"Kiss my cock, Victoria."

She hadn't expected the blatancy to come so soon and it took her by surprise. Her mental preparation had been severely inadequate. She could not bear to look at his erection. For a moment, she held back.

"Please, Victoria, suck my cock."

She forced herself to ignore her profound sense of personal humiliation and shame. I am not me, she told herself. I am invisible. She pressed her lips against his flesh. Pig, she thought, forcing herself to speak.

"I want more than an understanding, Gordon. I want your word that Michael will not be expelled."

"You have my word, Victoria."

"That he will not be expelled. Say it Gordon."

"He will not be expelled," he muttered. "Now get on with it, please. Blow me baby." Stay focused, Victoria, she begged herself. Then she stopped abruptly and lifted her head.

"Don't stop please?"

"Say it again Gordon. No expulsion for Michael."

"No expulsion for Michael. I told you. For crying out loud ,Victoria. Suck my cock."

She forced herself to concentrate on the mechanics of the deed. Tears filled her eyes. Get it over with, she shouted inside herself. It was the reason for her selfless sacrifice on the altar of his perfidy. She saw herself now as the woman before King Solomon, ready to deny her maternity to save the life of her baby. At that moment, over the void of five thousand years of history, she knew exactly what the woman must have felt. No sacrifice was too much to spare her child.

"Jesus Victoria. I love it."

He began to groan.

"I'm coming," he cried. "Swallow. Swallow."

She wanted to vomit, faking it now, using the tissue. He put his head against the backrest and smiled.

"God that was great Victoria."

She turned away, wiping her tears, breathing deeply to chase her nausea. She remained silent for a long moment as he straightened his clothing.

"That was something," he murmured. He leaned over and kissed her on the cheek. The touch of his lips froze her flesh. "We have got to do this again."

"You mean on a regular basis?"

"More or less," he chuckled.

"I just want to know what the deal is," she pressed, her legal training kicking in.

"A nice blow job once a week, say. Is that too much to ask?"

"And my boy is never to be harassed again?"

"Didn't I give you my word?" he said, transforming himself again to his role of the dignified head master. Then without another word, he started the car and headed back to the parking lot.

There was no more talk of the wonders of spring. She had the impression that he was no longer aware of her presence. What she needed now was to muster her courage, prepare herself for the denouement.

"Have you any idea of what risks you've taken?" she asked him as they pulled into the parking lot. "You've extracted a sexual favor from me by threatening my son's future."

"Now that is a bit dramatic, Victoria. We had consensual sex. Big deal. We're both married."

"You're not afraid of lawsuits? I'm a lawyer, remember. And what about the press?"

"Why would you do that, Victoria?" He had tensed suddenly and his voice rose. "Why would you want to jeopardize the school, your son's gateway to success? You're not a fool, Victoria. What's the bottom line here? Your child's education. His future. Sure, I've put myself at risk. The fact is that I do trust your good judgment. I know people, Victoria. Where is the harm here? I've just done you an enormous service." He smiled thinly. "I've bent the rules in favor of your child. I rarely have done that. I did it for you, Victoria. And I don't make a habit of this."

"You mean I'm a special case."

"That's exactly what I mean. I'm very attracted to you. You should be flattered."

"God summons," she snickered. "And I obey."

"You called me. You met me. You came for a ride with me. Really, Victoria. No one is the wiser. No one is hurt." He shook his head. "Michael lied. In our school culture that is a capital offense. There are hundreds of parents who would do a lot more to get their kids into Pendleton. Come now. No conscience, please. Consider yourself lucky that I've agreed to keep Michael."

"I do," she murmured. "I do."

"You see," he said, laughing. "Victoria, as we agreed, let's say this time next week." He bent over and kissed her again on the cheek. "Please, no more nonsense." She marveled at his cool self-confidence.

She got out of the car and fished in her pocketbook. Then she moved to the driver's side and asked that he lower the window. At that point she removed the small recorder she had placed inside, fiddled with it, praying that its technology had not let her down. Earlier, she had tested and retested the device.

"What's that?" he asked, confused. Then it hit him. "You didn't."

She pressed the play button, relieved to find that it had done its job. She flipped the volume switch to its loudest point. It wasn't exactly a boom box, but it was loud enough for him to hear the message. He turned ashen. When it came to the part she wanted most, she brought it close to his ear.

"Suck my cock, Victoria," his voice barked over the silence of the parking lot. She let it run for a moment more, then clicked it off and put it back in her pocketbook.

"Harass my child, ever, and you're a dead man, Tatum. And don't worry. This isn't a crusade and I'm not a reformer. Play your little sex

games all you want. I've already done my share. Frankly, it was revolting. But don't, under any circumstances, ever threaten my son with
expulsion or fail to give him the recommendations that he deserves.
Get my drift?"

"Rotten bitch," he muttered through trembling lips. His face had
gone ashen.

"And here's something to comfort you on the way home." She
threw a Milky Way through the window. It landed on his lap.

He opened his mouth, but could not speak. Then he gunned the
motor and, wheels squealing, sped away.

Back in her own car, she slumped over the wheel. She felt drained.
Worse, it was something she would have to live with all by herself.
Neither Josh nor Michael must ever know.

She admitted to herself that her focus was narrow in this case. She
had told Tatum the truth. She was not a crusader. Her only cause was
her children, their future. Weighed against that, who cared about his
sick peccadilloes? What she had done was to checkmate his power
over her and her child. Despite her revulsion and shame, she could
take comfort in the outcome.

Chapter 8

This time Josh had prepared himself for the confrontation with Dominic Bocci. His mind was clearer and he had developed some semblance of a plan.

By then, he had assessed his situation. He was ready to pay for his mistakes and willing to capitulate. Although he had disdained any knowledge of their personal finances, his experience with his parents' estate had given him some minor understanding of the basics of finance. He was certain that he had good credit and, once he knew where his assets were, he would find a way to borrow his way out of this situation. Of course, it was, as yet, a vague plan.

From his perspective, the only major fallout would be Victoria finding out. From panic had come realism.

Dominic Bocci came into his office seething with anger. Josh had been prepared for that. He was wearing the same outfit he had worn the day before, but anger had erased all pretension to charm.

"You're lookin' for trouble, man," Dominic said. "Here I thought we had a deal."

"We do."

"So where's the bread?"

"I've committed myself to your plan, Dom," Josh said. "So cool down. It's not as easy as you originally contemplated."

"I just want the bread and the signed paper. Don't tell me no sad stories."

"Let me explain."

"The hell with this, man," Dominic said, moving toward the door.

"I'm going to the company."

"Your prerogative. But first hear me out. Sit down. Please."

Dominic hesitated and shook his head. Begrudgingly, he seated himself in the same spot he had taken the day before. Josh sat facing him.

"I'm listening. It better be good."

Josh felt stronger than he had felt yesterday.

"No confrontations, Dom. I'm not negotiating. I'm fully prepared to meet your demands. This has nothing to do with morals or ethics or whatever. It's strictly business. All this has to do with is access."

"What the fuck are you talking about?"

"I don't handle the family exchequer."

"Shit, man. Talk American."

"My wife handles the money, Dom. Sorry, but all I know is how to work the ATM machine."

"What kind of crap are you handing me, Rose?"

"It's the truth, Dom."

He watched the blood drain from Dominic Bocci's face.

"But everything will be okay. Tonight I'll know exactly where everything is. With a little luck we can conclude this deal tomorrow."

"You gotta guarantee on that?"

"Once I know what's what, I'm sure I can get you the money without any problem."

"By tomorrow?"

"Hopefully."

"What's this hopefully shit?"

"Look Dom. I'm not going anywhere, and I'm not foreclosing on any of your options. Considering my situation, your time frame was unrealistic." He cleared his throat. For some reason, the insecurity that he had felt yesterday had returned.

"I don't like this," Dominic mused. He offered Josh a hard-eyed glance.

"Dom. I know the stakes here. I just need time."

"I ain't got time."

"What difference would a day or so make? I've agreed. Raising cash takes time. I have to borrow and I don't want my wife to know."

He felt Dominic's eyes studying him.

"You better not be playing games."

"My God, Dominic," Josh said. "You're playing with my life. And you know exactly what I have to lose."

He was immediately sorry for the outburst. He was showing weakness, an exploitable emotion.

"What happens if I come here tomorrow and get this same song and dance?" Dominic asked. His threatening demeanor retreated, but Josh could see he was cooking up some plan.

"It won't happen," Josh said, trying to maintain a stance of total confidence.

"You say your wife handles the dough?"

He seemed to grow thoughtful.

"I've already told you that, Dominic."

"Doesn't sound very smart. Never let them handle the money."

"In our case, it works. My wife has an extensive accounting background. I'm practically an illiterate when it comes to finance. Victoria, I'm sure, has invested very wisely."

"But you don't know where the dough is?"

"No, I don't."

Dominic was silent for a long moment. Finally, he spoke.

"So you could be worth a lot more than you think you are?"

Once again, Josh felt blindsided.

"I doubt it."

"But it's possible?"

"Anything's possible."

Dominic nodded as if he was satisfied with the response. Josh could see he was still pondering the situation.

"Tell you what," Dominic said, allowing a long pause of silence to ensue. Josh waited expectantly. He hated the idea of being at this man's mercy. "Double the deal."

"What are you saying?" Josh asked. He was sure that something had been lost in translation. He noted that Dominic's face was suddenly free of tension.

"I'm saying four hundred thousand," Dominic said. "No big deal. We change one number is all."

"Now you're pushing the envelope," Josh muttered.

"Right. Good way to put it, Josh man. I was fishing around for a way to make up for my disappointment of today. Four hundred thou…" He shook his head and chuckled.

"Don't be ridiculous," Josh sneered.

"You said it's possible."

"I said anything's possible."

"I'll buy that."

"Two hundred thousand and not a penny more. What do you take me for? You'll never be satisfied with any sum you get, paper or no paper. You're a goddamn cheap little blackmailer." He knew he was throwing caution to the winds, but he couldn't help himself. "And don't be so sure you'll be able to get custody of your kids." Again he had blurted out something he regretted.

"So you and she had a nice little chat?"

"Yes we did," Josh said retreating slightly.

"And what did the little bitch have to say?"

"She wants me to pay up and sign the paper."

"Good advice."

"She's scared shitless," Josh said. "Who could blame her?"

Josh could tell from the way the man's eyes glared that he was on the verge of explosion. Dominic stood up. Unlike yesterday, he reared himself back and came at Josh with a hard one-two combination to the body that knocked the wind out of him and brought him to his knees. Holding his stomach, Josh retched with the dry heaves.

"I'm raising the ante another hundred thou, man. Half a mil. And I don't give a shit how it comes."

As if to emphasize the point, he lifted his foot and pressed Josh in the butt. He collapsed supine on the floor.

"Two hundred thou. No more," Josh managed to say.

"Fuck you."

Josh heard Dominic leave the office and the door slam behind him. He lay on the floor for a long time trying to contemplate his options. He had miscalculated everything. The fact was that he had proven himself incompetent.

Left in limbo, he wasn't sure how to proceed. He had to assume that the man would be back at him tomorrow, but there was no way he was going to give him a half a million dollars, even if he had access to that amount. If Victoria found out, how could he possibly explain it?

In the end, he decided to stick with his original plan. He would find out tonight where their principal accounts were and take it from there.

Chapter 9

Victoria rushed to the bathroom and brushed her teeth and used a whole bottle of mouthwash to get the taste of Tatum out of her mouth. Then she showered for a long time, soaping herself furiously. While she was in the shower the phone rang, but she ignored it. The voice mail would pick up the call. Finally, she felt totally cleansed and uncommonly exhilarated. Now, she vowed, she must find a way to tuck this episode into the dark recesses of memory.

She went into the garage and got into the car. It was then that she remembered she still had the tape in her pocketbook. At first, she thought she might put it in the strong box at the bank where she kept their birth certificates, insurance policies, and other important documents. Although she had the only key, she felt it was the wrong place both on moral grounds and the fact that if she died suddenly, a thought planted in her mind last night, Josh would have access to the box.

She got out of the car and roamed through the house looking for a suitable place where Josh or the children were not likely to discover it. There was a box on the top shelf of her closet where she kept old letters and mementos of her girlhood. It seemed a like a safe place and she dropped the tape there.

Thankfully, she had a great many Mommy chores to do that day. Before leaving the house, she checked the answering machine to see who had called while she was in the shower. It was Josh. He sounded harried.

"Tried your cell. No answer. We've got a great communication system going. I just wanted you to know I'll be holding you to your

promise on the financing issue. Tonight for sure. I'll be home for dinner. Oh yes. I love you more than I can find words."

Her eyes misted at the message. She was delighted by the idea.
Especially that last part. It offered just the right soothing touch to the
psychic bruises she had sustained earlier.

On the matter of the finances, she was amused by his concern.
Why now? Perhaps Evie's plight frightened him. She was delighted by
his interest. For years, she had tried to persuade him to take a more
active role in their finances. He was, at that moment, the sole family
breadwinner, although she had added to the family coffers through
her skilled financial management. She would never give up her role
in the process. She was the one with the expertise. Of course she
would keep her promise to him, eagerly.

By such a gesture, perhaps, she might dismiss any residual guilt for
her action. Under no circumstances could it be defined as infidelity.
In fact, by most legal and moral definitions, it was the equivalent of
rape. Yes, she assured herself, she had been raped.

The strange events of the day had made her slightly manic. She felt
an uncommon high as she continued to rationalize what she had
done. It was not easily exorcised from her thoughts. She had endured
humiliation, but she had prevented a monster from harming her
child.

Despite her initial sense of disgust and degradation, she felt, in the
end, that she had won a great victory. It was worthy of celebration,
and she was determined to mark the event with a commemorative
feast.

After driving Emily and her friends to their ballet class, she
stopped at a florist and bought flowers for a centerpiece. Then she
went to a liquor store and bought two bottles of Dom Perignon.
What was a celebration without vintage champagne? After that, she
went off to the supermarket to get the ingredients for a spectacular
family dinner.

She would roast a turkey and cook a wonderful array of vegetables.
Brussels sprouts, carrots, peas. For starters she would make a Waldorf

salad and end with a bouquet of fresh fruits and a scoop of fat-free ice cream. A healthy feast for her beloved family.

A brief image of Evie intruded suddenly, but without malice. Poor Evie. She was to be pitied. Josh's worries about her future were certainly understandable. But the sad fact was that poor Evie probably hadn't much of a future. If only she didn't proselytize her half-baked theories about the psychic power of food. Nevertheless, Victoria's antagonism of yesterday had faded. Josh should be a loving sibling. She would want nothing less for her own children.

She couldn't wait to explain their finances to Josh. She hoped he would be surprised by their good fortune. By any measure, they were rich. They were millionaires, three times over, which put them in the .0005 percentile of Americans in terms of net worth. All in all, their lives were blessed with wonderful things. Josh had a satisfying and lucrative job. They lived in a great house in a lovely area. They had their health. Their children were lovely and smart. They all loved each other.

Yet, this exercise of counting blessings always required acknowledging that they had been lucky to escape the consequences of their past and had by courage, discipline, and self-awareness risen above their early traumas, she as a child of divorce, he as a premature orphan. She felt a great deal of pride in that achievement. They were, after all, a statistical miracle.

After preparing the turkey and putting it in the oven to roast, she went to her computer and called up their finances. As she looked over the various listings of their assets, the front door buzzer sounded. She moved to the hallway. Feeling secure and content, she opened to the door.

Before her stood a pleasant-looking man with dark curly hair, immaculately dressed in a blue blazer and gray flannel slacks.

"Mrs. Rose," the man said. "My name is Dominic Bocci. My wife Angela has worked for your husband. May I come in?"

Chapter 10

After a long drive in which his mind raced with a plethora of conflicting scenarios, Josh entered his home and was greeted by delicious cooking smells. Michael ran to greet him.

"Hey, Dad," Michael said, embracing his father.

"Quite a greeting, son," Josh said. His son's greeting seemed to chase the blues.

He went into the kitchen where Victoria was basting the turkey and Emily was mashing the sweet potatoes. Seeing him, Emily came over and hugged him.

"To what do I owe this honor?" Josh asked.

"Because you're my daddy, that's why."

Victoria looked up from her work and offered a smile.

"What's the occasion?" Josh asked.

"Family party," Victoria said.

"Smells okay to me."

In the background, he could hear the mellow strains of Mahler coming over the stereo.

He went upstairs, changed to jeans and a sport shirt, and came downstairs. The horrors of the day seemed dispelled and all his optimism came rushing back. He had his family. What else mattered? He would solve the problem with Dominic Bocci and never allow himself to get screwed up like this again.

When he came down, the table was set. An ice bucket containing a bottle of Dom Perignon sat beside the table.

"Remember grace," Victoria said, and the family joined hands. It was not an unusual occurrence, but there was a sense of something of importance in the air. Before Josh could assemble his thoughts, Victoria began:

"We thank the Lord for the blessing of this food and we ask his indulgence to help us cope with whatever struggles we face ahead. Grant us the wisdom and the insight to make the necessary decisions for our peace of mind and, above all, to keep and protect our lovely children. Amen."

Josh felt oddly discomforted by her words, which made no specific mention of him. Nevertheless, he shrugged it off and busied himself with uncorking the champagne bottle, which made a large pop, much to the delight of the children. He poured Victoria and himself a glass.

"Can I, Mom, please?" Michael said.

"Just a little drop, please?" Emily whined.

Josh and Victoria exchanged glances and Victoria nodded. Josh poured a thimbleful of the champagne into each of his children's glasses.

"Might as well start them on the best," he said, lifting his glass. "To the greatest family in the world." He clinked glasses with Victoria and the children. Victoria smiled and drank. He noted that she drained her glass in one swoop, which was unusual for her. He drank half his glass, then filled both glasses again.

"There must be an occasion," he said. "Come on, you're holding back. Something good has happened, hasn't it?"

His question sounded more like a plea than an inquiry. Above all, he needed something good to happen. The air of celebration felt surreal. There was simply nothing obvious to celebrate, which was disturbing. It made him feel alien and left out.

"Not missing an important date, am I?"

His question was met with confused shrugs. Victoria avoided his glance.

"Champagne? Roast turkey and all the trimmings?" Josh persisted. "Mahler on the stereo? Must be something."

"I guess I felt festive," Victoria said, draining her glass again.

"It sure looks like it," Josh said, disturbed by his own touch of sarcasm. Victoria held out her glass and he poured her another.

"What was your day like, Michael?" Josh asked suddenly, determined to deflect any overt signs of irritation.

"Super," Michael said, turning to his mother and nodding.

"And Emily?"

"Fun day, Daddy. The teacher hung my drawing on the bulletin board."

"How wonderful," Josh said, turning to Victoria. "And yours?"

"Best ever, Josh. Best ever."

Oddly, she seemed less than enthusiastic, but he let it pass. His own concerns focused on a single issue.

"After dinner, we'll go over the financial situation, won't we, Victoria?" he asked.

"Of course we will, Josh. Don't I always keep my promises?"

He nodded, surprised by the faint hint of sarcasm in her remark. He looked at her. She winked, raised her glass again, and drank.

The dinner seemed long. Perhaps it was his impatience. When they rose from the table, Michael kissed his mother and went up to his room while Emily came into the kitchen to help her mother with the dishes.

"Why not leave that 'til later?" Josh asked his daughter, anxious to get on with their financial discussion.

"It won't be long," Victoria said, as she continued the process of cleaning up.

But it was long, longer by far than Josh had calculated. By the time Emily was sent off to bed and he had kissed her goodnight, it was nearly ten.

"Now?" he asked.

"Now."

Josh followed Victoria into the den, but instead of her sitting down in front of the computer she sat on the couch and stared at him. He was confused by her sudden change of attitude.

"What's happening?" he asked, his agitation growing. He was genuinely confused.

"This," she said. She reached behind her, and then held up what looked like a small trinket of some sort. She held it up and dangled it in front of him. His stomach lurched and he felt his chest tighten. Then she stretched it between fingers of two hands and read the inscription.

"My delicious whore. J." She snickered. "J? Now who do you suppose that stands for?"

A wave of nausea washed over him. He began to sweat profusely.

"J for Jackass," she cried, flinging the ankle bracelet in his face.

He tried to speak but couldn't. His mind went suddenly blank. It was as if he had fainted and remained conscious.

"How about O for Over," Victoria snapped.

"Over?"

The other shoe had dropped. He felt as if it were a horseshoe that had landed on his head.

"I had a wonderful conversation this afternoon with Dominic Bocci," she said, her face remarkably serene. Naming Dominic made things clearer. It actually served to restore him to a feeling of equilibrium. The initial shock quickly dissipated. He knew exactly where he was now. In deep shit.

"That dirty little bastard," Josh hissed.

"I agree. But I have to assume that his allegations about you and his wife are correct." Her arms were crossed over her chest and she seemed strangely calm. "Nevertheless, you do have a chance of rebuttal."

"Okay, what did he tell you?" Josh asked, his throat constricted.

"Come now, Josh. Don't be cute. He told me that you and his wife were... how shall I put it...sexually involved for the last six months, though he put it a tad more crudely."

Her calm demeanor was disconcerting and he felt a terrible hollowness inside of him.

"I...I broke it off. I couldn't bear the tension. It was against the grain, Victoria."

"Against the grain?" Victoria sneered. "What crap."

"It's not as cut and dried..."

"Betrayal is betrayal. No getting around that, my darling husband."

"I've never done anything like this."

"Spare me," Victoria said without emotion. She paused and shook her head. Her expression seemed one of utter disgust. "I see no legitimate reason why this marriage should not be terminated."

"Terminated? Just like that? You make it sound so..."

"Final."

"Cold-blooded."

"It's my reactive choice, Josh. I'm trying to feel nothing except a desire for..."

"Termination," he whispered.

"Exactly."

"There's so much at stake here, really Victoria. A little compassion is called for. I made a mistake. I admit it. I understand how you feel."

"I told you, Josh, I'm trying to feel nothing. And I must admit, I'm succeeding. Frankly, I don't want to feel anything. You violated our contract. The fact is, I no longer want to be involved with you. I can't trust you, and without trust, marriage is nothing."

"Jeez, Victoria. You sound so..."

"Lawyerly?"

"That, too."

"Rational is the word, Josh. Above all, this must be a time for reason. I would not want this little betrayal to disintegrate into something similar to what your parents went through."

"Or yours," he said, trying to recover some semblance of poise through this weak try at a counterattack.

Studying her, she reminded him of the first day they had met in her office. There was the same purposeful look in her eyes, the same single-mindedness. He knew she meant what she was saying. Hadn't he predicted it to Evie? He was genuinely frightened.

"Our first consideration must be the children," she said.

"Would you expect anything less of me? They're my kids, too." Despite the predictability of her reaction, he had secretly hoped that the gloomy fate that awaited the children might soften her stance when it came to their marriage. It hadn't.

But it did explain her conduct during dinner. She had opted for performance over reality, a kind of protective cover for the benefit of the kids. Projecting such actions into the future, he understood the tactic. An angry scene would have devastated them.

"We must do what's best for them," Victoria said with conviction. He shook his head and pursed his lips.

"I could have solved everything for two hundred thousand dollars."

"You would never have gotten away with it, Josh. Never. Like your six-month peccadillo. Sooner or later these things come out."

"I was such a damned fool," he muttered.

"Worse, Josh. Far worse. Beneath contempt. When I think of all the lying you had to do...it makes me want to puke. Coming to my bed after being with her. Who was the damned fool here? How could I have not known?"

"What can I say? I can't even believe it was me doing these things. And doing them to you, Victoria. You of all people. My wife..."

She put her hands to her ears.

"I don't want to hear it, Josh. Please. It's too revolting. I want to avoid this scene at all costs. Do you understand? Just shut up. Please."

Never in his life had he felt such contrition. His stomach was in knots. He wished he could will himself to disappear.

"I'm so, so sorry," he said, feeling a sob begin deep inside of him. "I'll do anything." The sob surfaced and tears brimmed over his eyelids and slid down his cheeks.

"You're pathetic," Victoria sighed.

"That I am," he managed to croak. He wiped away his tears with the back of his hand.

"Unfortunately, we have to consider the practical implications. As much as I hate to do it, we have to save your job. If I had my druthers I'd let them fire your ass."

"I wouldn't blame you."

"The fact is, it's too lucrative to toss away. You are, for the moment, still the family breadwinner."

Still? The connotation was loud and clear. She was going back to work.

She looked at him without the slightest expression of understanding or sympathy. Then she bit her lip and sucked in a deep breath.

Lifting her eyes, she said, "You're right about one thing. I couldn't believe you ever again. I just can't live with that. The idea that you and that woman..." She paused and shook her head. "It just repulses me so much to think about it. Six months, Josh. Six months. How can I get it out of my mind? My God! Sharing such profound intimacy with another woman. I'm sickened by the idea of it. It was dirty, disgusting."

She suddenly shivered as if hit by a cold wind "And dangerous. Living such a lie. How could you? I feel utterly violated. Is it a male compulsion?" Her nostrils dilated as she seemed to ponder the question for a moment. "You know, I never subscribed to my mother's paranoia on that issue, but I can see her point, and it does frighten the hell out of me. I'm sorry, Josh. I've weighed all the factors, including the impact on the children. The fact is that it can never be the way it was before. Never."

Her logic was chilling. Worse, he could not disagree with her. He knew he would have reacted in exactly the same way. She was deliberately cutting him off from his moorings.

"I love my family," he whispered. "It's everything to me." In the face of her clear-eyed explanation, he felt utterly helpless.

"No, only our children are the issue. That's all I've been thinking about ever since that wonderful Mr. Bocci arrived on my doorstep. I'm not going to wallow in self-pity or regret. Disillusion will pass. I guess I put my money on the wrong horse. Let's try to work out this...this disentanglement...with a minimum of trauma for us, and especially for the children. Do you understand what I'm saying?"

He wasn't sure how to respond. He had pleaded. He had begged for mercy. Suddenly another thought crossed his mind. Suppose the shoe was on the other foot. Would he forgive and forget? Forgive, maybe, he conceded. Forget, never.

"I do understand, Victoria."

She nodded.

"I've also been thinking about what approach we should take."

"Approach? You'll have to be clearer."

"I hope you'll go along with me on this, Josh. I'd like us to have joint custody. It's the closest thing to the situation we have going for them now. Two loving parents sharing their children's lives."

He was instantly wary.

"I'd like to do what in family law is called 'bird nesting.' It's not the usual approach. But I remember the expression from my law school days, my course in family law."

"I would like to soften the blow for the children by maintaining the household. I would like their routine to continue in the same environment with a minimum of change.

"I haven't a clue to what you're suggesting, Victoria."

"I really don't mean that we should continue to live together. What I'm suggesting is that we share our domicile. There I go with that legalese. I'm suggesting that we each take charge of the household for a couple of weeks at a time. We rotate. Two weeks on and two weeks off. That way the children will feel a lesser sense of desertion or loss. They'll have their dad and their mom in their own environment, in their own space, but at different times. In that way, they'll understand that they're the priority for both of us."

She had averted her eyes as she told him this. And she was right. It did sound radical and he hated the prospect.

"That sounds like a ridiculous idea. If you'd like, I'll move out. Why should you have to have a separate place? You can live here. Just as long as I have access to the children."

"Of course, you're going to have access. Above all, I don't want them to feel…well, deserted by their father. Maybe I'm just reacting to my own experience, but I know what it means to grow up as a fatherless child."

"You sound so…sensible, Victoria," he said grimly.

"We have to be, Josh. Both of us. Of course, there's no telling how long it must last. But it seems a logical way to transition them."

The conversation between them seemed stilted, too matter-of-fact, too rational. He would rather have had shouts and curses, recriminations, temper tantrums, cruel words, and angry diatribes. This was more like a contract negotiation, bloodless and without feeling.

His mind suddenly filled with confusing details. How will they get through the night? Will they sleep in the same bed? What will they tell the children and when? How will the children react? Will her idea about a transition period really work? There was no question that Victoria was dead earnest and determined.

At that point he suddenly remembered the original impetus for the meeting with Victoria. He was supposed to get a rundown of their financial status. At the very least, he was entitled to know the amount and disposition of their assets. He reminded her of this.

"All in due time, Josh," she replied. "All in due time."

He felt impotent, powerless, and devastated.

Chapter 11

They met in the storefront office of Alfonse Bocci, Dominic's brother, on the Lower East Side of Manhattan. Josh came with her with strict instructions to remain silent.

The office was seedy and consisted of a reception area manned by a fat receptionist and a cluttered inner office with a desk piled high with papers. Behind the desk sat Alfonse, who vaguely resembled his brother. He wore no tie and a shirt that looked as if it had not been laundered for weeks.

Dominic sat in one of the mismatched chairs assembled in a semi-circle around Alfonse's desk. He was cross-legged and upright, cautious of his pressed clothes. He had actually shaken Victoria's hand as if they had established a friendly relationship during their earlier meeting.

Josh sat in another chair looking ashen. He had slept in the spare room. Victoria, wearing a gray businesslike lawyerly suit, sat beside him.

Contrary to her expectations, she felt oddly unburdened. She had been up all night, her mind filled with thoughts and various ideas on how she was going to conduct her life from that day forward. From the moment of her confrontation with Dominic Bocci the day before, she knew that she would have to prepare for profound changes in her life.

She was, of course, shocked and disgusted by Dominic's revelations. When Dominic had suddenly appeared at her door yesterday and then unburdened himself, she managed to contain her fury over Josh. The miracle was that she was able to hold herself together, to freeze her emotions while this smooth bastard blandly told her his story. Despite her immediate detestation of the man, she knew his allegations were true. He was hardly subtle. She even forced herself to maintain a cool demeanor when he made his monetary demands. He struck her as less the outraged husband than a greedy predator. Did the fool really believe that she would consent to part with half-a-million dollars?

He had explained that he had forgiven his wife, implying that she had submitted to Josh's sexual demands under duress. That part of it somehow did not ring true. Under duress or not, she had succumbed and confessed. That was more than enough validation for her.

"You think I don't know your pain?" Dominic asked her. "I got the same condition. It ain't easy to know that your spouse is cheating on you."

"Apparently not," she agreed coldly, trying to recover from the sudden shock. Now she directed her thoughts to coping with the catastrophe this evil man had brought into her life.

"You should thank me for coming here," he said.

"Don't think I'm ungrateful," she replied, forcing a tight smile.

"I wouldn't have come," he told her as if he were confessing true reluctance. "But your husband said you handle the family finances. So I had to come direct to the source. I figured he was too chicken to come clean."

"You did come to the right place," she agreed, continuing to be guarded about her demeanor. Survival had suddenly taken on a different meaning. At that point, she had put both him and her husband into the same category. They had now been transformed in her mind into her mother's devil fantasy, venal male predators, her ultimate self-fulfilling prophecy.

Dominic seemed to be enjoying his role as a messenger from hell, although he was, she suspected, confused by her reaction.

"To me, it seems like a cheap price to pay," Dominic continued. "He keeps his job, his big income. Hell, you'll make up the money in a couple of years. No hassles."

"Makes sense," she mused aloud. But her thoughts were moving in another direction.

Instantaneously, the door had closed on her marriage and another had suddenly opened. She was going through this second door now, compelled by a new idea. The objective now was to prevent or severely limit any trauma to her children. Divorce was inevitable now. She had discovered that she possessed no capacity for forgiveness.

"What's that saying?" Dom said, screwing up his face in mock contemplation. "What's good for the goose..."

"Is good for the gander."

"Gander is the lady goose, right?"

He winked, his motive clear. She wished she could find the courage to choke the bastard to death.

"Maybe when all this is over..."

She forced a smile. With a knife in my hand, she thought.

"So tomorrow we get it all squared away," he said, writing down the address of his brother's office. "Just bring the you-know-what and we'll put this all behind us."

"Yes," she nodded.

"That's using the old noodle, Mrs. Rose. It's all gonna be nice and legal."

He started toward the door, stopped, and turned.

"I like you," he said. "You're open-minded. I like that in a woman. Yeah. Maybe you and I...you know..."

"Fuck you," she said.

"Well, well. Finally got to you."

He stood in the doorway and pointed a finger.

"Just be there, lady. *Capisce?*"

He walked out the door. She dropped to the floor and on her knees cried for a long time. Finally, with her emotions under control, she rose and began to plan her next move and her new life.

She had, of course, accepted Dominic's Bocci's challenge. In her previous law practice, she had always been good at lawyer-to-lawyer confrontations, especially when she was angry. Thus, her state of mind coming into Alphonse Bocci's office was militant and aggressive. Her objective was clearly defined. Preserve Josh's job and hold down the price of the Bocci bastard's blackmail.

"I hope we can resolve the situation as quickly as possible," Alfonse Bocci began. Just as he spoke, the fat receptionist came in with Styrofoam containers of coffee and bagels and cream cheese.

"On the house," Alfonse said, setting the bagels and coffee out in a semicircle at the edge of his desk. He unwrapped a bagel and pulled the top off of a coffee container.

"Now," he said, his mouth full. "We are asking five hundred thousand dollars and, of course, a signed document by Mr. Rose admitting his guilt." He looked toward Josh and smiled thinly. "Naturally, this will be filed away, never to be used, unless..."

"We understand that, Mr. Bocci," Victoria said, glancing toward Josh, whose complexion had turned dead white. She turned toward Dominic and offered a thin smile. He smiled back, obviously secure in the knowledge that he had made the deal with the source.

"Then I assume you've brought the certified check for the amount specified."

"No, I haven't," Victoria said calmly. "Nor do I intend to."

"Shit!" Dominic cried, partially spilling the coffee on his creased gray flannels. He tried absorbing the stains with a napkin, but they seemed to make things worse. "Fuckin' broad. What's she trying to pull?"

"I don't understand," Alphonse said. His face had reddened. "Dom said the purpose of this meeting was to finish the deal."

"That's exactly correct," Victoria said. "And I intend to do just that."

"So where the fuck's the money?" Dominic sneered.

"Oh, we're prepared to make a settlement, gentlemen," Victoria said, "but not on your basis. I've prepared my own letter for you both to sign and, of course, Angela Bocci."

She had pulled out a letter from her briefcase that she had written on her computer the night before. Alfonse took it, opened it, and read it.

"You outta your fucking mind?" he shouted at Victoria, tossing the letter to his brother. "Read it, Dom. She wants us and Angela to sign it. Angela denies any sexual harassment and admits that she seduced this *jaboni,* and we sign as witnesses to money passing hands in lieu of any future harassment suits on Angela's part. Hey lady, you people are at risk. Not us."

"Wrong," Victoria said crisply, smiling slightly, staring directly into Alfonse Bocci's beady eyes. "You people are at risk. You're the blackmailers."

"Why waste time, Al. Let's go to the firm."

"No one is stopping you," Victoria said. "Go ahead."

"He's history there, lady. You want that?"

"Doesn't bother me," Victoria said. "We're getting divorced anyway."

"What the fuck is going on here?" Alfonse Bocci asked.

"Blackmail," Victoria said. "That's what's going on."

"Listen to this broad," Dominic said.

"I don't think you can get away with that characterization, Mrs. Rose," Alfonse said, assuming a lawyerly role. "As my brother's lawyer, you could be in real trouble with that allegation."

"Sue me," Victoria said.

"You mean that? You know what it will cost you if you have to go to court?"

"Time, Mr. Bocci. Time. You, too. Lots of time."

"You know what your legal fees will cost you?"

"I'm a lawyer, Bocci. You fuck around with me, I'll keep your brother and his bitch in court for the rest of their lives if I have to. I'm good at it. As a matter of fact, I'll make it so that you won't have room on your schedule for any other cases."

"Are you threatening me?" Alfonse Bocci said. It was, Victoria concluded, a macho knee-jerk reaction. She noted that Josh had remained, as she had instructed him, totally silent.

"Now you're getting the message."

"Why you lousy bitch," Dom said, jumping from his chair, reaching out to grab Victoria.

Josh stood up protectively and pushed Dom away. Alfonse rose swiftly from his chair and restrained his brother.

"Don't be an idiot, Dom," he cried, wrestling his brother back to his chair.

"Let him strike me. Give me more ammunition," Victoria said.

"Who the fuck does this cunt think she is?" Dominic cried, his face flushing beet red.

"You'd better watch your language," Josh shouted.

Victoria cut him a glance that silenced him, then addressed both brothers in turn.

"As I told you, I really don't care if you go to Josh's firm. True, Josh could lose his job. Tell you the truth, I wouldn't want that to happen. He makes good money, although I'm sure they'll give him a great severance package. But it won't help your wife, either. Nevertheless, I'm willing to be reasonable, providing you both and she sign that document."

She paused, looking silently from one brother's face to the other. "If you don't, I am going to take you to court. Great country, America. Due process. Anybody can sue anybody. Believe me, I'll find the statutes that apply. Who knows, maybe a complaint to the District Attorney's office might be appropriate. Up to you. I'm willing to make a deal."

"Talk about blackmail. This is a holdup," Dominic sneered.

"How much are we talking about?" Alfonse said, maintaining his lawyerly pose.

"Fifty thousand," Victoria said without pausing.

"Fifty thousand? That's 10 percent."

"If you don't sign, you get nothing but trouble. Fifty thousand will be small potatoes after I get myself charged up."

"You're lookin' for trouble lady," Dominic said menacingly, looking toward his brother. "We got connections."

"Please. Don't pull that Mafia macho shit on me. What are you going to do? Hire somebody to break my kneecaps?" She paused. "As for trouble, you haven't got a clue."

Suddenly Dom turned toward Josh.

"Ain't you got nothin' to say? Got any balls left?"

"Apparently enough to do your wife for six months," Victoria snapped, looking Dominic Bocci dead in the eyes.

"Maybe he wasn't getting enough at home," Dominic said.

"Could have been the same problem over at your house," Victoria said. She turned toward Alfonse. "What will it be, Counselor?"

She watched Alfonse Bocci grow thoughtful, rubbing his chin, wetting his lips.

"Bitch has us by the short ones," he hissed, a remark meant for his brother's ears alone. Then, louder, as he put up his hands and looked pointedly at Victoria, "I don't think we can fuck with her, Dom. Broads like this get you by the *cojones*. They squeeze until they crush you. I seen enough of them in my life." He turned toward his brother. "You got a big problem back at the barn, brother. Your Angela can't keep her legs crossed? You know what I say? Take the fucking fifty grand. Sign the goddamned paper. Get her to sign it. She ain't gonna use it." He turned toward Josh. "She's keeping your job for you, buddy. Maybe she's doing you a favor dumping you. I couldn't live with a hardass like her for two minutes." He turned toward his brother. "Take it, Dom. We overreached is all. Better get what you can."

"Good advice, Counselor," Victoria said.

"Fuck her," Dominic said morosely.

"Here's the game plan. We don't have to meet again." She reached into her briefcase and pulled out an envelope. "The check is post-dated for a week from now. But if I don't get the letter back signed by all three of you and properly notarized, I stop it. Understand?"

Alfonse shook his head and looked toward his brother, who was obviously fuming. Dominic snarled and nodded.

"I'll have a messenger pick up the paper tomorrow. If it's in order, you can cash the check. And I'd appreciate if you henceforth eliminate yourselves from our lives. *Capisce?*"

"Fuckin' bitch," Dominic mumbled as Victoria and Josh stood up and, without another word, left the office.

Chapter 12

The children sat together on the couch in the den, wide-eyed and expectant. This was the usual place of family conferences, the truly serious stuff, and their father knew they were concerned and somewhat confused. Josh studied them, his progeny, Michael and Emily, two beautiful children, his hope and his future. Mustn't show his pain, he implored himself, trading glances with Victoria, whose cool visage, he knew, hid her own consternation. In the brief time since yesterday, she had shown him the full extent of her determination. As a husband, he had been unceremoniously amputated from her, body and soul.

"We have something to announce, children," Victoria began. He noted that her cheeks had reddened and he could hear a reedy tremor in her voice. The children looked from one parent to the other, still unsuspecting, although it was clear that they could read in their parents' expressions something ominous.

Emily reached out for Michael's hand. Josh understood their need to touch for solace. He had experienced a similar reaction following his parent's demise. The urge to touch his sibling's flesh was overpowering.

"Nothing is going to change for you children," Victoria began, then hesitated, looking imploringly toward Josh. For the first time since she had been informed of his betrayal, she was vacillating.

"What your mother is trying to say," Josh said, taking courage from her faltering voice, "is that we, your mother and I, are planning to divorce."

He watched the expression on his children's faces run the gamut from confusion to disbelief. They exchanged stunned glances. Michael's face became ashen and frown lines appeared on his forehead. Emily's eyes glazed, then moistened.

Josh continued, barely able to find his voice. Droplets of sweat were heading down the sides of his body and sprouting on his back. "Nothing will change for you guys. We love you both very much."

His words sounded trite and foolish. Nothing will change? It was an outright lie. Their lives were going to be changed forever.

"Daddy and I are just unhappy living together anymore," Victoria said.

"It has nothing to do with you children," Josh added quickly, clearing a lump from his throat. Huddled together on the couch, the children looked pitiful and forlorn. This was much harder than he had expected.

"Is Daddy going to leave us, like Bobbie's father?" Emily asked. Tears began to stream down Emily's cheeks, and she tried wiping them with the back of her little hands. It was heartbreaking. Josh turned helplessly to Victoria.

"Is this worth it?" he whispered.

Victoria ignored him and turned to the children.

"No, darling," she said. "Daddy is going to stay here."

"Does that mean you're going away, Mom?" Michael asked, desperately trying to hold back his tears.

"That's not the way it's going to be, children," Victoria said. "We love you both too much to hurt you in any way. Actually, the way it will work is that Daddy will be here with you for two weeks, then I'll take over and be with you for two weeks. You see, nothing is going to change for you."

"Where will you go, Mommy?" Emily asked nervously, her eyes shifting from one parent to the other.

"Oh, I'll be fine. I'll be staying in Manhattan during those two weeks, but this will be my home. I'm also going back to work as a lawyer." She looked toward Josh for help.

"It'll be like your Mom and Dad will be taking a vacation every two weeks."

"But it won't be a vacation, really," Michael protested.

"I said like a vacation," Josh said, feeling foolish.

The children once again exchanged glances. It was obvious that they were dissatisfied and uncomfortable with the explanation.

"It will work out fine," Victoria said. "I promise you."

Josh looked at her and shook his head. Promises? How could she possibly promise such a thing?

"The important thing," Josh said, hesitating, knowing he was being a hypocrite. "Is that we'll still be a family."

"Absolutely," Victoria said.

He could tell that the children were buying none of it, going along, trying to cope with this new impending reality. He wished he had the guts to tell them the truth. You're getting screwed, kids. It won't ever be the same for you.

Emily insinuated herself into Josh's arms. He held her on his lap and kissed her tears away.

Michael remained seated on the couch. He was putting on a good show of bravery, but it was obvious that he was devastated.

"Is it because you don't love each other anymore?" Michael asked.

Victoria shot a confused glance at Josh and shrugged. He saw it as a wordless cry for him to answer the question. It did, after all, go to the heart of the matter. The question was an honest one, but he knew he would have to give a dishonest answer.

"You might say that, son," Josh said, caressing his daughter's thighs, holding his cheek next to hers. "It happens to parents some-times."

He turned toward his boy. "We're not divorcing our children, Michael. Only each other. When you grow up, you'll understand."

Another lie, Josh thought. They understand now. As grownups they would be confused.

"There are people at Pendleton whose parents are divorced, Mom. I understand. Sure I do. It'll be okay for Emily and me. You'll see."

"Of course it will," Josh said, his voice breaking.

"Mommy and Daddy," Emily said, her sobs had turned to hiccups. "Is this going to be for..." She hiccupped again, then said, "Always?"

"Hold your breath, darling, and count to ten," Josh said.

She tried to do so, but it didn't work.

"Nothing is forever," he managed to whisper, looking at Victoria, who avoided his glance. She knew the situation had not gone according to her expectations. He hoped so. It was certainly worse than he had expected.

"I promise you both, children. Everything will be all right," Victoria said. For the first time since their talk had commenced, Josh detected a note of uncertainty in her response.

"But will it be for always?" Emily persisted between hiccups.

"I'm afraid so," Victoria sighed. Josh averted his eyes and did not respond.

"So Dad will stay with us first, Mom?" Michael asked, obviously trying to show his acceptance of their solution. It was a valiant try.

"For the next two weeks," Victoria replied. Apparently her equilibrium had returned. "Then I'll come home and take care of you guys. No problem. We've already worked it out, haven't we, Josh?"

"Oh yes. We've worked it out." He sounded tentative and quickly adjusted his response. "But you guys will have to help me through it."

"Your dad's a very creative fellow. He'll do the job just wonderfully," Victoria said.

"Betcha life," Josh said.

"And I'll call every day and talk to both of you. I promise. Cross my heart." More promises. It sickened him to hear them.

"Me, too," Josh said with forced enthusiasm. "When Mom is here."

"Will that be for always, too?" Michael asked. "Changing places every two weeks?" It was, Josh noted, a subtle abridgement of Emily's question. It seemed more a question of process than a deeper look into the future.

At that point, Emily wriggled out of Josh's arms and went to her mother, who hugged her with equal fervor.

"I love you, Mommy," Emily said.

"And I love you."

"How come you don't love each other anymore?" Emily asked. Her hiccups had disappeared.

"I don't think I can explain it in any way that you'll understand, sweetheart."

"I thought Mommys and Daddys are supposed to love each other always."

"Don't be silly, Emily," Michael said. "Remember what Gramma said when she came to visit last Christmas?"

"Gramma?" Josh snapped, turning to Victoria. "What did Gramma say?"

"Sometimes she says things she doesn't mean," Victoria quickly countered.

But Emily was not to be thwarted.

"She said that Grampa Stewart was a bad man and was very mean to her and left her all alone with Mommy."

"She told you that?" Josh said angrily.

"Yes she did," Emily persisted. "And she said boys could be mean like that."

"Christ, Victoria," Josh cried. "I thought you were going to shut her up about things like that. That woman is a menace."

"She promised," Victoria said defensively.

"Promised, did she?" Josh muttered, hating to hear that word again. "Just keep her away from the kids. I will not have her poisoning their minds about me."

"She won't. It would be contrary to my position." She looked toward the children. "There's no point in having this discussion now."

"It's as good a time as any, Victoria," Josh snapped. "She starts out with Grampa Stewart then works her way through my parents, then to me."

"Was Grampa Stewart really a bad man?" Michael asked.

"How did we ever get on this subject?" Victoria sighed. "My mother's opinions have always been off the wall. I know her faults Josh, but she is still my mother."

"And why did Gramma and Grampa Rose kill each other?" Michael asked. The question struck Josh as insidious, a dangerous time bomb planted by Mrs. Stewart.

Explaining what had happened to his parents was always a sore point. "They didn't kill each other. It was an accident." He shook his head in disgust. "Gramma Stewart is dead wrong."

They were getting off the track, and he feared that he and Victoria would find themselves in a confrontation in front of the children.

Victoria freed Michael from her embrace and drew Emily beside her, hugging her.

"I'll see you both in two weeks," she said.

Josh watched as the children again hugged their mother. He could see their reluctance to let her go, and he was certain that they were feeling the same sense of abandonment he was.

"That was tough," Victoria acknowledged after the children had gone up to their rooms.

"Very," he muttered.

"We'll just have to hope for the best."

"Any way you slice it, it stinks."

"Yes it does," she agreed, shrugging.

"It doesn't have to be this way," he said.

"Unfortunately, it does, Josh," she huffed, turning away. "I have to finish packing."

He was relieved when she left the room. He sat back in the chair, turned on the television set, and tried to eliminate all thinking, letting the flow of inane sitcoms and canned applause wash over him.

Later, she called from upstairs and asked him to help bring down her suitcases, which he did as the ever-dutiful husband. She had packed three suitcases and a hanging bag. He brought them into the garage.

Then she asked that he help her carry out her computer, screen, and printer, which he did. Knowing that the computer contained all the information about their joint finances, he resented the idea that he was participating in removing crucial knowledge from his own house. He made no comment as he loaded the baggage and electronic gear into the trunk of the Lexus.

Considering the importance of the occasion, he felt a strange sensation, a mixture of banality, intense grief, and simmering anger. The act itself seemed oddly benign, as if he was simply loading the car to go on a vacation instead of participating in this monumental moment of separation. But the hard slamming of the trunk suggested a symbolic explosion. For the second time, his life was being blown to smithereens.

He handed her the keys.

"The kids are asleep," she said. "I wouldn't want them to be around now."

"I'm glad you waited."

They exchanged glances. She was the first to turn away.

"No emotional good-byes, Josh. No tears. No last-minute pleas." She gave him a piece of paper torn from a yellow pad. "I've made a list of 'to dos' and 'no nos.' Try to pursue the game plan. Follow their regular diet and disciplines. I'll call every day. And I'll get the ball rolling about the divorce. Hiring a lawyer is your option." She paused for a moment. Their eyes met briefly. "Well then, I'm off."

He watched her get into the car. The garage door rose and the car headed into the night.

Evie arrived by cab in mid-morning. He had managed to get the children off to school with a minimum of mishaps, trying desperately to put a happy face on the situation. When he mentioned that Evie was coming to help them, the children exchanged frightened glances.

"Mom won't like it," Michael said.

"She'll be mad," Emily said.

"What about you guys?" Josh asked. "How do you feel about the idea?"

Again they exchanged glances and shrugged.

"Aunt Evie is fun," Emily said.

Michael nodded agreement. Josh was relieved. But there was a still a loose end to consider.

"Mom said she was going to call every day," Michael said, the import of his comment obvious. "We tell her that Aunt Evie's here she'll really be upset. You know how she feels, Dad."

"Yes I do. But Aunt Evie is my big sister and I trust her to do the right thing for all of us. Frankly, kids, I need the help."

Both children were silent for a while, then Emily said: "Let's not upset Mommy, then."

"Good thinking Emily," he said. He would not have asked them to lie.

Josh spent the morning on the phone with his office, conferring with his staff and the various account executives. Nothing seemed amiss. Angela was no longer an employee. No one in the firm was the wiser. All was well, as far as his job was concerned.

As he spoke, he noted the dust outline on the desk where her computer had sat. Again he felt resentment at the removal of their records. Granted that some of the money was what she had pulled out of her law practice, but the fact was that most of their net worth was money he had earned through his talent and hard work.

The cab driver, sweating profusely, followed Evie into the house lugging two cartons, one under each arm. He had to make four trips to carry the remaining cartons and two suitcases. Evie led the way, carrying only Tweedledee.

Josh had forgotten about the cat. Her presence did violate his caveat about not having pets in the house. The ban, of course, had stemmed from his memories of his parents' terrible conflict in which their pets had become tragically involved in their battle. Both had become, as they say, collateral damage. But Evie had rejected such a ban, and he had no choice now but to accept the visitor.

"I don't believe this," Josh said. He paid the cab driver and embraced his flushed and excited sister as she waddled into the kitchen.

"I've come as fully prepared as possible," she said, taking a knife and slicing open the cartons. He watched in awe as she removed pots, pans, knives, and other appliances he recognized from his mother's kitchen. There was a food processor, electric mixer, vegetable mill, drum sieve and pestle, bulb baster, poultry shears, spatulas, scrapers, wire whips, whisks, and a complete set of knives.

"If Victoria saw this, she'd have a fit," he said, actually enjoying the display. Of course, he was concerned about the meals she had in mind, but he didn't have the heart to discourage her. He'd go along, he decided. He was in charge.

"But Victoria is not here, Josh," Evie said, laughing, as she emptied another carton filled with food. She removed packages of thick bacon, butter, cheese, cream, candied fruits, flour, oil, cuts of beef, fresh chickens, duck, veal chops, shallots, and truffles.

"We'll fill in from the supermarket," Evie said, opening the cupboards and refrigerator and loading up the goods she had brought. "These are just the basics."

"The basics?" he laughed. "Must have cost a fortune."

"What is money against what must be accomplished in this house?" she replied, waving her hand over the kitchen in a possessive gesture.

"Funny, I was just mulling over such a thought. For me, Evie, you are an investment in hope." He felt his lip tremble with emotion.

She turned toward him and laid a chubby finger on his lips, stilling them.

"Now you're getting the message. Big sister is here to bring happiness and love."

He chuckled, feeling good, the earlier wave of depression dispelled.

"You remind me of Mom," Josh said, feeling a lump grow in his throat.

"I hope so, Josh."

"Everything looks wonderful," he sighed, surveying the items she had brought with her.

"We're going to feast away all hurt, brother dear. Teach your children the power of the palate, ingestion of God's true gifts."

"Food is love," he said, smiling, shaking his head in awe.

"Absolutely. Of the purest kind."

He wished that Victoria could be present to observe what was happening. He wanted to see her cool reserve penetrated and would have been delighted to see her truly infuriated.

Evie bustled around the house, organizing the kitchen. Then she went upstairs and unpacked her clothes in the spare room. When she came down again, she was dressed for going out.

He drove her to the supermarket to get, as she put it, the "extras." Going through the aisles, she loaded up on items that he had rarely seen in Victoria's kitchen, gallons of ice cream and bars of candy in large quantities.

"Milky Ways, too," he cried, recalling Michael's ordeal at school.

"Absolutely. And Snickers, Baby Ruths, Reese's Peanut Butter Cups, Good and Plentys, and Tootsie Rolls. These are to be shared with their little friends. Candy means friendship and giving it is the essence of sharing."

She put whole milk in the cart, the real thing, not skim milk, then whipping cream, exotic cheeses, three dozen jumbo-sized eggs, a large ham, and a bag of very large potatoes. Also apples, oranges, bananas, pears, persimmons, and every conceivable kind of vegetable.

"All earth's bounty," she said as she carefully inspected each item.

Josh noted that, contrary to Victoria's practice, Evie never looked at the nutritional values on the food packages. But he withheld any criticism.

The children seemed excited and overjoyed to see her in the kitchen when they arrived home. She embraced each of them in turn. When Emily spied Tweedledee, she squealed with delight, embraced her, and cradled her in her arms.

"We're going to have one high time for the next two weeks," Evie said. "Aunt Evie's on the case." She gave them each a Snickers bar. Josh noted their cautious glances in his direction.

"It's okay with me," he said. For a moment the health aspects of Evie's influence cast a brief shadow over his thoughts. He quickly put it out of his mind. After all, it was only a temporary situation. The more pleasure they had, the better.

He helped each of the children with their homework. Tweedledee was now ensconced in Emily's room, her litter box already installed in her bathroom. When he had finished with them, he peeked in at Evie working in the kitchen. She was dicing vegetables.

"What's for dinner?" he said playfully.

"Never you mind," Evie said. "It'll be a surprise."

He went into the den and poured himself a Glenfiddich over ice, which he sipped slowly. He put Mahler on the stereo, closed his eyes for a moment to let the delicious sound waft over him.

His eyes roamed over the various objects of her Victoriana collection, the ink wells and vases and porcelain objects, her leather-bound sets of books by Victorian authors, the large-brimmed straw hats lining the walls above the shelving. Her stamp was everywhere in the house, reminders of her influence, her presence, and her authority.

When Evie called him into dinner, the children were already seated. Tweedledee sat on Emily's lap. He hadn't the heart to separate them. The beautifully set table was bathed in candlelight, and the aroma from the food was tantalizing. In the background the Mahler played softly. He promised himself that he would taste everything and try his damnedest to set an example of enjoyment.

Evie came in to the dining room from the kitchen carrying a tureen of soup.

"Ta da," she cried, placing the tureen on the table and ladling out the soup.

"Looks yummy," Emily said.

"What is it?" Michael asked.

"Potage veloute aux champignons," Evie said giggling. "To you, cream of mushroom soup."

Michael tasted it cautiously.

"Pretty good," he said, smacking his lips and dipping his spoon in again.

"Delicious," Josh said.

The soup course was followed with another ceremonial entrance, and the clarion "Ta da." Evie described the offering on the platter as Braised Filet of Beef stuffed with Foie Gras and Truffles, which the children had never tasted before. There were also side dishes of vegetables. Thankfully, Josh noted, she had served each child a sensible portion.

"Not your usual kid's food," Josh said.

"Pace yourself, children," Evie said. "Let your palate grow used to this wonderful food that God has given us."

"I'm not sure I like it," Emily said. From time to time she had nipped off little pieces and popped them into Tweedledee's mouth.

"You will eventually," Evie said. "It took Tweedledee a while to savor my cooking."

"I love it, Aunt Evie," Michael said.

Evie had selected a fine Bordeaux. Josh found the wine delicious.

"Leave some room for dessert, children," Evie said, going into the kitchen.

In a moment, she returned carrying a dessert that looked like a miniature white mountain. Beside it on the tray was a bottle of cognac.

"Baked Alaska," she announced. "The king of desserts. Now we must make it light up the world."

She poured a puddle of cognac into an indentation at the peak of the confection. Then she took a box of matches from her apron pocket.

"Now who wishes to light up the world?" she winked. Both children raised their hands.

"It's very dangerous," she said, offering a tongue-in-cheek warning. "Depending on how much cognac one pours into it. We don't want a volcano."

"Let me, Aunt Evie," Emily pleaded. "Let me."

She looked toward Michael, who shrugged his consent.

"You'll do the next one, Michael. I promise."

She kissed him on his head and then gave the match to Emily. She rubbed it against the box, ignited it.

"What should I do now, Aunt Evie?" Emily said, holding the burning match. Evie guided Emily's hand to the indentation in which she had poured the cognac, then lit the liquid. It burst into flames. Josh blinked, then all four of them clapped.

"Bravo," Josh said, watching the flame die down. The desert looked like a snow-capped mountain with hot lava flowing down. When the flame had expired, leaving the mountain burnished, Evie cut into it and gave each of them a big slice.

"Now this is delicious, Aunt Evie," Emily said, lapping it up. Michael agreed.

Calorie-wise, Josh noted, it was more than they had ever had for dinner. His stomach felt a trifle queasy, but he was happily surprised to see that the rich food had no harmful effects on the children.

"Did you like the dinner Aunt Evie cooked for us?" Josh asked. They each nodded approval and embraced Evie, whose eyes suddenly clouded with tears.

"I want so much to make you all happy," she said.

"You did, Aunt Evie," Emily said, kissing her on both cheeks.

"Yes you did," Michael said.

"That is my mission, children."

Suddenly the telephone rang. Josh and Evie exchanged glances.

"Probably Victoria," Josh said. He felt his heartbeat accelerate.

"I'll get it, Dad," Michael said. "Emily, you get on the phone in the kitchen."

Josh concentrated on listening to their one-sided responses, mostly short answers, and was gratified to learn that neither child mentioned Evie. Yet, he did have mixed feelings about that. In effect, the children were participating in a conspiracy of silence. Victoria would be furious if she knew. Suddenly, Michael called for him to pick up the phone.

"Everything seems to have gone very well," Victoria said, sounding crisp and efficient.

"Very."

"Have you had any luck on help?" she asked.

"I expect I'll be able to handle that," he said, deliberately vague.

"Good. I'll call again tomorrow."

"Fine."

She showed no interest in anything beyond the children. He assumed it was deliberate on her part. She was, after all, withdrawing from their relationship. Their common bond, the children, was to be her only interest. Understanding this fact, he made no inquiries about how things were going with her.

"Everything okay with Victoria?" Evie asked when he came back to the kitchen where she was now cleaning up.

"Apparently," he said.

"No mention of me?" she asked.

"Looks like we're home free on that, Evie. The kids seem to be with us."

After breakfast, on the morning of the Sunday that Victoria was scheduled to take over, the four of them moved cartons of Evie's kitchen equipment and whatever staples that would not spoil, including the boxes of candy bars, into the storage room in the basement along with some of her clothes. Josh had bought a combination lock for further security.

"Remember the numbers, kids," Josh said, letting them both open and close the lock a few times.

They checked the cupboards and refrigerator for any leftover foods that might meet with Victoria's objections and carefully scrutinized the spare room for any sign of clothes that Evie may have forgotten.

This done, Josh and the children went off to the supermarket to stock up on those foods that were Victoria's normal fare, cereals, fresh vegetables, organically grown free-range chickens, and whatever else was listed on nutritional labels as fat free, low sugar, and low sodium. No red meat, no butter, no eggs, nothing smoked or spicy. No candy. The children, expert in their knowledge of Victoria's purchases, led the way to her choices.

"Good work, guys," Josh said as they loaded the groceries into the van.

Back at the house, they put the food in the proper places.

"This isn't real food," Evie muttered, reading some of the labels. "This is survival rations."

"We're changing gears is all," Josh said, offering a smile to the children who smiled back.

"Remember kids," Josh warned when they had finished stocking the kitchen. "You listen to Mommy. When she's in charge, whatever she says goes. That goes for what she serves and all the other rules. Promise?"

Both children nodded agreement. There was no need to mention the part about Evie. What they had done to hide any sign of her presence was more than enough to send that message.

Victoria arrived precisely at eleven. The children greeted her affectionately with hugs and kisses. Victoria wore jeans and a cashmere sweater and, despite his growing antagonism toward her, he could not deny a tug of attraction. She looked radiant.

When the embraces and greetings had run their course and they had said good-bye to Josh, the children asked her permission to watch television and she consented. It was, after all, Sunday night, early prime time, and they knew the game plan of what was acceptable for their mother. There had been no such restrictions during their father's tenure. They knew, too, that the transfer of authority had occurred the moment Victoria entered the house, which increased his antagonism and considerably diminished his sense of attraction.

"Can I get you a drink?" he asked when the children had gone upstairs to watch television.

"No thank you," she answered politely.

They were standing in the living room. His suitcases were packed and had already been placed in the garage prior to loading into the car. Her suitcases, which she had carried inside herself, stood in the hallway at the foot of the stairs. He noted that she had brought her laptop computer. For a moment, he contemplated asking her once again to go over their financial situation, but he demurred. It didn't seem the right time or place.

"Is there anything I should know, Josh?" she asked.

"Nothing I can think of," he shrugged. "Things at school are fine. They're adjusting remarkably well to the..." He hesitated. "To the situation. I hope it goes as well on your watch."

She let a long moment go by as her eyes roamed the room.

"What is it?" he asked.

"The children seem different," she said, her eyes landing on him finally.

"Different? How so?"

"I can't put my finger on it," she said thoughtfully. "They appear...I don't know...different."

"How?"

"I'm not sure."

He was confused by her observation and wondered if she knew more than she was letting on or had decided to build a case against the idea they were pursuing. The children certainly did not look different to him. Had they forgotten something? Left a trace of Evie? Or did she sense his sister's presence?

"Is there an implication here that I haven't done right by them?"

"Not at all, Josh," she said quickly. "Maybe it's only my imagination."

"You can see they're quite happy and content."

"Yes they are," she agreed, but she looked tentative.

Then she shrugged and picked up her computer. She unstrapped the protective case and removed an envelope from one of the pockets and handed it to him.

"The papers we talked about," she said.

He contemplated the envelope in his hands.

"Aren't you rushing things a bit, Victoria?" he said.

"I told you I was preparing them, Josh."

He nodded and looked at the envelope dumbly.

"No sense procrastinating. We have, after all, agreed on a divorce."

It struck him as a one-sided agreement, but he did not protest.

He dreaded reading the agreement. It meant hassle and conflict, and he suspected that her idea of fairness would be terribly biased. Besides, he had just begun to assess his own position. He sensed that his perspective was changing. During the past two weeks, he had felt the initial pain of the prospect of divorce dissipate. Perhaps he had begun to adjust to his single state, missing her less than he might have expected.

He thought he had successfully erased the pain from his mind, but seeing her now face to face recalled the hurt. He remembered that the first few nights of sleeping alone had been awful. Reaching beside him in the bed, he had felt the cold empty space and an overwhelming sense of loneliness. And he could not deny the missing aura of her presence and her scent, the absence of her voice and movement. There were other inchoate yearnings as well, physical and mental.

"Read the documents carefully, Josh," she said crisply.

"I will."

They exchanged glances and she was the first to turn away. She did not volunteer any more information about how she had spent the two weeks. Accept it, he urged himself. She is creating a life without him.

"I'll take the Lexus. You'll need the Explorer."

She nodded.

"You'll call every day, of course," she said.

"Absolutely."

He went into the garage.

"Do you think this is going to work?" she asked.

"I do," he said, averting her eyes as he moved toward his suitcases. "See you in two weeks," he said, feeling empty and alone.

As he drove out of the garage, his eyes misted. He could barely see the road and had to calm himself and blink away the tears.

Chapter 13

During the long lonely nights in her new studio apartment on the East Side, she had weighed the pros and cons of the invitation to her mother. Josh, she knew, would be furious, and it would probably endanger the entire project. But Victoria was busily engaged setting up a new practice and might be called on to meet with clients in Manhattan. She did not want a surrogate mother to be in charge during this critical time and a grandmother was definitely in a different category.

"You must refrain from expressing any negativity to the children," Victoria had explained. "This is a delicate time for them."

"Don't you think I know that?"

"And no belligerent outbursts."

"Me?"

"I want them to think of you as a loving Gramma, a person that they will always remember with affection and warmth."

"What's a Gramma for?" she chuckled.

"Do it for me, Mother."

"What about Josh? Will he object?"

"Never mind Josh. Even a big girl needs her Mommy when she's in trouble," Victoria said with an air of amusement, knowing her words would have their softening effect.

Victoria arose early to make a solid healthy breakfast for the children. She cooked the oatmeal and put out toast and sugar-free jam, orange juice and skimmed milk.

"So it went well the last two weeks?" she said to the children as they ate their oatmeal. They did not seem particularly hungry.

"Very well," Michael said, glancing at his sister.

"We had a real good time with Daddy," Emily said. Victoria sensed that Emily was forcing herself to be cheerful, saying things her mother wanted to hear.

"I'm so glad," Victoria said, pausing, hoping that this would be the best time to tell them about her mother.

"I've got another surprise for you. Gramma is going to stay with us."

The children turned to each other and shrugged. Emily looked suddenly sad.

"She loves you very much," Victoria said. "I'd like you to get to know her. You may be seeing a great deal of her from now on."

"Sure, Mom," Michael said. Emily nodded, but without enthusiasm.

"I may have to be going to Manhattan on some days," she explained further. "With Gramma here I'll feel a lot better." She paused and studied their faces. "Did Dad have good help for you guys?"

"Very good," Michael said, looking at his sister, who averted her eyes.

"Was she reliable? I mean, was she here when you came home from school?"

"Yes she was," Michael said.

"Did she help cook?"

"Yes she did," Michael said, turning to his sister, who nodded.

"Gramma is a great cook. She really knows her nutrition. She's also very smart and can help with your homework. Did Dad help you?"

"Dad always helps us with our homework, Mom," Michael said. Again Emily nodded.

"Of course he does," Victoria said, realizing that they might interpret her questions as too probing. She did not want them to think that she disapproved of the way Josh had taken care of them. So far, she hadn't, although she still could not get it out of her mind that things were somehow different.

She could not put her finger on the difference and it puzzled her. There were certain expectations. Growing children changed rapidly and it was possible to miss a growth spurt or some subtle swift change. They did seem healthy and full of cheerful spirits that belied the break in their routine. Perhaps she had imagined that they would be more withdrawn and introspective. Dismissing her bafflement, she attributed it to her own faulty observation.

"Gramma will be here when you come home from school. And, of course, she'll drive you to your other activities. I know you'll both be very obedient and respectful to her."

"We will, Mom," Michael said, rising from the table. Emily also rose. "She's our Gramma."

"Your only Gramma," Victoria said pointedly.

She studied the children as they got up from the table and gathered their backpacks.

"Is something wrong, Mommy?" Emily asked, noting her curiosity.

"No dear. Nothing," she replied hastily.

Both children kissed her and went out the door. It was at that moment that she suspected what might have made them appear different. Was it her imagination? They looked more cherubic than when she had seen them two weeks ago, more filled out. And their clothes seemed tighter.

When they had gone, she inspected the refrigerator and cupboards. There weren't any signs of no-nos. Perhaps it was only her imagination. Children grew fast. She had never been away from them for two weeks before.

She spent the morning roaming the house. Even the den, after a cursory inspection, had a different feel, which was the only way she could describe it. She would have to spend at least a day during the next two weeks dusting and cleaning the place. Perhaps then she might find out what was giving her this feeling.

Everything looked remarkably neat, which gratified her at first, then began to trouble her. The children's rooms were never in such a tidy condition. Had Josh urged them to show their mother how neat they had been? That was the only explanation that made any sense.

Finally, she decided that it was only natural that she would feel this way after a two-week absence. She had removed herself from the routine of the household. Of course it had to "feel" different.

Shrugging off her odd discomfort, she checked for any messages at her new office. She had made a series of telephone calls to her old contacts. Things had begun to happen. Clients were coming on board.

Despite the net worth of her investments, she wanted to quickly establish her financial independence from her husband. It was less the money than the concept. She did not want him to have any psychological advantage over her.

Victoria had carefully researched the question of custody, discovering that they could agree legally to a joint custody agreement that kept parenting as intact as humanly possible under the circumstances. This is one time, she vowed to herself, when children of divorce will not grow up mistrustful, insecure, and generally screwed up. Like herself, she chuckled. Action and reaction. She knew what a split family had done to her.

Mrs. Stewart arrived early in the afternoon. She was a tall, lean woman, the vestiges of early beauty still visible, although bitterness had cast a pinched look around her lips and eyes. She looked no worse for wear since Victoria had seen her at Christmas time. She came laden with gifts for the children and a carefully chosen present for Victoria, a brand-new leather briefcase. Victoria got the point at once.

"Well, here I am," Mrs. Stewart said. "Prepared to do the loving Gramma bit."

Victoria embraced her, thankful for her presence. In crisis, her mother always came through.

During the afternoon, she carefully instructed her mother about the children's routine, handing her a schedule of their activities and the various no-nos that had been proscribed. No television during the week, no junk food, a strict homework schedule, and neither of them up after nine.

"Above all, Mother, I want them to get used to your presence. And I don't want them to hear one bad word about their father."

"Why would I do that?"

"Guard you tongue, Mother. That's all I ask."

The children came home from school and greeted their grandmother with what Victoria felt was obedient affection. She wished her mother was a more cuddly type, but that wasn't in the cards. Respect was good enough at this juncture, and the children seemed to understand that.

Victoria and her mother prepared a dinner consisting of a fruit cup, broiled chicken, baked potatoes, boiled carrots and string beans, sourdough bread and jam, and fat-free chocolate ice cream, their favorite flavor. In the background the music of Chopin played on the stereo. Neither Michael nor Emily exhibited much of an appetite, which troubled Victoria.

"What's going on here?" she asked, watching them playing with their food. Emily ate almost nothing.

"Just not hungry today, Mommy," Emily said.

"Gramma helped make this wonderful dinner," Victoria said. "The only way we can acknowledge that is by eating it."

Michael seemed to make an effort in that direction, but, she noted, without relish. As they were about to start the ice cream course, the telephone rang.

"That's probably Daddy," Victoria said as the children exchanged glances.

Michael got up and ran to the phone while Emily hurried to the kitchen. Michael picked up the phone, but before speaking, he covered the mouthpiece and looked at his mother.

"Shall I tell him that Gramma's here?" he asked.

"What do you think, Michael?"

"I will if you want me to," he said.

"It can wait," Victoria said gently, trying to dismiss the idea as being of little importance.

She listened as Michael spoke to his father, noting his change of mood. He seemed animated and enthusiastic. She had wanted that, of course, but it did give her a stab of jealousy. Had they spoken to her with the same enthusiasm? After what seemed like a longer conversation than they normally had with her, they came back to the table and began to eat their ice cream with more appetite than they had shown earlier.

"How is Dad?" she asked.

"Fine," Michael said.

"Did he mention where he is?"

"No," Michael said.

She hadn't expected him to ask for her, but the fact that he didn't annoyed her. This failure was not lost on Mrs. Stewart.

"Did he ask to speak with your mother?" she inquired with more snappishness than Victoria might have wished.

Michael shook his head and averted his eyes as he continued eating his ice cream.

"It wasn't required, Mother," Victoria said.

"One would think that your common interest in the children would have."

"Never mind, Mother. I didn't speak to him more than once or twice during his stay."

"I'm sorry I mentioned it," she said with peevishness.

After dinner, the children went upstairs to do their homework, but before doing so both Victoria and her mother demonstrated their affection with hugs and vocal expressions of devotion.

"Love you kids," they said, embracing both children in turn.

"Me too, Mommy and Gramma," Emily said going from one to the other.

"Love you guys," Michael said as he kissed and hugged both women.

Victoria was well aware that she needed this demonstrative validation as much as the children did. The more repetitive, the better. Mrs. Stewart, too, despite her colder nature, seemed to enjoy the ritual.

"Do the children look different?" Victoria asked as they both cleaned the kitchen.

"How so?"

"Bigger. More filled out."

"Now that you mention it," Mrs. Stewart said, observing her daughter curiously, "you're right. They're busting out of their clothes."

"Then again, children grow fast," Victoria reflected. "Two weeks is a long time in a child's life."

"Yes it is," her mother agreed.

"There's more," Victoria muttered after a long silence. "But I can't put my finger on it."

Her mother shrugged.

"It's perfectly natural. There's a life change going on. Everything will probably seem different."

Victoria carefully maintained the routine that they had followed during the days before the separation. Her mother was enormously helpful, driving the children to extra-curricular activities, helping with the cooking while Victoria followed up on her search for clients. She went into Manhattan a number of times to check on her office and apartment but was always home for dinner.

Josh called every night at dinnertime and the children talked with him, their conversations animated and cheerful. She still resented not being asked to talk with him, but felt good about the children maintaining the bond with their father. Her mother continued to prod her.

"You'd think he would at least ask for your assessment of how things are going," Mrs. Stewart told her.

"I assume the children are giving him that information."

"I hope they haven't mentioned me."

"So do I."

In the middle of her second week of taking care of the children, Victoria sent her mother to the supermarket, planning to spend the entire day dusting and cleaning the den with special emphasis on her books and Victoriana collectibles. She climbed the book ladder and removed some of her large hats for dusting. It was then that she discovered that one of them was missing, a straw hat with a green ribbon around the crown.

"That is strange," she whispered aloud. She assumed that all the hats were in place before she had left the house two weeks ago. But she couldn't be certain, since permanent objects often went unnoticed. The inescapable fact, however, was that the hat with the green ribbon was among the missing.

Could it be that the woman that Josh had employed had taken a fancy to the hat and helped herself to it? Women were often tempted to try on the hats. Sometimes she had actually let them do just that, but always under her careful supervision. She allowed herself no conclusion, but made a mental note to discuss it with Josh when he called that night.

Soon after learning of the hat's disappearance, she discovered that one of the prized inkwells in her collection was not in its proper place on an end table. Had it been moved elsewhere? She carefully searched through the collection. She knew each piece, having carefully chosen every purchase. It was nowhere to be found. Still, she was not ready to make a concrete conclusion.

But when she could not find a pink vase, one of her very first acquisitions, in its usual place above the mantelpiece, it began to dawn on her that this was something that demanded greater attention. She went through the collection, noting that not one but two inkwells were gone. A second pass at her collection showed a cobalt-blue bell also among the missing.

Her mind was rife with speculation and annoyance. She walked up the stairs and checked the fashion plates and other knickknacks that were scattered throughout the house.

Everything seemed intact until she went into the spare room, which she had cursorily inspected earlier. This was the room she had given her mother. She had hung three fashion plates on the walls and one was clearly missing, since the outline could be seen on the wall. She hadn't noticed it before.

What she had discovered was both curious and disturbing, and when her mother returned from the supermarket she discussed it with her.

"Why would anyone want to steal them?" Mrs. Stewart asked. Victoria knew she was offering an opinion just short of saying what she really meant, namely that the knickknacks in her collection were, to her mother's way of thinking, merely junk.

"Because, Mother, despite your opinion, they had value. Even the fashion plate that is missing from your room."

"So that's it. Your mother's a thief."

"I hadn't noticed it before," Victoria said, ignoring her mother's remark.

"Why would I want it?"

"Mother, stop it. I'm not accusing you."

"Maybe it was the work of your wonderful Josh," her mother speculated sarcastically.

"Why would he do that?"

Mrs. Stewart shrugged. "Spite."

"Don't be ridiculous. What would be the point?"

"Get you riled up." Her mother inspected her. "Like you are now."

"Mother, don't."

"Just a thought. He attacks the material things you care about. Runs in the family," her mother said, winking, as she directed her attention to emptying the bags of groceries.

Victoria went back into the den, inspecting it yet again. She directed her attention to the leather-bound books by Victorian authors. The books were by Dickens, Thackery, Hardy, Goldsmith, Trollope, and others. She had always tended them with great care, treating the leather and dusting them periodically. She counted the various volumes. In each set, one book was missing. She checked them three times. Every book had been in sequence, the volume numbers marked on the spines.

There was no pattern to the missing numbers. In one set Volume Two was missing, in another Volume Eleven, in another Volume Four. Books were valued by complete sets, and missing a volume considerably reduced the value of the set.

She did not bring this information to her mother's attention since it could validate her suspicion that spite might, indeed, be involved. At that moment, she did not want to deal with Mrs. Stewart's smug surety. She felt heartsick about such a possibility. However he had betrayed her, she could not conceive of Josh as spiteful. Such conduct could completely destroy their attempt to properly share the rearing of their children. Dismissing such a possibility, she fixated on the person he had hired to help him during his two-week tenure.

At dinner that night, Victoria tried to subtly probe the children about the person Josh had selected. Not wanting to upset them, she avoided any mention of the thefts.

"What kind of a person was she?" Victoria asked casually.

"Very nice," Michael muttered without interest.

"Young, old?"

"I don't know," Michael shrugged looking at his sister. "Medium."

"Medium," Mrs. Stewart chuckled. "What does that mean?"

"Plain medium," Michael said.

"When she went home did she carry things?" Mrs. Stewart asked. The children exchanged glances and shook their heads.

"We never saw," Michael said.

"No, Mommy, we never saw."

When the telephone rang the children rushed to the phone.

"When you're finished, tell Daddy I'd like to speak with him," Victoria called to Michael. As usual, Emily used the kitchen phone.

"Above all, I don't want a confrontation," Victoria whispered to her mother.

"Good luck," her mother sneered.

The children talked to their father for what seemed an inordinately long time. Then Michael summoned her and she went into the kitchen to take the call, making sure the children had gone back to the table.

"Everything seems to be going well with the kids," Josh said. His tone struck her as icy.

"Yes fine, Josh," Victoria said drawing in a deep breath.

"I read your papers," Josh said. "Your concept of fairness leaves much to be desired."

"Not now, Josh. I have something else to ask you."

She told him about her discovery of all the missing things.

"Are you sure?"

"Absolutely."

"Makes no sense," Josh said after a long silence.

"Could it be the person you hired?"

"Who?"

"The person you hired."

"No way." He seemed irritated.

"How can you be so sure?"

"I'm sure. Believe me. Why would anyone want to take those things? One book from each set. Ink wells. Vases. Fashion plates. The one in the spare room. Are you hallucinating, Victoria?"

"I'll ignore that remark," she said coldly. "Just take my word for it."

"Look, Victoria," Josh said, "I don't know anything about this. Frankly it sounds...well...ridiculous."

"Ridiculous?" she said, her voice rising. "Something is definitely wrong here. I hope..." She tried calming herself, measuring her words. "I hope this is not some kind of spitefulness on your part, Josh."

"Spitefulness!" Josh shouted. "What are you talking about?"

"It's perfectly natural, Josh," she replied angrily. "You've got to admit that your credibility is certainly suspect."

"I don't believe this," Josh cried.

"It's not such a leap of faith," Victoria said, feeling her insides heave with anger, "to jump from fornicator to thief."

"I guess not. Jesus, you sound just like your mother," Josh said after a long pause. "Where will I go from there, Victoria? Embezzlement? Drug smuggling? Perhaps rape, pillage, even murder? Have you checked to see if there's a mustache painted over the lip of Queen Victoria? Now that's a crime for you. Can't you see how ridiculous your accusations are?"

"Maybe we should drop the subject," Victoria said, feeling suddenly foolish. Emotion was clouding her judgment.

"Amen."

"The fact is, these items are missing," Victoria said.

"Meaning I'm not off the hook."

"Meaning that you keep a watchful eye on your help or whoever else comes into the house."

"Whatever you say."

"We'll talk again," she said.

"Fine."

After she hung up, she realized that nothing had been resolved, that she was as much in the dark as ever.

The question kept reoccurring. Why not spite? A man who could keep an illicit love affair a secret for six months was capable of anything. Subjecting her to confusion and uncertainty could be quite gratifying to an antagonist. He could derive great pleasure from observing her aggravation.

On Sunday, Victoria was to turn over the house to Josh. She helped her mother pack. Despite occasional lapses in which she would unleash her poisonous tongue, Mrs. Stewart did seem to gain the children's confidence. She drove them to their respective after-school activities, took them to the movies, and generally behaved grandmotherly, at least to the limit of her capability.

"I hope you'll come again when my turn rolls around," Victoria asked when she was ready to go.

"Didn't I play the Gramma part well? Of course I will."

They embraced and her mother waved good-bye and got into a taxi.

-◆⊱══◑

When Josh showed up at the house, the children embraced him eagerly, perhaps more eagerly than they had embraced her when she had arrived two weeks ago. Tamping down her jealousy, she noted to herself that they had been very affectionate during her two-week stay, often hugging and kissing and telling her frequently how much they loved her. After their few moments of greeting, the children went up to their rooms.

"Remember the rule, children," Victoria called after them. "Listen to your dad."

"Of course they will," Josh said. "Anything I should know?" He did not offer much eye contact.

"No problems," she said. "The children were well-behaved and from all indications both seem to be doing well at school."

"Good."

"I bought them some new outfits. They seem to be filling out fast. Not to worry. I bought them on my dime."

"How generous."

His sarcasm seemed pointed and she tried changing the subject.

"No problems at the office?"

"None."

"Good." She paused, then tried to get off the next question casually. "Did you go over the divorce papers?"

"Not now, Victoria."

"I told you to get a lawyer, Josh. A lawyer can explain how I reached my conclusions on the settlement."

"I intend to."

Noting his tight-faced reaction, she said: "I don't want this to get contentious."

"I'm trying, Victoria."

She sucked in a deep breath.

"On that other matter."

"Must we?"

"I'm not imagining things, Josh. Let me show you."

He made a face and with obvious reluctance followed her into the den. She showed him the books first. He looked at them with little interest. Then she pointed to the end table and the mantelpiece.

"They were there. There are two inkwells and one vase missing, and in the spare room there is a fashion plate gone. You can still see the outline of where it was hung."

"Look, Victoria," he said impatiently. "I'd rather concentrate on getting the kids set. I don't know what happened to those pieces. Furthermore, I don't care. As far as I'm concerned, you can take them with you."

She was stunned by his sudden belligerence.

"This does not bode well," she snapped.

"No it doesn't."

"Somebody took them."

"Call in the house dick."

"This is not funny, Josh."

"Do you see me laughing?"

"How well do you know this person that is helping you with the children?"

"Not that again."

"I'd like to pursue that angle, before raising the other."

"Jesus, Victoria."

"All right. All right," she said raising her hands palms up. "But I'd strongly suggest that you watch her carefully."

"Who's going to watch you?"

"What does that mean?"

"It means that maybe this is all a ploy to further discredit me."

"Believe me, Josh. I don't need a ploy for that. Don't try to make me the culprit here, Josh. I'm the victim remember? The betrayed, faithful wife."

"I guess I'll be paying for that for the rest of my life," Josh sighed.

"I hope so."

He shook his head and turned away.

"Will you help me load the car?"

He nodded and went up to the room they had once shared. As he had done two weeks earlier, he loaded the Lexus.

"The kids know their schedule. I'll call them every night."

She got into the car, started it, and let the window go down. He had started to go into the hallway, but her voice stopped him.

"Note, Josh. Only *my* things were stolen. Not yours. Why is that, do you suppose?"

She rolled up the window and drove the car out of the garage.

Chapter 14

The past two weeks had been a trial for Josh. He had slept badly on Evie's couch, which meant he would arrive at his office in a state of irritation, adding to the tension of his job. For the sake of his digestion, he took most of his meals out, much to his sister's consternation. Two weeks a month was as much of her food as he could take.

So far there had been no signs of repercussions. Angela had officially turned in her resignation in writing and, as far as the agency was concerned, it appeared to be a closed matter. He did wonder about how she had fared with her husband, but he managed to push the thought from his mind. Their entanglement had been a disaster for both of them.

As much as he adored his sister and her lavish generosity, there was no question that he would have to get his own place, which reminded him of the matter of expense. It could not be avoided. He and Victoria would have to maintain three separate domiciles.

"You've been wonderful, Evie, but living here won't work."

"I understand, Josh."

"Besides, you need to have your own private life."

"I'm perfectly content the way it is, Josh. I like being around you and, of course, I love it when I'm with the children."

He wondered how long this situation would last. To make matters worse, he had finally read the divorce papers. She had allocated to him thirty-five percent of their assets as a settlement. The net worth of the percentages was to be determined by an independent accountant. Nevertheless, the uneven split was patently unfair. She had allocated sixty-five percent to herself on the grounds that she had lost ground on her career path by being a full-time mother and, therefore, was entitled to more as "compensation."

"No fucking way," he cried aloud when he finished reading her so-called "fair" papers, which he flung across the room in anger.

A single interview with a lawyer, a Harriet Franken, confirmed his misgivings.

"You need a nut-cutter," an old friend who had had a divorce told him. His friend had recommended Franken, a hard-boiled little woman with dyed red hair and a deep masculine voice.

"The fuck she will," Franken said when she had finished reading the papers. He had filled her in on his affair with Angela but had omitted all references to the Bocci settlement. "Your wife has set you up, Mr. Rose."

"I just want everything to be fair," Josh had muttered. He detested the woman lawyer on sight.

"Fair!" Franken exclaimed. "According to these papers, you've been castrated. She can't take the house just because it's in her name. The court will rule it's community property and the split she suggests is outrageous. Also, she's got you paying the whole load on custody. Screw her." She studied him over her half-glasses. "Don't be a *neb-bish*, Rose. You'll live to regret it."

"I don't want the children to be hurt."

"Then don't get divorced," Franken sighed.

"She's the one that wants out."

"Can you blame her?"

"It was an aberration. I was stupid."

"Not stupid, Mr. Rose. You let your cock rule your brain."

He was startled by the roughness of her language.

"I love my wife and family," he sighed.

"Listen to me, Rose," Franken said. "You're an adulterer, espe-cially in the eyes of the family court judge. We might be able to negotiate a reasonable settlement, considering that its your wife who wants out. As the main money person in the family, she'll probably hide some assets. You might have to pay for a forensic accountant. In any event, prepare yourself for some screwing and lots of contention. You say she's a lawyer handling her own case. Tough shit for you. She could make it expensive on your end. But custody will be tricky. She'll paint you as a man who puts pussy before parenting."

"But I don't. And she knows I love my children."

"All the better, from her point of view. It's the only weapon she has to punish you for the betrayal."

"But she believes in fathers having a strong role." He told her about Victoria's rearing with an absent father and an embittered mother.

"Double bind, Mr. Rose," the lawyer explained. "She doesn't trust you. And she probably hates her father for deserting her. At the same time she knows the kids need a daddy. She's on the horns of her own dilemma. I know the drill. We have to use it in our psychological warfare."

"Do you think this so-called bird nesting will work?" he asked, frightened by the prospects ahead.

"Don't bank on it, Mr. Rose. It could get too competitive."

He nodded, unwilling to elicit any further explanation. The whole process was demeaning. He felt her studying him.

"Divorce is a dreary business. Nobody wins. The best case scenario is a draw." She lifted a finger and waved it in his face. "Advice. On the money and property angle, don't fold your cards too soon. I'll get you close to fair. As for the kids, don't let it get sticky. Money, after all, is a replaceable resource. Kids aren't. The majority are fucked by divorce. I'm sorry to say this. But I've seen too much pain in this racket." She slapped the desk. "There. I've done my good lawyer's job of trying to talk you out of it."

"I hate this," Josh said, standing up. She put out her hand and he took it.

"It's a living," she said, offering a shrug. "Think about it."

He moved toward the door, but her voice recalled him.

"Take yourself in hand, Mr. Rose. It'll be a lot cheaper."
He didn't laugh.

Later, he and Evie went through the refrigerator and the cupboards to remove whatever foods Victoria had purchased that were subject to spoilage.

"This isn't real food," Evie said as she removed containers of skim milk and packages of fat-free cheeses, sour cream, and margarine from the refrigerator and threw them into a plastic bag to be consigned to garbage.

"Imagine the food industry selling these ersatz products under the false idea that it is actually food," she railed. "Where is the nutrition? Where is the caloric content? They might as well package sawdust."

She evangelized so often about the joy and comfort of food that he no longer found it in his heart to contradict her or openly criticize her obesity as a health risk.

"Food creates an attitude, Josh. Bad food, a bad attitude. Good food, a good attitude. A good attitude means a higher quality of life. If longevity suffers, and there is some reason for doubt, so be it. One day someone may even offer conclusive scientific proof that fat in food is healthier than no fat."

Considering the happy state of her mental health and her joyful attitude toward life, he would often speculate that there might be a lot to say for the quality of, perhaps, a shorter life of sensual pleasures than a longer one of deprivation and self-discipline.

After one of Evie's usual dinner ceremonies, and when the children had finally gone to sleep, the two of them sat in the den. He had poured out a brandy for himself and a crème de menthe for Evie. He hadn't talked to her about Victoria's proposed settlement, but he had mentioned the strange disappearances she was alleging.

"She has two suspects in mind. One is the so-called help," Josh explained, chuckling.

"Meaning me?"

"She doesn't know it's you, Evie."

He found it strangely gratifying that the children had apparently kept their secret about Aunt Evie. He knew firsthand the insidious pressure of keeping secrets.

"But what is missing is, nevertheless, missing," Evie said, sipping her crème de menthe.

"I'm not so sure I'm ready to buy that yet," Josh said, upending his brandy. "Could have happened a while ago. They could have been misplaced, broken. The kids' friends could have done it in some roughhouse way. She might have forgotten. As for the fashion plate in the spare room, she probably hadn't been in there in a couple of years. She also might have taken the objects herself."

"Why would she do that?"

"So she could accuse me. I'm the other suspect."

"You!" Evie exclaimed, pouring herself another crème de menthe.

"Spitefulness is the way she put it. I didn't quite understand what she meant at first. She cited Mom and Dad. Doing things to each other for pure spite. It's ironic." He shook his head. "The fact is I had this urge to smash some of her precious pieces. I really did. But I managed to kill the urge or, at least, contain it." He picked up one of the inkwells, then quickly replaced it. "I'd break them all if I had the guts."

"Poor Josh," Evie sighed.

"Anyway." He shook off his gloom, reached out, and took his sister's soft fleshy hand. "Thank God I have you, Evie."

As during his first two weeks of bird nesting, the household operated in a similar routine. Josh went to the office while Evie supervised the home. Evie continued to cook her elaborate meals. The children loved them, especially the desserts. Evie was a marvel. She made soufflés every night, of every variety, vanilla, chocolate, orange, praline, almonds, and whatever else struck her fancy.

She made mousses and custards and all types of molds. Often they would have two desserts at dinner. Sometimes she would actually cook two main dishes, poultry, fish, or meat. What she did with eggs

and potatoes were works of art. The house was never free from delicious cooking scents, and there were always plates of exotic cookies
available at all times.

To cope with all the rich food, Josh kept a secret cache of pre-
scription antacids within easy reach, a fact that he would never dare
reveal to Evie. The children, on the other hand, never seemed to fal-
ter, their young digestive systems able to cope without discomfort
with Evie's cooking repertoire. Watching them revel happily in her
creations, he could be convinced that her theories on food might
have more merit than he had earlier speculated.

The children appeared to thrive on the program. Or so he assured
himself. They ate whatever they wanted, went to bed at all hours, and
lived without any of the constrictions their mother had laid down. It
amazed him how smoothly they moved from one plan to the other.

Then, a few days before Josh's two weeks were up, his own obser-
vations about the children's so-called adjustment was called into
question. Emily brought home an alarming school report, her
progress rendered by comment rather than by grades.

"Emily seems to have lost interest in school," the teacher's report
read. "She has also lost her concentration and is not as friendly and
cooperative with both teachers and her fellow students as she had been
earlier in the term. Her reading skills seem to have deteriorated lately
as well. In general, I would say that more help at home is warranted."

Josh was shocked and Emily was embarrassed by the report. Josh
soothed her by blaming everything on the circumstances of her parents' separation. He assured her that once the tension passed and they
had all made the emotional adjustment to the new circumstances, she
would regain the will to study and get better grades. But he did insist
that she read the teacher's comments to her mother over the phone.
Victoria, as he had expected, asked to speak with Josh.

"I hope you didn't scold her," Josh said.

"I did tell her that I was disappointed," Victoria said.

"I would have preferred you didn't," Josh said. "It was completely
predictable."

"Is she very upset?"

"Of course she is. Who wouldn't be? Her regression is obviously a consequence of what's happening between us."

"It's just one more thing we'll have to deal with, Josh."

"Yeah," Josh muttered. "One more thing."

It turned out to be two more things. Michael, too, presented him with a terrible report card. It was Saturday, the day before Josh was to relinquish the house to Victoria. Josh noted that Michael had held off a full day before showing it to him.

"Why didn't you show it to me yesterday?"

"I was scared and Emily had just got hers."

"I see the point," Josh said, gloomily looking over the report. "This is surprising," he said. Michael had flunked both math and science, which had been his best subjects.

"I guess I screwed up, Dad."

"Everyone is allowed at least one screw up," Josh said gently. Although he was genuinely alarmed, he thought it best, as he had advised Victoria, not to show too much disappointment.

"Should I tell Mom when she calls tonight or wait until tomorrow?"

"I'd suggest you tell her tonight. After all, you did get the report on my watch. I wouldn't want her to show up and get a big surprise."

"I guess she'll be pissed, especially after Emily."

"I hope not," Josh said diplomatically. "We all know this is just temporary. You're a smart kid. You'll get back on track."

Again, after hearing about Michael's report, she asked to speak with Josh.

"It's a double whammy, Josh," she said with obvious irritation.

"It is very incongruous, Victoria."

"Incongruous, Josh? That is a very odd comment."

"He does his homework. He's not withdrawn or depressed. He seems happy and content. I don't understand it."

"It could be a form of protest," Victoria said. "For both of them."

"Maybe. How would you propose to handle that?" Josh asked, hoping she would see it as a challenge.

"I don't know. We're certainly giving them more than most parents in this situation."

"If you say so," Josh mused bitterly.

"Maybe they need a good talking to. Both of them."

"As of tomorrow, you're in charge."

"Josh, this has to be a joint decision."

"My take on it is that they've got enough on their plate without further scolding. They know they blew it."

"It simply is not acceptable."

"You're telling me. If Michael keeps going down like this, Pendleton could choose to let him go. Their standards are pretty high."

"You mean expel him?"

"It hasn't reached that point yet, Victoria. But it could."

"Never," Victoria snapped, her voice rising. "They had better not."

He was surprised at her militancy.

"It's their right."

"Never mind their right. They will never expel him. Take my word for it."

Her comment was puzzling. He could hear her hard breathing at the other end of the line, which seemed strange.

"Are you all right, Victoria?" he asked, genuinely concerned, as if they were still devoted spouses.

"I'm fine," Victoria said belligerently. "Why do you ask?"

"Never mind," he sighed, waiting through another long silence. "Are you still there?"

She cleared her throat.

"I was thinking about that other matter...the thefts."

"They are only objects, Victoria. Things."

Shades of his parents, he thought suddenly. Just things. In the end it killed them.

"You're being self-righteous, Josh. It doesn't become you."

"Victoria," he muttered, angered by her words and his memories. "I really don't give a shit about your fucking ink wells or hats or whatever."

"I'll ignore that remark. And I'd advise you to watch your help. She could be pulling the wool over your eyes."

From where he stood, he could see Evie bustling around in the kitchen.

There was another long pause at both ends of the line. He had no wish to pursue the matter further. Not now.

"You're a hard woman, Victoria," he said.

"I tried the other way. A lot of good it did me."

The phone went dead.

Later, he sat alone in the den while Evie cleaned the kitchen. His expression gave him away and Evie had suggested that he might need some solitude. He was thankful for her sensitivity. Thinking about the situation, he felt mired in frustration and failure. Worse, he sensed that a profound depression was beginning to afflict him. He wanted to cry but the tears would not come.

"Was Mom angry?" It was Michael's voice. He had come downstairs followed by Emily, who carried Tweedledee in her arms. From their rooms came the sounds of television.

"A little," he sighed.

"At us?"

"That's only part of it, children," he said, reaching out and embracing them both.

"We're sorry, Daddy," Emily said, still holding Tweedledee. "We talked it over. We're going to work real hard, aren't we, Mikey?"

"Real hard."

"I know you will."

He continued to hold them, wondering how it would all turn out in the end. He was not optimistic.

"It's only natural, kids. Probably a consequence of what you're going through. Things were much better when we were all together."

Josh felt comforted by their presence and this show of affection. There was also another factor becoming more and more apparent to him. Their solidarity. It reminded him again of the bond between Evie and himself.

"You'll make it, guys," he said. "I know it."

"We'll get better, Dad," Michael said. "You'll see."

Emily nodded and kissed Tweedledee on the head.

"I'll never let you down, guys." He drew in a deep breath. "Neither will Mom."

"We know that, Dad."

"But we do have a question, Daddy," Emily said.

"Maybe I should ask it, Emmie," Michael whispered.

"No. I want to ask it. You said I could."

"It's a very hard question," Michael persisted, raising his voice.

Josh braced himself.

"Why don't you and Mommy live together anymore?" Emily blurted.

"We told you. Because we were unhappy living together," Josh said. It was the party line that he and Victoria had agreed to.

"No you weren't," Michael said.

"Now how would you know that?" Josh asked gently. It was obvious that the explanation hadn't made its point.

"We live here too, Dad," Michael said.

"Yes we do," Emily seconded.

"Did something happen?" Michael asked.

"What happened was...well, she got to be unhappy is all," Josh replied, realizing that his answers were becoming more and more evasive.

"We think you should get together again," Michael said, glancing at his sister as if they had scripted the remarks.

"If you really love us, like you say you do, then you should do that," Emily said. Both children were serious and unsmiling.

"Easier said than done."

"We should all get another chance, Dad," Michael said.

"Maybe we all deserve another chance. Mommy, too," Josh said, surrendering to the idea. He gathered his children to him and embraced them.

"We need for all of us to be together, Daddy," Emily said. "Like it was before."

A lump began to grow in Josh's throat.

"I couldn't agree more."

"Then why don't you make it happen?" Michael said, his words firm, as if it were an order. "You're the father."

He felt as if his heart would break.

"Maybe I have to go back to Daddy school," he replied quickly, swallowing hard. At that moment, an idea popped into his head. "Maybe you should be having this discussion with Mom."

"We're going to, aren't we, Emmie?" Michael said.

"Yes we are, Daddy," Emily said firmly.

"Good."

He gathered the children together in a tighter embrace, kissed their heads, and then patted them both on their rears.

"Now get on upstairs and stop trying to figure out the weirdness of adults."

When they had gone, Evie emerged from where she was standing nearby.

"I heard, Josh," she said. "It broke my heart."

"How do you respond to such an appeal? I feel so helpless."

"Josh. They're part of this family. They had every right to have something to say about what is happening to them."

"Unfortunately, divorce is about adults, not kids. The sad fact is that they don't get to vote, Evie."

"Maybe they should."

"We didn't," Josh sighed, his vision blurring with tears.

Chapter 15

One evening during their two-week stint, Victoria, her mother, and the children went to the performance of *Annie* at the Pendleton Hall auditorium, which they all seemed to enjoy. After the show, the audience gathered in an adjoining room and Mr. Tatum, looking his usual patrician self, made a short complimentary speech about the performance. Victoria listened with a combination of amusement and disgust, recalling the image of him in the car, penis aroused, demanding sexual favors. At one point, their eyes met and she could see the sudden stab of fear in them as he quickly diverted his attention.

As Tatum mingled with the crowd, she felt him observing her, and soon he was moving in her direction. It struck her as odd, since she thought he would have gone to great lengths to avoid her.

"How are you, Mrs. Rose?" he asked.

"Very well, thank you," she said without expression, noting that her mother and her children were a safe distance from them.

"We've got a problem, Victoria," he whispered. He was unsmiling and seemed genuinely anguished. "I was going to call, but I feared your reaction."

"You were very wise," she said belligerently.

"We have to talk," he whispered.

"Not again, Tatum."

"It's serious, Victoria."

"He'll improve. I guarantee it."

"It's not that."

"Not that?" She was startled.

"I've been trying to keep a lid on this," he said, looking genuinely upset. "I can't any longer. It's out of hand."

"What is?"

"Not here," he said quickly. Mrs. Stewart came to join them, and Victoria introduced them.

"I loved the play, Mr. Tatum," she said.

"Thank you," he said, turning to Victoria. "So nice seeing you again, Mrs. Rose." Then he moved away.

She felt her mother inspecting her.

"My God, you've turned ashen. What's wrong?"

"I'm fine, Mother."

Later, after they'd gone home, Victoria came into Michael's room.

"Mr. Tatum wants to talk to me," she said. "Is there anything I should know?"

Michael looked up at the ceiling, as if he were mulling possibilities. Finally, his eyes met his mothers.

"I'm gonna do better, Mom. I told you that."

"It wasn't about your report," she said, closely observing him.

"It wasn't?" Lines of concern creased his forehead.

"Is there something I should know, Michael?" she asked.

"About what?"

"Must be something," she mused aloud.

He shook his head and shrugged. She kissed him and left the room.

In three days, she would put the household back in Josh's hands. For the first time since they had put the system into effect, she was having second thoughts. She was tempted to call Josh at the office and discuss the situation, but she decided against it. In her present state, she knew she would get emotional and accusatory.

Tatum called early the morning after the play and she agreed to meet with him, but only in his office.

"Of course in my office, Mrs. Rose," he said officiously. "This is school business."

"I've heard that before," she said with a sneer before hanging up.

She was ushered into his office. Instead of directing her to the chair in front of his desk where he had made his initial proposition, he directed her to the conversational grouping where they had had their meeting with the Crespos.

"I'm in a bind, Mrs. Rose," he said, his voice barely audible. She noted that he looked fearfully toward his office door.

"That's pretty obvious, Gordon."

"Please, Mrs. Rose, let's keep this formal."

"Whatever you say. Now what's this all about?"

"Believe it or not," he paused and offered an expression of total frustration, "it's about candy."

"That again."

"Can you believe it? My world hangs in the balance over..." He leaned over the desk, his eyes meeting hers, "damned candy."

"The Crespos..." she began.

He nodded and shrugged.

"Them and every other parent."

"You're not making much sense, Gor..." She checked herself. "Mr. Tatum."

"At first it seemed so trivial." He shook his head. "Someone was just handing out candy bars. Simple as that."

"Milky Ways," Victoria said in a kind of knee-jerk reaction.

"Yes." He paused and offered a wry but joyless chuckle. "And Snickers. Mars Bars, Tootsie Rolls, Good and Plentys. Look how expert I've become on the confection industry. Call it the attack of the candy bars, Mrs. Rose. Somebody was handing them out on a daily basis."

"To whom?"

He paused and swallowed hard as if it were painful to articulate.

"The children in Michael's class."

"Free of charge? Just handing them out?"

He nodded.

"Is that an infraction of the rules?" she asked with some sarcasm.

"Not exactly. At first I thought this was just a passing trend. I didn't like the idea, of course. It's the very reason why we do not have candy vending machines in the school. But we've been through all that, haven't we, Mrs. Rose?"

"I'm afraid so."

She suddenly felt as if she had entered a surreal world as far removed from reality as the earth from the nearest star. What does this have to do with me, she wondered? Or was this another of his subtle ploys?

"As you know there is no specific rule barring candy bars from the school, and it goes without saying that we do not encourage our students to eat candy per se. Nor do we restrict students from eating candy bars in the cafeteria."

"Get to the point, Tatum," Victoria snapped.

"It starts as a trickle, then accelerates and becomes a flood."

"What does?"

"Parental complaints."

"If I'd known, I'd be the first to object. They're absolutely right. I think I've made myself very clear on the subject."

"Yes you have."

"Am I here because I've been chosen to lead the charge against the practice?"

"Not exactly."

"Then what?" Victoria said, wondering again if the man was brazen enough to begin his little game again. It crossed her mind that perhaps he had developed some sexual obsession about her, some uncontrollable impulse.

"I'm afraid the benefactor of all this candy largesse is, as you might have guessed, your Michael."

"Michael!" she cried. "You can't be serious."

Was this déja vu? Candy? Was this a monstrous joke being played on her?

"Considering the situation," Tatum said, lifting his chin and scratching his neck in contemplation. "I thought we should talk. The truth is, Mrs. Rose..." He paused and whispered: "Victoria. I'm being pushed. Look, I'm completely at your mercy. I've been a fool. Worse. I've put my career and my family on the line. You can destroy me, Victoria."

"Have you talked to Michael about this?" she asked, ignoring his appeal. His pleading embarrassed her.

"Yes, I have. Very tactfully, of course. Not accusatory. I did not tell him about the pressure I'm getting from the parents."

"What did he say?"

"He admitted to giving out the candy. He hadn't intended it to be a secret."

Victoria was astonished.

"Did he say why?"

"Proudly, he said: 'Food is love. Candy is sharing and friendship.'"

"Evie!" she cried, rising to her feet.

"I don't understand."

"My sister-in-law."

"I still don't understand."

"This practice will stop, Tatum," Victoria said. "I guarantee it."

"And you're not angry that I brought it up?"

"Hell no," Victoria said.

"I'm greatly relieved," he said.

"I'm not."

She felt the full fury of this revelation. Evie! Of course. Fat little Evie. This explained why the children were gaining weight. Evie was the help and Josh had deliberately kept it from her. It was an outrage, exposing the children to Evie's destructive obsessions and influence.

For years she had tolerated her cultish madness about food, her erratic and repugnant lifestyle, her stunted philosophy and behavior. Long after she had forbidden the children to visit with her she had tolerated Josh's sentimental attachment with this obviously unbalanced woman.

She berated herself for her naiveté. Once again, Josh had betrayed her. Worse, he had enlisted the children in this conspiracy. To her, that was the most terrible infraction of all. He had used them, abused her own magnanimity and fairness to corrupt her teachings and rearing principles.

Driving home, she tried to work out some way of extracting them and herself from the dilemma she had unwittingly created. There seemed no point now in ignoring what she saw as the evil being perpetrated against her and her offspring. Josh was deliberately alienating her children from her, creating subtle animosities and, she was certain, stealing for the sheer pleasure of aggravating her.

"What's going on?" Mrs. Stewart asked when she arrived home. "You look like you've been through the wringer."

"Leave me alone, Mother," Victoria snapped. "I'm too furious to talk." She went into the den and poured herself a stiff drink.

"Must be serious business for a belt like that," her mother said.

"I've been fucked," Victoria cried, blurting out the story in bits and pieces.

"That fat bitch," her mother said. "And the kids were in on it." She shook her head.

"They won't get away with this," Victoria cried, upending her glass.

When the children came home from school, she had already worked up a good head of steam. She summoned them to the den and they came obediently with odd expressions of curiosity on their faces as they exchanged glances. She ordered them both to sit on the couch. She did not sit down. Instead, she paced the floor in front of them while Mrs. Stewart observed her.

"Above all, children, I want the absolute truth. No more lies. No more denials. I've had enough." She looked pointedly at Michael. "Do you understand what I'm saying?"

Both children looked at each other in confusion.

"Who has been living here and helping Daddy?"

She had expected a thunderbolt reaction. None came.

"Aunt Evie," Michael said calmly.

"Yes, Mommy. Aunt Evie," Emily said.

"Why haven't I been told?" Victoria scolded.

"Because we know you don't like Aunt Evie," Michael said as if it were merely a passing comment on the weather. "We didn't want to upset you. Did we, Emmie?"

"No, Mommy."

"And what has she been stuffing into your fat little mouths?"

"Ragout," Emily began. "de Veau..." She looked helplessly at her brother.

"What are you trying to say?"

"Aux champignons," Michael added in bad French.

"Rich French food," Mrs. Stewart sneered. "She's been feeding them that slop."

"I don't believe this," Victoria cried.

"Lots of sweets and cakes and pies, right?" Mrs. Stewart said, raising her voice. "You were keeping it a secret from your mother, weren't you, children?"

"Mommy doesn't like Aunt Evie," Emily said, looking at her grandmother with obvious disdain.

"She's been brainwashing them about food being love and candy sharing a sign of pure friendship and nonsense like that," Victoria fumed as she paced in front of them.

"It's disgusting," Mrs. Stewart sneered.

The children frowned and looked at each in confusion.

"I spoke to Mr. Tatum today," Victoria said, directing her attention to Michael. "He informed me about your little candy caper. How could you defy me in that way, especially after that other episode with the Crespo girl?"

"All I did was give candy to my friends," Michael protested.

"Their parents are complaining, Michael. Mr. Tatum says he may be forced to take some action. Hasn't my teaching meant anything to you? I thought we had an understanding. You were taught the difference between right and wrong."

"Ask him where he got the candy," Mrs. Stewart interposed.

"That's pretty obvious, Mother," Victoria said, pausing and shaking her head. "What I can't understand and what boggles my mind is how you conveniently neglected to tell me about Aunt Evie being here."

"We didn't tell Dad about Gramma," Michael said with an air of defiance.

Victoria observed her son curiously. Suddenly she saw him in a strangely different light and it startled her. What had earlier been merely disappointment was now compounded by another more frightening vision. He seemed a complete stranger, someone who was not at all like the child she thought she knew.

"I think this child hasn't got a clue to what's going on here," Mrs. Stewart said. "And I believe he ought to be told."

"Told what, Mother?" Victoria said, her mind still dealing with the unanswered questions of her parenting.

"About why this is happening, Victoria," Mrs. Stewart said, rising from her chair. "If you won't tell them, Victoria, I will."

She was unstoppable now, and Victoria was too psychologically exhausted to make the effort. Mrs. Stewart faced the children, her eyes wandering from one face to the other.

"Your father betrayed your mother," she began, pausing to watch their reaction. Victoria agonized over the revelation, but said nothing. "He broke up his family by violating the marriage contract, having sex with another woman. You may not yet understand what I'm saying now. But someday you'll remember what I said, and you'll know what I meant. He was unfaithful to your mother. He lay with another woman. He is a selfish, evil, bad man."

"Good God, Mother," Victoria shouted. "They don't know what the hell you're talking about."

"Oh yes they do," Mrs. Stewart snapped. "Don't fool yourself."

Emily's expression was one of total confusion. She began to cry hysterically. Victoria rushed to comfort her with an embrace.

Michael sat stone-faced, lips pursed, his expression contemptuous, his reactions curiously unchildlike. She had the impression that Michael knew exactly what his grandmother had meant.

"Your father is evil," Mrs. Stewart shouted.

"This is getting out of hand," Victoria cried, tightening her embrace of Emily.

Michael looked at his mother with eyes blazing. Victoria saw in them something she had never seen before. Pure rage.

"I'm going to tell Dad about Gramma," he shouted, then turning to Mrs. Stewart, "My dad is not an evil man."

"He's not," Emily cried, tears streaming down her cheeks.

"You're a very bad woman," Michael blurted, still facing his grandmother.

"Don't you dare talk to your Gramma like that," Victoria screamed, releasing Emily and slapping her son hard across his cheek, his skin quickly reddening with the imprint of her fingers.

Emily ran to her brother and clung to him screaming. "Mommy, stop it. Please."

"I don't care what you tell your father, Michael," Mrs. Stewart shouted. "What he can't change is the fact that I'm your grandmother. I don't care if he does despise me. I hate him, too."

"Stop it. Stop it. Stop it," Victoria said, reaching for her son, overwhelmed by contrition over what she had done.

"Please forgive me, Michael. Please. I didn't mean it. My God, what has got into us?" She kissed his reddened cheek. "Forgive me, my baby. Please."

"He deserves it, Victoria," Mrs. Stewart shouted. "Why are you coddling him?"

"I didn't do anything, Mom," Michael said, caressing his mother's arm. "All we want is for you and Dad to love each other and stay together."

"Fat chance," Mrs. Stewart hissed, turning to her daughter. "We know where the source of all this trouble is coming from, don't we Victoria?"

"I wish you would shut your mouth, Mother," Victoria yelled. "Just shut up. Shut up. Please shut up."

"Don't talk to me like that, Victoria."

"I just don't want to hear any more," Victoria snapped, fighting for control. She and her mother exchanged fiery glances.

"You've got a big problem here, Victoria," Mrs. Stewart said, turning and with obvious indignation leaving the room.

When her mother was gone, Victoria tightened her embrace on both children. Emily continued to sob.

"Please forgive me, kids. I don't know what got into me. I love you both so much." She gently caressed Michael's cheek. "I'm so sorry, Michael," she sighed. "Can you ever forgive me?"

Her plea for forgiveness seemed to have the desired effect. Both children kissed and hugged their mother and remained in her arms until they had all calmed down. After a while, she released the children and sent them upstairs.

On further reflection, although contrite and thoroughly ashamed of her outburst, she began to have second thoughts about her mother's revelation to the children. Despite the bad timing and acrimony, sooner or later they had to know. Maybe they did not understand what sexual infidelity meant, but surely they knew the meaning of disloyalty and betrayal. Perhaps her mother's mean-mindedness did serve a useful purpose after all.

This incident made it increasingly apparent that she and Josh were competing against each other for the love of their children. She didn't have any illusions about who was winning. Josh and Evie were indulging them with food. But that was only one manifestation of their technique. As the disciplining parent, she was playing the less-attractive role and suffering the consequences.

It was obvious that this "bird nesting" arrangement was not the solution she had hoped it would be. She had not foreseen that Josh could be so devious when came to the children. Once again, she had been naïve in her assumptions. She was now convinced that Josh's cooperation in this venture had been a pose.

It was time, she decided, to take another tack, one more aggressive and considerably less trusting.

Chapter 16

Josh got the call from Michael in his office. He sounded panicked and upset. It was late Friday and he would not be back at the house until Sunday evening.

"Mom knows about Aunt Evie," Michael said almost in a whisper, as if he feared discovery.

"How did she find out?"

"Emily and I didn't tell her. She..." He hesitated. "She went to the school. I...I was giving away candy to the class."

"That wasn't too smart, Michael."

"I'm sorry, Dad."

"What was her reaction?"

"Not good, Dad. She slapped me."

"Oh my God. Emily, too? Did she?"

"Just me. Then she said she was sorry."

It was out of character for Victoria to ever hit her children. In fact, she had railed against such disciplinary measures, and he had never lifted a hand to them in rebuke.

"And Dad..."

Again he could hear the hesitation in Michael's voice.

"What is it, son?"

"Gramma said bad things."

Mrs. Stewart's sad face surfaced in his mind, bringing with it all the aura of her mean spirit. How did she get into the picture? The truth dawned on him with explosive force. His rage erupted.

"What is that monster doing in my house?" he screamed into the

phone. He immediately regretted the outburst. Both he and Victoria
had been scrupulous in not defaming Mrs. Stewart in front of the
children and were extraordinarily tolerant of Victoria's love-hate
attachment to her. A lot of good all that caution had achieved. His
rage accelerated and he had to pause and take deep breaths to com-
pose himself before he was able to speak again.

"Are you okay, Dad?" Michael asked.

"I'm fine, son. It's just...well never mind. Tell me what kind of
things your grandmother said about me."

It took Michael some seconds to get the words out.

"Bad things," Michael said, his voice suddenly hoarse.

"Tell me, son," Josh said.

"About laying with another woman. About betraying Mom."

Josh was stunned. Then it occurred to him that she might not have
spared Emily.

"Did Emily hear these things?"

"Yes, Dad. She made Emily cry."

"Bitch," Josh muttered, inflamed by the idea that this bitter
woman, who had preached her hatred of men as a solemn cause
could be let loose to spew her poison over his children.

"And this all happened today?"

"When we came home from school."

"And now? What is it like now?"

"Mom and Gramma are making dinner."

"And Emily?"

"She's standing right here."

Emily took the phone.

"I love you, Daddy," she said. He could hear the sadness in her
voice. "Gramma said bad things."

"I know, darling. I love you, too. But it's all going to be all right.
Cross my heart. I promise."

"Okay, Daddy."

He was at a loss for words. What could one say to a nine-year-old
who had just heard her father was a bad man?

"I'm not a bad man, sweetheart."

"I know Daddy."

"Honey, let me speak to Michael again."

It was obvious that they were using a telephone extension out of earshot of his wife and her mother. Michael got on the phone again.

"Does Mom know you're talking to me?"

"No," Michael said, but his reply seemed tentative. Then he said: "But I did tell her I would tell you about Gramma."

"And what did she say to that?"

"She was very angry."

"Was Mom there when your grandmother said those bad things?"

"Yes."

He felt as if a hot poker had been shoved into his guts. He began to shake.

"And she did nothing to stop her?"

"After...after she told Gramma to shut her mouth."

"After?" he repeated calmly, understanding Michael's hidden message. Victoria had let it be said and her mother had been the instrument of the revelation.

"So Gramma has been there all along?"

"Yes, Dad."

"And you didn't tell me?"

"It was like Aunt Evie, Dad. I didn't tell Mom about that, either." Michael again paused in his explanation. "I know you don't like Gramma and I know Mom doesn't like Aunt Evie."

"It's alright, son. I'm not blaming you. I understand."

"Are you mad at me, Dad?"

"God no, Michael. And you did the right thing about telling me."

"I figured that since Mom knew about Aunt Evie it was all right to tell about Gramma."

"You shouldn't have been asked to bear that burden." He wondered if his son understood what he meant. He was a fool not to understand that Victoria would reach out for her mother in a time of extreme stress.

"Do you believe your dad is a bad person, Michael?" he asked gently.

"You're my dad. Of course not."

"But it's true that I did a bad thing to Mommy." He felt a sob begin in his chest. Did he really understand what it meant to lay with another woman, he wondered? "But I do love her and am very sorry for what I did."

"And you did promise you wouldn't do it anymore. Didn't you, Dad?"

Michael's comment did not surprise him. Josh was learning fast. Children could ferret out lies and misdeeds a lot better and faster than adults. He was also certain that they understood in some primitive but compelling form the "bad" things that Mrs. Stewart had said about him.

"Yes I did, son. I promised I wouldn't ever do it again."

What he needed most of all was time to think this out. It was obvious to him that conditions had changed and the children were caught in a parental crossfire.

"I want you to promise me something, Michael."

"Sure, Dad."

"Be a good boy. Try not to make things worse than they are. When I come Sunday, we'll straighten everything out. And tell Emily to be a good girl."

"I will, Dad...and Dad?"

"Yes?"

"Are you going to bring Aunt Evie?"

He felt caught short by the question and pondered it for a few moments.

"Of course, Michael. Aunt Evie will be there."

As promised, the phone conversations with the children on both Friday and Saturday were short and deliberately routine. He had half-expected Victoria to call him at Evie's, but no calls came, which he interpreted as ominous. Victoria could not let the information about Evie's presence in the house during his two-week stay go unchallenged.

On the other hand, he was immersed in what he considered a far more serious dilemma. His mother-in-law was a menace. She was obviously bent on alienating him from his children at all costs and continuing her sick influence over Victoria. The irony was that Victoria knew her predilections, had fought them all her life, and yet was trapped in the relationship and unwilling or unable to sever it.

To keep the peace, he had tolerated the relationship. She was, after all, Victoria's mother. His feeling, heightened by the fact that he had lost own his mother at an early age, was that there was something sacred about the very idea of motherhood. And he interpreted Victoria's attachment to her, however strained and neurotic, as a natural need.

Victoria had confided to him about the emotional meeting she had had with her father before he died. She had also explained that she could not find it in her heart to forgive him. It seemed to weigh on her heavily, although she had admitted that she could not summon up anything approaching her mother's hatred of him. In fact, all she had felt was pity. The poor man had married the wrong woman and it had obviously ruined his life.

With a great deal of trepidation, Josh drove the Lexus into the garage. Victoria, looking paler than when he had seen her last, met him in the hallway as he brought in his suitcases. Normally, her baggage would be packed and ready to load. There were no suitcases in sight.

"You're late," she said.

"Traffic," he replied.

Her annoyance was palpable, but he ignored it.

"I hope it was a good two weeks," he said pleasantly.

She did not offer an answer. Instead she said: "We have to talk."

"About what?" he asked.

"The situation."

"I thought things were going well," he replied, offering what he hoped was a look of total innocence.

"Hardly," Victoria said coldly.

"Where are the children?" he asked. Normally, they would be present to greet him. This was, indeed, an ominous sign.

"I sent them to the movies," Victoria said coldly.

"Alone?"

"With my mother."

He followed her to the den, where she moved to the bar and poured herself a stiff drink.

"You?" she asked.

He shook his head in the negative and she moved to one of the chairs. She took a deep sip of her drink. He was standing in the center of the room, waiting for her to make the opening comment.

"I can't trust you, Josh," she said. "Aside from being an unfaithful bastard, you're a sneak, a liar, and a cheat. You disappoint me in all respects. But the very worst thing you're guilty of is using our children as pawns in your little game. In my opinion this alone would disqualify you as a fit father."

He listened with his eyes averted. He had expected something of the sort, although the depth of her anger and the suddenness of her attack stunned him. It had caught him off guard.

"I think I will have that drink," he said, pouring himself a stiff scotch in a highball glass, then taking a deep swallow.

"You must think I'm a naïve fool," she said, her lips tight, her look hard. "Tell me, Josh, when does the fat girl arrive? And don't look startled. I'm sure your little partner in the conspiracy has already informed you of my mother's presence when I'm in charge."

"Makes us even, Victoria," he said, inflamed by the derisive way she portrayed Michael.

"Hardly even. My mother obeyed my rules to the letter. Madame Obesity and you violated all of them. How could you, Josh? How could you possibly have allowed that to happen? She's made gluttons out of our children and it shows. Food is love, is it? I'm sure he told you what he did at school. I don't believe we've heard the end of this. It won't be like the other. This time I'm going to let the chips fall where they may."

"What does that mean?"

"Never mind that," she said, sipping her drink. "It is obvious that things can't go on the way they have been."

"Quite obvious," Josh said.

Victoria tossed off the rest of her drink. Anger and bitterness had transformed her. His affair with Angela had wounded her in a way he could not have imagined, and for that he was sorry. There was no way to rationalize that. She was on her way to becoming a harridan like her mother. But he forced himself to hold back much of his anger.

At that moment, he heard sounds coming from the front door and the voices of his children.

"Did he put up much of a fuss?" Mrs. Stewart said as she entered the den. When she saw Josh, she stopped in her tracks.

"Well, that answers that question," she snapped just as the children came into the room and embraced their father.

"Where's Aunt Evie?" Emily asked.

"She'll be here soon," Josh said.

"Children," Victoria said. "Why don't you go upstairs? Dad and I have lots to talk about. Okay, kids?"

"Okay, Dad?" Michael asked his father.

"I've already given you permission, children," Victoria said harshly. He could feel Emily observe his reaction.

"Sure, kids. You go upstairs and watch TV. We'll talk later."

The children exchanged confused glances with their parents and with each other, then turned and moved slowly out of the room. He was struck at that moment with the realization that the removal of the children from their proximity in no way hindered their knowledge of what was transpiring. They were deluding themselves if they believed that the children were not fully aware of the conflict going on in their home. In fact, he was beginning to believe that they were more highly active participants in their fate than he had imagined.

"There's no need for you to stay," Josh said to his mother-in-law, who looked to Victoria for guidance. "This doesn't concern you."

"You stay, Mother," Victoria said. "He has no authority in this house. In fact, legally speaking, he has no ownership."

"I have no intention of leaving," Mrs. Stewart said with haughty disdain, glancing at her daughter who seemed to offer confirmation of her stand.

Victoria paced the room, turning finally and facing him.

"Really, Josh, your presence here is very disruptive. It does not bode well for an amicable settlement between us. You've caused enough difficulties already."

"Difficulties? You and your mother are the culprits here. The children were perfectly happy during their stay with me."

"Happy? You mean indulged."

"I know what I mean."

"I'd call the police if I were you, Victoria," her mother said smugly. "He's trespassing."

"Good idea," Josh said. "Let them be the judge of who is really trespassing."

"Well then..." She turned to her daughter. "Call it spousal abuse."

"What role would you like to take, Victoria? Abuser or abusee?"

"You really should go, Josh," Victoria said, apparently adopting a more conciliatory tone. "This entire discussion is counterproductive."

By then, Josh had mentally dug in his heels. He was not, under any circumstances, going to leave the house. If Victoria sensed that, she showed no signs of retreating. Shrugging, she moved toward the bar and poured herself a third drink.

"My daughter is right," Mrs. Stewart said. "You're not needed here. Haven't you done enough to hurt this family? Tell you the truth, I knew this would happen someday. It was completely predictable."

"Please, Mother. Not now," Victoria said. Her face had flushed and her articulation seemed to be getting thicker.

"I was the only one who saw it coming," Mrs. Stewart continued. "Aside from your dubious background, Josh, I could sense that you were on your way to infidelity. Experience is a valuable teacher."

"Can't you shut her up, Victoria?"

"She has a right to her opinion," Victoria snapped. Josh sensed that her response was more emotional than logical. She was simply letting her mother be the battering ram. Josh turned to Mrs. Stewart.

"Your rights are irrelevant," Josh said, sucking in a deep breath. "You are a bitter woman with a hateful, twisted mind. At this juncture, you are beyond toleration." He turned toward Victoria. "I will not have my children exposed to this terrible woman."

"It's in their blood, Victoria. Heed my words. Your father's own infidelity and desertion proved the point. Never once had he ever inquired about us. Never once did he ever see his child again," Mrs. Stewart said, her bitterness permeating her speech. Her face, Josh observed, seemed to have turned to stone. "Actually, it was probably a blessing."

She was comparing him to a deserting father, which inflamed him.

"Victoria, why don't you tell this woman the truth?" he asked casually. He saw the fear in her eyes.

"What is he talking about?" Mrs. Stewart snapped.

"The truth about seeing her father." He turned toward Victoria. "Tell her, my dear. Tell her the little secret you kept from her."

Josh walked calmly over to the bar and poured himself another drink.

"What is he talking about, Victoria?" Mrs. Stewart asked, pointedly searching her daughter's face. "Your father? What secrets?"

"You rotten shit," Victoria said through pursed lips.

"I don't understand. What is going on here?" Mrs. Stewart asked, frowning.

"He's making up stories. Don't listen to him."

"What stories?" Mrs. Stewart probed.

"The story about your daughter's visit to her father. Tell her, Victoria."

"I won't listen to this," Victoria said, moving to an opposite corner of the room, turning her back on both of them.

"You see, he was dying in this hospital in Boston," Josh said with a quick glance at his wife. "According to Victoria, he had some rather unpleasant things to say about you, Mrs. Stewart."

"You saw him, Victoria?" Mrs. Stewart asked angrily. The blood had drained from her face. "And you never told me?"

"What purpose would that serve?" Victoria replied, turning to face her. "It would only have upset you."

"But you knew how I felt!" Mrs. Stewart persisted.

"He was still my father. He found me and asked me to come."

"He abandoned you is what he did. You had no right to see him without consulting me."

"You would have said no, Mother."

"You're damned right I would have," Mrs. Stewart snapped, her voice croaking with anger. "You had no right to reward him with your presence. He never sent a dime for your support. He was a disgusting, fornicating, unfaithful bastard." She was fuming with rage now, on the point of hyperventilating. "And you were an ungrateful daughter to have honored him with your presence. You should have cursed him, spat on him, insulted him."

"He was dying, Mother."

"You were disloyal, Victoria. You betrayed me."

Victoria turned to Josh.

"Look what you've done. Was that necessary?"

"You're the big truth monger here, Victoria," Josh said.

"You are beneath contempt," Victoria hissed, turning to her mother, whose anger remained at white heat.

"Your cheating husband corrupted you," Mrs. Stewart cried, her anger reaching white heat. "He probably put you up to it."

"Tell her how long ago it was when you saw your father, Victoria," Josh said, chuckling. He turned toward Mrs. Stewart. "She was still a college girl, Mommy Dearest. I wasn't even in the picture."

Mrs. Stewart's bottom lip began to quiver. Josh had never seen her cry and was actually looking forward to it.

"Mother, please. He wanted to see me. We spoke. He told me that I was named after Queen Victoria. I felt nothing for him. And I never forgave him. Not in my heart. Not now. Not ever. I swear it."

Mrs. Stewart collapsed into a chair. Victoria ran to the bar and poured a glass of water, which she brought to her mother. Mrs. Stewart waved it away.

"And I never for one moment stopped hating him," Victoria said to her mother.

"That is a lie, Victoria, and you know it. You told me yourself. You didn't hate him. You pitied him," Josh said.

"Must you?" Victoria screeched.

Josh turned toward Mrs. Stewart and continued.

"He told your daughter he couldn't live with you. He had to escape from you. Who could blame him for that? How bad was he really?" Josh paused, knowing that his next statement would inflame her. "After all, he did make an honest woman of you."

Mrs. Stewart looked as if she would erupt and fly through the ceiling. But the energy of her anger quickly collapsed and she seemed to crumple into the chair.

"You didn't have to do this," Victoria said.

"Yes I did. She has attempted to turn my children against me. And you allowed that."

"All she did was tell the children the truth about their father," Victoria cried.

"I was unfaithful to you, not to them."

"You savaged all of us. Can't you see that? You're the one who destroyed this family. Not her."

Victoria knew exactly where his vulnerability lay. He had no illusions about his guilt. His penance was unfolding before his eyes and would haunt him until the day he died. But it was unfair to scar the next generation with his offense. Just as it was unfair for him to be scarred by the actions of his parents and, he thought magnanimously, unfair for Victoria to be scarred by the actions of her parents.

"She has to share the guilt, Victoria."

"That is ridiculous."

"That woman has destroyed your ability to ever forgive me."

"You betrayed me. She never did. At least she's been consistent. I've always known where she stood. In your case, I was deceived."

Even in the midst of this bitter exchange, he could contemplate the consequences of his act. But he knew the rock-bottom irrevocable truth: he and Victoria were the walking wounded, still in pain from the festering unhealed scar tissue caused by the injuries inflicted by their parents. What he was seeking, he knew, was some way to prevent this from happening to his children.

"You are one vindictive bastard," Victoria said, suddenly erupting. She walked across the room and with her fist bashed aside the glass case that held the lone Staffordshire of the boxer Cribb. Both the glass and Cribb crashed to the floor, breaking into a thousand pieces.

"That was a childish outburst," he told her calmly, showing no visible hint of outrage for what she had done.

"You haven't seen anything yet, Josh," she sneered. "I won't rest until..."

"Hello, everybody!"

It was Evie, offering her cupid's smile, oblivious to the hatred that had permeated the room. She was cradling Tweedledee in her arms.

"Well, well," Victoria said. "The blimp has arrived." She turned to Josh. "And her little pussy."

"They're being cruel, Evie. Pay no attention."

"It's all right, Josh. Really."

Evie's presence seemed to have also energized Mrs. Stewart. Even the color had come back to her cheeks.

"My God. She's put on a hundred pounds since I saw her last."

"Mrs. Stewart," Evie exclaimed, her smile in place. "So nice to see you again."

Then Michael appeared suddenly and embraced his aunt. She smiled broadly and returned the affection. Josh felt certain that the children had heard their entire argument.

"I told you children to stay upstairs," Victoria snarled.

"We just wanted to see Aunt Evie," Emily said. "And Tweedledee."

"Well, you've seen her," Victoria said. "Now you can both go back upstairs."

"Listen to your mommy, children," Evie said, her smile intact.

"No need to go up just yet, kids," Josh said.

Evie, still smiling, appeared caught in the middle. Her glance darted between Josh and Victoria.

"Tell you what," she said sweetly, "I've brought the makings of a delicious Baked Alaska. You remember how much you loved it. I've done most of it at home and all I have to do is the finishing touches. How does that sound, everybody?"

"Great, Aunt Evie," Michael exclaimed.

"Can I help?" Emily squealed.

"Both of you can help," Evie told them.

Victoria and her mother exchanged glances. Mrs. Stewart, as indomitable as granite, seemed to have fully recovered her equilibrium, and both mother and daughter appeared to have united again, energized by their common enemy.

Evie seemed suddenly lost in thought, her chubby little forefinger caressing her chin.

"Hmmmm. All I'll need is confectioner's sugar, a sieve, and some cognac."

"I know where the confectioner's sugar is and the sieve," Emily blurted, immediately sensing that she had inadvertently revealed secret information. She slapped a little hand over her mouth.

"It's okay, darling," Victoria said, shooting her mother a sinister half-smile, confirming their alliance. "Where is the confectioner's sugar and the sieve?"

"Don't worry, honey," Josh said reassuringly. "We have no secrets here."

"Not anymore," Victoria said.

"You'll all love it. That I guarantee," Evie said, offering smiles all around. "Of course, we'll need a little time, but it will be worth the wait. There is nothing like a delicious flaming Baked Alaska to bring joy and harmony into our lives."

He could see Victoria winding up for a comment, but before she could get it out, Michael spotted the broken glass box and the figure of Cribb.

"Look, Dad," he cried.

"We know, Michael. It was an accident."

"A real accident?" he asked.

"Yes," he said, looking at Victoria, "a real accident."

"You didn't answer my question, darling," Victoria said, directing her attention to Emily. "I asked where the confectioner's sugar and the sieve are stored."

Emily exchanged glances with Michael.

"I'll get it," Josh said.

"Let me, Dad," Michael interjected.

"Why don't I go with you?" Victoria said.

"It's all right, Mom," Michael said nervously. "I'll go myself. I know where it is."

He ran swiftly to the door to the basement and they heard him clambering down the steps.

"You'll get the cognac, won't you Josh?" Evie asked. Holding Emily's hand, she started out the room, then stopped.

"We must do everything we can to keep this lovely family together," she said with a winning air of optimism, then moved with Emily out of the room.

Victoria nodded while her mother could not resist a sneering insult.

"That woman sounds retarded."

"That woman is a saint," Josh said, glaring at Mrs. Stewart. Victoria's mind seemed elsewhere.

They heard Michael coming up the basement stairs, then heading for the kitchen.

"So that's how they did it," Victoria said after a long silence. "That storage room in the basement." She turned toward Josh. "You son of a bitch, making your children a party to this travesty. I want that woman out of here, along with that dirty cat and yourself."

"Is that an order?" he mocked. He saw her hesitate for a moment. From the kitchen came the sound of children's voices and pots clattering.

"After this disgusting little ritual. Just as soon as they go off to bed."

"I appreciate the dispensation, Victoria. But I'm not leaving this house," Josh said. "I have no intention of putting those children in harm's way." He waved his finger at Mrs. Stewart, who squared her shoulders and sneered at him. The woman was impervious, Josh thought, with grudging admiration and disgust.

"And I'll insist that you take the contents of that room with you. I assume you used it as a store room for the creation of her love objects and a larder for fat-creating concoctions like the one she is now making, which I have no intention of eating."

"Your loss," Josh muttered.

"Now if you don't mind, I think I'm entitled to see exactly what is in that room."

"Christ, Victoria. It's only kitchen stuff. Maybe some food and Evie's clothes. No big deal." Josh said.

"A hidden cache," Victoria smirked.

"The intent was hardly as sinister as that. We knew you'd be upset if you found out that Evie was helping out. There were practical concerns as well. Taking things back and forth. I wouldn't be surprised if you had a special place to store your mother's things...a hidden room somewhere."

"Here we go again. Tit for tat. No such luck. Mother left nothing." She looked at him with an angry stare. "This is my house. Now show me what's in that damn room."

Josh shrugged and started toward the hall corridor. Looking behind him, he saw Mrs. Stewart following in Victoria's wake.

"Does she need to come?" Josh asked.

"You're not going to leave me here by myself," Mrs. Stewart said.

"This is stupid, Victoria," he said as they proceeded down the basement stairs.

"Not to me, it isn't."

He led them past the furnace and the hot water heater, stopping in front of the storage room door. He looked at the combination lock, then grasped it and began to roll the dial, discovering after a few attempts that he had forgotten the combination.

"I don't remember it," he said finally.

"I'll bet Michael does," Victoria said.

"Leave Michael out of it," Josh snapped.

Victoria walked to the bottom of the basement stairs and shouted her son's name.

"Yes, Mom," Michael cried from the top of the stairs.

"Come down here this minute."

He walked halfway down the stairs, looking wary and uncomfortable. Then he stopped.

"I want that door open," she said, pointing to the basement door.

Josh watched his son's face. It had turned white, accentuated by the dull basement light. His expression was oddly defiant, the nostrils dilated, the eyes blazing with anger. Michael said nothing, staring at her.

"Don't you hear me?" Victoria screamed. "Do you want me to come up there and drag you down here?"

"What is it, son?" Josh asked, moving toward the stairs.

Victoria turned to face him.

"What have you done to this child?" she shouted. She looked up at Michael again. "You come down here, Michael. Right now!"

"I won't," Michael cried.

"Oh yes you will," Victoria yelled, starting up the stairs.

"No. I won't," Michael said, his voice breaking. Suddenly he turned and ran up the stairs. Victoria followed him halfway up, then stopped and came down again, gasping. She turned to Josh.

"You fuck," she cried. "What have you done to him?"

"It's you who's making him crazy, Victoria."

"What the hell's in that room?"

"I told you," Josh replied. He, too, had been stunned by Michael's reaction. He wanted to go upstairs and comfort his son.

But Victoria's sudden movement prevented him. She grabbed an axe hanging on the basement wall that Josh had occasionally used to split fireplace wood. As a reflex, he moved away. Mrs. Stewart, too, seemed uneasy with her daughter's action and shrunk out of her path.

Victoria paid no attention to either Josh or her mother and moved instead to the door of basement room. Josh watched in stunned silence as Victoria lifted the axe and swung it toward the lock. The force of her blows was astonishing and it took no more than four swings to smash away the lock and break the door hinges.

Victoria kicked the door open and, still holding the axe, entered the room. Josh and Mrs. Stewart exchanged nervous glances, but did not follow.

"Is everything okay down there?"

It was Evie's voice cheerfully calling from the top of the basement stairs.

"Okay, Evie," Josh called back. "No problem."

"Won't be long, kiddies," Evie replied. "I'll call you when it's ready."

At that moment, Josh saw a white shape bound down the stairs.

"Tweedledee," Emily called.

The cat moved along the basement floor and through the door of the basement room.

"Don't come down, Emily," Josh called. "You help Aunt Evie."

"What about Tweedledee?" she cried.

"We'll bring her up. Go with Aunt Evie now, sweetheart."

"Okay, Daddy."

The door was hanging on its hinges. He could hear Victoria inside but made no move to go in.

"Victoria," he called into the room.

There was no answer. He moved forward cautiously.

"Victoria," he called again.

Suddenly he heard a loud clatter from inside the room, and a shriek.

Rushing into the room, he stopped in his tracks. Victoria was swinging the axe at Tweedledee as she darted in and out of the various clutter of pots, pans, boxes, cans, and suitcases that were piled up there.

"Stop it," Josh shouted. "Have you lost your mind?"

Undeterred, she took another swing. Josh grabbed the handle, wrestled it out of her grip, and threw it to the other side of the room. Tweedledee bounded out of her hiding place behind a suitcase and scooted up the stairs.

Victoria looked at him in horror.

"Jesus," she said, shaking her head. Their eyes met briefly, then she turned away and her gaze seemed to freeze.

"What is it?" Josh asked.

"That," she said, pointing to various objects that lined the floor along the wall, their hiding place revealed by the displacement of suitcases and other large items. The fracas with the cat had scattered their protective cover.

The sight stunned him. There were the missing Victorian inkwells, vases, blue bells, Victorian hats, and leather-bound books. In fact, all the missing items in her collections.

"So this is where you hid them?" Mrs. Stewart croaked.

"Don't be ridiculous," Josh replied. He knew, of course, who had put them there. It explained Michael's reluctance to open the door.

At that moment, they heard Evie's cheery voice calling from the top of the basement steps.

"We're ready," she called. "Come see Emily light the mountain."

Josh searched for Victoria's eyes and held her glance for a long while. Had she understood?

Without thinking, they obeyed Evie's call for their presence. Their reaction was inexplicable. They moved slowly up the basement stairs. To Josh it felt like a funeral procession. Upstairs, they were greeted incongruously by Evie's happy face. She held a tray on which was perched the white confectionery mountain she had created. Emily stood beside her holding Tweedledee.

"Isn't that just beautiful?" she said, smiling broadly, oblivious to the gloomy faces confronting her.

"Where's Michael?" Josh asked.

"Isn't he with you?" Evie replied.

Josh and Victoria exchanged panicked looks. Josh went to the top of the stairs and shouted "Michael! Michael!"

There was no answer.

"Michael," Emily shouted.

Still no answer.

"I better put this on the dining room table," Evie said, moving into the dining room.

Suddenly, they heard loud voices emanating from the den. Josh recognized Victoria's voice and looked at her puzzled and confused.

"*I need to know your decision, Gordon. It's very important to me.*" Victoria's voice boomed from the den.

"*I think we are heading for an understanding, Victoria,*" a male voice said in counterpoint. The voice was vaguely familiar.

It was soon obvious that the voices were coming through the stereo speakers.

Victoria erupted.

"Stop," she screamed. "Stop that at once."

With an expression of extreme panic on her face, she dashed toward the den. Josh reacted in tandem, reaching her just as she lifted her arm toward the stereo. Pinning her arms back, he held her tightly. She struggled to be released, but Josh continued to hold her.

"*He will not be expelled. Now get on with it, please. Blow me, baby.*"

"*Say it again, Gordon. No expulsion for Michael.*"

"*No expulsion for Michael. I told you. For crying out loud, Victoria. Suck my cock.*"

"*Jesus, Victoria. I love it.*"

"Please, I beg of you," Victoria shouted, struggling in Josh's arms.

"*I'm coming,*" the male voice cried from the stereo. "*Swallow. Swallow.*"

"Stop, please," Victoria shouted. Josh held her with all his strength, mesmerized and utterly confused by what he was hearing. He slapped her hard across the face. She shook with sobs as her strength ebbed and she made no further moves to free herself.

Surveying the room, he could see the ashen face of Mrs. Stewart and the stunned and confused expressions of Evie and Emily. He wondered suddenly if Emily actually understood what was being said.

In the earlier melee, he had missed some of the words, but as he concentrated he picked up the thread of what was happening. By then, Victoria had collapsed in his arms. *"God that was great, Victoria,"* the male voice said, the words clear, the situation unmistakable.

Victoria's sobs became louder. For a tiny moment his concentration wavered, then returned. He felt too astonished to react.

"That was something. We have got to do this again."

"You mean on a regular basis?" Victoria's voice asked.

"More or less."

"I just want to know what the deal is."

There was no mistaking the implication and the event. But beyond the shock of it was the nagging question. How did this recording arrive here at precisely this moment in time? Who had put it in the stereo?

"A nice blow job once a week, say. Is that too much to ask?"

There was a pause.

"Shut it off!"

Victoria's shriek reverberated through the house. It was primal, a furious testimony to her pain. Josh was so horrified by her scream that his grip loosened. Victoria darted for the stereo and slammed the power button. The recorded conversation was silenced. She collapsed in a heap on the floor, hysterical, beating her fist into the carpet.

Josh felt rooted to the spot. Questions poured into his mind. Victoria had made this recording, had offered herself for the cause of her child. That deduction and the use for which it was intended were clear. Suddenly he turned and surveyed the people in the room. One person, Michael, was clearly among the missing.

But before he could calculate his response, something else was happening in the house.

His nostrils quivered with recognition. Panic seized him. Something was burning.

Chapter 17

When Victoria heard her own words floating through space over the speakers, she thought she was caught in some hideous nightmare. She felt helpless, trapped in a whirlpool, unable to tear free, struggling against a relentless downward pull that carried her into a bottomless black hole. Then reality intervened and she fervently wished that she *were* back in the hole.

She felt the intense agony of mortification, discovered as she performed some shamefully obscene act, which, of course, she had. Her first instinct was to obliterate the sound, but Josh had restrained her, forcing her to endure the horror of her humiliation.

Everything was awry, her emotional and mental state barely endurable. She had been responsible for three blatant acts of mindless violence, all totally out of the mainstream of any previous personal experience. She had struck her beloved son, and then lashed out at a symbolic plaster figure as if it had a living presence. Finally, she had deliberately, with malice clearly in her mind, sought to murder an innocent cat. What had she become? These acts went to the heart of her identity.

Worst of all, she found it difficult to recognize her own children. They seemed to have evolved into hostile strangers. Even the weird alliance with her mother was more aberrational than natural.

It was only then that she was distracted by the odor of burning. She heard her name being called, and then a hand grabbed her arm and lifted her along violently. Josh, holding Emily, was moving past the dining room. She noted that the lace curtains had caught fire.

"It was Michael," Evie cried. "He must have poured too much cognac on the Baked Alaska."

Victoria's mind barely grasped the idea. A house being burned by Baked Alaska?

"Michael! Where is Michael?" It was Josh's voice, echoing through the house. It brought her back to reality.

"Michael," she screamed. "Michael."

"Everybody out," Josh shouted.

Emily started to cry, and Victoria saw Josh caress her head and kiss her cheek. He handed her to Victoria.

"Take her out," Josh ordered. "I'll call the fire department."

Emily screamed.

"Mikey!"

"Just leave." His look was pleading. "Please, Victoria," he added gently.

She ran out the front door and deposited Emily with Evie, who was standing and watching the flames, tears streaming down her cheeks, her body shuddering with sobs.

"He wasn't supposed to light the cognac," she blurted. "Emily was going to light the cognac. God, Victoria, I'm so sorry, so terribly sorry."

"Don't, Evie," Victoria said. "It's too late for that."

"It was no accident," Mrs. Stewart snapped. She stood beside them watching the flames spear out of the dining room window. "It's all her fault. Her and that stupid concoction."

"Dammit, Mother, won't you ever quit? Even now?" Victoria cried, shaking her head in despair.

"Whose side are you on now?" Mrs. Stewart shouted. "And don't think I'm ever going to forget about your little Boston caper."

"I hope not, Mother," Victoria said, her heart pounding with fear for her son. "I hope you never forget."

"You see what's happening here? Do you see what's happening here?" Mrs. Stewart exclaimed. "This is a direct result..."

"Will you shut up, Mother?" Victoria shouted, almost on the point of another act of violence. In the distance, she could hear the screech of sirens.

"Find Mikey, Mommy," Emily screeched hysterically. "Find my brother."

"Please, God. Find my little boy," Victoria wailed.

"He's probably already out of the house, hiding somewhere. He knows what he's done," Mrs. Stewart said between pursed lips.

She saw Josh running from the house. As he came closer, she could see the glistening sweat on his face and his expression of agitation.

"Is Michael here?"

Victoria felt her stomach lurch.

"Oh my God," she cried. "You didn't find him?"

"I looked everywhere," Josh said. "I called out. He didn't answer."

He cupped his hands and shouted in all directions.

"Michael! Michael!"

Emily aped his action, her little voice calling out in futility.

"Mikey! Mikey!"

"He's still inside, Josh," Victoria screamed. "I'm sure of it. You didn't look hard enough."

The sirens came closer, drowning out their shouts. Then the big trucks careened down the street and the firemen leaped from the trucks before they ground to a halt. Some ran into the house carrying axes and other equipment. Others unloaded the hose and dragged it to a nearby hydrant.

Victoria sprinted over to one of the firemen, Josh following. The flames were spreading through the lower part of the house and gusts of smoke poured out of the windows.

"My son is in there," she shouted.

"We'll find him," the fireman barked as he joined the others to pull the hose toward the house. He shouted to the men inside.

"There's a boy in there."

One of the firemen raised his hand and made an "O" signal of understanding with his fingers.

The lead fireman pulling on the hose pointed it toward the house and soon a heavy spray was blasting its way through the dining room window.

"Find my son. Please," Victoria screamed hysterically. The force of the water drowned out her screams. Unable to stand about without taking action, she ran through the open front door into the house. Josh followed swiftly behind her.

The fireman who was pointing the hose shouted a warning to the men inside. Ignoring him, they moved further into the house. The smoke was intense as Victoria and Josh stumbled and coughed through the downstairs hallway.

"Michael!" Victoria screamed as loud as she could.

"Michael!" Josh shouted in unison.

A fireman brandishing an axe spotted them.

"Get the hell out of here!" he cried. Then he turned to one of the other firemen, who had now grabbed the nozzle of the hose and was directing the spray onto the dining room walls that were now on fire.

Josh grabbed Victoria by the arm and pulled her into the den, shouting Michael's name. They moved through the smoke. The flames were beginning to crawl up the doorpost at the den's entrance and were making their way forward toward the bookcases like some glowing snake.

For a fleeting moment an errant idea passed through her mind. Save the Victoriana. She looked up at the painting of Queen Victoria over the mantle, and then squinted through the smoke at her leather-bound book collection, her wide-brim hats, and the various knickknacks that had once been her pride. They had little relevance now. Her mother's dictum ran through her mind. At that moment they seemed mere useless objects, junk.

"Michael," she yelled as they moved through the den. "Where are you? Please, darling. I forgive you, sweetheart! Mommy forgives you. Daddy, too. Where are you?"

"Michael!" Josh shouted beside her as they moved through the room. "Answer us. Please, Michael."

Again and again they called his name as spears of fire reached the bookcases and ignited the books. She saw her leather-bound sets erupting into flames. Josh's collection of advertising art books joined the inferno. It took only seconds for the straw of her large-brimmed Victorian hats that lined the walls to explode and quickly disappear in the holocaust. The destruction made only a minor impact on her emotions as if it was somehow a necessary act to validate an inevitable ending.

"They're in here," someone shouted. Then she heard footsteps behind her and two burly firemen blocked their path.

"You have got to leave now," one of the fireman shouted.

"We have to find our son!" Josh screamed.

"If he's here, we'll find him," the other fireman said, grabbing Victoria's arm. She tried to shake loose.

"I want my son."

"Please, you're endangering yourselves," the fireman who held her pleaded.

She squirmed out of his grasp and ran through the room to the hallway. One of the firemen held Josh in a tight grip and began dragging him, kicking and protesting, out of the room.

"Get her," he cried as they pulled him through the door. "Get my wife."

Victoria was halfway up the stairs before she felt the pull on her ankle.

"Michael, where are you?" she screamed, panicked beyond reason now, kicking wildly, trying to tear herself loose from the fireman's grasp.

"You can't, lady," the fireman cried. "Be reasonable."

She held on to the banister, still screaming her son's name. Another fireman came forward and grabbed at her hands, loosening her grip, finger by finger.

"You're not helping us, lady," the fireman pleaded. "You have got to get out of here."

Finally, her grip on the banister was loosened and she felt herself being pulled down the stairs. Once she began to face the reality of being overpowered, she stopped all resistance.

The fireman led her out of the house to the front lawn, where the others were waiting. He put his arm around her shoulder. She did not shake him away. She looked toward the house. The flames had spread to the kitchen and smoke poured out of the now-smashed windows of the upper floors. She noted that Emily, embracing Tweedledee, was whimpering in Evie's arms.

"Please God, find him!" Victoria cried. "Find my son." She felt hollow and inert as she continued to observe the burning house.

"I'm sure he's okay," Mrs. Stewart said as she moved closer to them. "Probably just scared and feeling guilty and hiding somewhere around here." She waved her arm to take in the street.

"Guilty?" Victoria said, suddenly energized. She turned to her mother.

Her mother looked at her and nodded her head.

"Of course, guilty," Mrs. Stewart said. "Is there any doubt about that?"

"I can't listen to this, Mother. Can't you just stop?"

"I'm merely saying what is obvious to all of us."

"I can't stand anymore," Victoria cried, turning her gaze from her mother.

"Where are your brains? Haven't you the slightest bit of sensitivity and understanding?" Josh said angrily. He was enraged. "Our son is missing. He could be in there, in terrible danger. What kind of an unfeeling bitch are you?"

"I hadn't meant..." Mrs. Stewart began making a futile effort at contrition. Failing that, she shook her head. "You men..." She sucked in a deep breath and blew it out, staring at her daughter. "The truth always hurts."

Suddenly, Victoria could not stand it for one moment longer. She balled her hand into a fist, and in blind fury, swung out. She struck her mother full on the side of her head. The woman went down like a rock. Not satisfied, Victoria started pummeling her on the ground and Josh had to pull her away.

"No, Victoria," he said. "No."

He bent down beside Mrs. Stewart. The woman sat on the grass rubbing her head.

"Did you see that?" she cried.

Josh tried to help her up.

"Get your hands off me," she cried.

"Okay. Then just sit there and keep your goddamn mouth shut," he ordered.

She struggled to her feet. Victoria felt no pity for what she had done. Instead, her eyes were glued to the burning house.

The fireman continued to fight the blaze. It was dying down now. The lower floor appeared in shambles. Smoke continued to pour out of the upper floors.

"It's all my fault," Victoria said. She had moved closer to where Josh was standing now. "It's punishment for doing what I did." A sob escaped her. "For making that stupid tape."

"Not now, Victoria," Josh muttered. "This is not your fault."

"I'd forgotten I hid it in my closet where you found it. I'll never forgive myself," Victoria sobbed. Josh looked at her archly.

"For God's sake, Victoria. Not now." Josh cried.

She glanced at him, her eyes flickering with pain, then turned away, her gaze concentrated on the house. The area was filled with the acrid smell of dampness, burnt wood, and smoke. In the distance she could make out the sound of an ambulance siren. Then she saw a fireman come through the door cradling a small body in his arms. They both rushed toward him.

"Michael!"

The fireman kneeled to the ground and gently laid the child on the grass. Michael lay lifeless, his face cherry red, his upper body wrapped in what she recognized as her plaid pleated skirt, the one she had worn during that fateful day with Mr. Tatum. The memory assailed her like a kick in her chest.

"Found him hiding in an upstairs closet. Damnedest thing, as if he didn't want to get found," the fireman said, removing his hat and wiping perspiration from his forehead with the arm of his coat. She reached over to touch him. The fireman held her back as the crew from the ambulance came forward.

"Please," the fireman said gently. "Let the medics take charge."

"It's the carbon monoxide that makes his face red," the fireman explained gently. "Smoke got him, but he is alive."

"My baby. My poor baby."

One of the medics clamped an oxygen mask over Michael's face. Another brought a stretcher. They lifted him cautiously and laid him gently on the stretcher.

"Will he be okay?" Josh asked the medic.

"We'll do everything we can," he replied as they moved the stretcher toward the ambulance.

Victoria and Josh followed beside the stretcher. In the ambulance, she kneeled beside her unconscious son.

"May I hold his hand?" she asked. The medic nodded.

She brought his hand up to her mouth and kissed it. It felt cold and lifeless. Josh, kneeling beside her, gripped her shoulder.

"Oh God, please," she cried, lifting her tear-stained face upward. "Have mercy on this child."

The ambulance door closed behind them. The siren began to blare and the ambulance moved down the street, picking up speed. They moved to the other side of the ambulance to give the medics room to work on Michael. One of them, a balding young man, pressed a stethoscope to the boy's chest and listened while another medic, a young woman, held the oxygen mask in place over his face. Victoria watched, whimpering, her cheeks wet with her tears. Josh sat beside her opposite the stretcher where the boy lay. The medic completed his examination, then prepared an injection and quickly plunged the needle into Michael's arm.

"What do you think?" Josh asked the young man. Victoria looked into the young man's eyes.

"The truth," she whispered.

"Touch and go," he answered, shaking his head.

"There's always hope," the young woman said with obvious sympathy.

Victoria looked toward Josh.

"I wish it was me instead."

"Not you," Josh mumbled. "Me."

The blare of the siren grew louder as the ambulance sped into the night. On the floor next to Michael's body she saw the plaid skirt, looking at it with horror. Then she remembered that she had wrapped the tape in it and placed it in the back of the shelf of her closet. Her eyes met Josh's.

"So it wasn't you who found it?"

He shook his head and both parents turned their gaze on their stricken son.

Chapter 18

Victoria and Josh sat in the waiting room of the hospital, barely speaking. Two days had passed and Michael was still in a coma. The prognosis was guarded, although the nurses who tended him 'round the clock were optimistic.

"I've seen them come out after weeks and be right as rain," one of the nurses, a gray-haired woman with a confident air, told them. Her remarks were soothing, but unconvincing. Josh stared at his son, helpless and still, a small white apparition under the sheets, tubes inserted in his nostrils, his tiny chest rising and falling with the rhythm of a respirator attached to him. A bag of liquid hung above the boy with an IV attachment to his arm.

Neither Josh nor Victoria could look at him without tears spilling over their eyelids. Guilt and despair gnawed at him. He blamed himself for igniting the fuse that led to this horror. Words failed him. Besides, he was certain that Victoria believed he had orchestrated the events that had led to this tragedy. And yet, through his grief he could not grasp the idea that it was without doubt the children who had set them in motion.

Despite his innocence in that regard, he could not shake the idea of culpability. He felt like a murderer.

Since their house was a shambles, they had checked in to a Holiday Inn within walking distance of the hospital. Josh had arranged for three rooms, one for Victoria and Emily, another for Evie, and one for himself.

They had packed off Mrs. Stewart without major complications.

The aftermath of Victoria's physical attack and his revelation about her meeting with her father had, inexplicably, made only minor dents in the woman's demeanor. It was obvious to both Josh and Victoria that bitterness had atrophied her emotions. Nothing could ever change her attitude.

The reality was that Victoria and her mother were bonded together in a love-hate relationship. Even Victoria's awareness of its destructive nature was not enough to sever it.

"Were you able to get any sleep?" he asked Victoria as they had breakfast with Emily on the third day of their ordeal. They were obviously in silent agreement to show no animosity in front of their daughter. For the first two days they had barely spoken, the shock of their circumstances too raw for any but the most mechanical dialogue, although their proximity as a family seemed to be comforting to Emily.

Emily, looking exhausted and pale, sat beside them, a bowl of oatmeal before her in which she was showing little interest. As on the previous two days, they had risen early. Josh was thankful that Evie was still asleep and Victoria would not have to observe her imbibing her usual hearty breakfast. Nothing, no joyful or tragic event, ever stood in the way of Evie's appetite.

Victoria answered his question with a negative shake of her head and offered no inquiry about how he had gotten through the night. Nevertheless, he volunteered.

"Me neither."

He had checked on Michael's condition at intervals, discovering in talking to the nurse on duty that Victoria had done the same. Both Josh and Victoria had assured Emily that Michael was recovering nicely, although they each suspected that she had her doubts. By then, he had lost all faith in the possibility that he could hide the truth from his children, any truth. Children knew. It had become an axiom in his mind. He had discovered through the experience of the last few weeks that the adult world hadn't a clue about what went on inside a child's mind.

"When will Michael be all better?" Emily asked them.

"Soon," Victoria replied.

"How soon?"

"Very soon."

"Tomorrow, Mommy?"

"Maybe."

"Is he still sleeping?"

Had they told her that, he wondered, exchanging glances with his wife?

"Yes, he is," Josh said, sensing that she was posing, hiding her awareness of the truth.

"When will he wake up?"

"Soon."

"Can I be there when he wakes up?"

"If we can time it properly. Yes."

"Promise. Cross your heart."

Both parents crossed their hearts in tandem. Josh felt like bursting into tears. Instead, he crossed his heart again, looking toward Victoria, who turned away, deliberately averting his gaze.

"His eyes are flickering," the gray-haired nurse said, smiling. She had come out of Michael's room to summon them and they had rushed to his bedside.

"Please, Michael. Look at us," Victoria begged. Josh's hand touched Victoria's shoulder. She did not shake it away.

They sat by his bedside for the next few hours, concentrating on every movement the child made, rarely speaking except to point out changes in him they had perceived or imagined.

"Come on, Michael, wake up," Josh pleaded, his mouth next to his son's ear. "You can do it. Mom and Dad are here beside you, waiting for you to greet us. Come on, Michael."

"Do you think he can hear us?" Victoria asked.

"Sure he can," Josh said, suspecting that he was probably wrong.

"Michael," Victoria said. She was bent next to the boy with her mouth placed, as Josh had done, as close to his ear as possible.

"Please, Michael. We love you and we need you. Mom needs you.

Dad needs you. Emily needs you most of all. I told her you were sleeping. She wants to be here with us when you wake up. God, there's so much that we're going to do when you get better."

There was no improvement in his response, although some fluttering continued behind the eyelids. Josh gripped Michael's hand and squeezed. Both of them had done this repeatedly and each time he had responded. He did so again.

"He must know we're here," Victoria said.

"Sure he knows."

Soon after midnight, a nurse suggested that they leave and get some sleep. They rose reluctantly and went back to the motel. Emily was sleeping in her mother's motel room and Evie was sitting in the one good chair reading a cookbook.

"Is he awake yet?" Evie asked, closing her book.

"Not yet," Josh said. "But he is showing signs. He'll be fine. You'll see."

Josh kissed his sister goodnight. Victoria pointedly ignored her. After she had gone, Josh bent down and kissed Emily's head and caressed it for a moment.

"Sleep well, love."

He stood up suddenly, feeling awkward. Victoria and Josh briefly exchanged glances. Neither spoke. For a brief moment, he thought she was going to say something. He toyed with the idea that she was going to ask him to stay, but her blank and stony expression told him otherwise. Then the moment passed and he turned away.

"See you in the morning," he said.

"If you hear anything, let me know."

"Of course."

He let himself out of the room and into his adjoining room. He called his office to pick up his voice mail. He went through message after message, trying to become engaged, but without success. He decided to try again in the morning. Suddenly he heard a familiar voice on the line and he froze. It was Angela.

"This is good-bye, Josh. You'll probably never hear from me

again," the message began. His heart thumped. In the brief pause that followed, suicide was the first thing that came to his mind. "I have left my family and am off to Italy to devote my life to my talent. I have a job in Milan and I will paint on the side." He was both stunned and relieved. "You see, I have discovered that I am a true romantic. I will never forget you for believing, above all, in my artistic talent. So I will always owe you for that. I will pour all my passion into this undertaking. I hope you will forgive me. I fully recognize that I am solely to blame for the terrible pain I have caused to everyone around me. Dominic and my mother will take wonderful care of my children. I am at ease on that score. You were wonderful and I loved every minute of our adventure. I thank you for that as well. Good luck and good-bye, my sweet love."

"And good luck to you," he mused aloud, tears rolling down his cheeks.

He lay down in bed and tried to reconcile what he had just heard with his memories of her. She had thanked him for the adventure and he silently returned her thanks. Now that it was over, he could acknowledge that it was the joyride of his life. He felt a lingering sense of possession remembering Angela in orgasmic fury, knuckles in her mouth to stifle her sounds of release. Angela, the sexual acrobat, the wild mistress, his whore.

He chased such images from his mind, but another took its place. Victoria and Tatum. He hadn't even thought about the revelation in a sexual context. Tatum's demands reverberated in his mind. The bastard! It was rape, pure and simple. He had abused a mother's love. For Victoria it wasn't sex. It was sacrifice.

He tried to sleep but couldn't. His mind continued to be a cauldron for his thoughts, mostly fantasies of doom. Images assailed him of Michael laid out in a white coffin being lowered into the ground, of his mother-in-law laughing hysterically, of Angela Bocci in a traditional nun's habit being repeatedly beaten by her husband, of Evie blowing up like a balloon, exploding, of Victoria chopping off Tweedledee's head with an axe.

Then he was running as fast as he could into his burning house, Victoria chasing him, screaming epithets. These were waking nightmares. His eyes were open.

The phone rang. Before it could complete another ring, he picked it up.

"This is the night nurse," a voice said. "He's coming out of it."

"I'll be right there."

His mind cleared and he called Victoria's room.

"Come quick. He's waking up."

"Thank God," Victoria said.

"Bring Emily."

In a few moments, they were dressed and ready and running as fast as they could to the hospital. Then they were by Michael's bed. He was blinking his eyes.

"We're here, sweetheart," Victoria said.

Josh lifted Emily so that Michael could get a better view of her.

"It's Emily, Michael. See?"

The boy's eyes flickered, and then closed again.

"Mikey, it's me, Emmie. Wake up, Mikey."

The sound of her voice seemed to trigger more of a response. His eyes flickered again, then stayed opened. He seemed to be squinting, getting his vision accustomed to the light.

"Here I am, Mikey," Emily said.

He stared at her as she moved her arms in a flaying motion.

"Here I am," Emily said again.

Then she made funny faces and used her hands to draw her cheeks down, forcing her eyes upward so that the pupils didn't show.

Michael smiled, tentatively at first, then broadly.

"It's us," Josh said, putting an arm around Victoria's shoulder. He felt her stiffen under his touch, but he did not remove his arm. "Your family."

Michael nodded, then closed his eyes again, and the smile disappeared. When his eyes closed, she shook free of Josh's arm.

"Is he off again?" Victoria asked. She reached out and took

Michael's hand. He squeezed back without prompting. His lips moved. He was trying to speak. Josh bent down and put his ear close to his son's mouth.

"I'm sorry," Michael whispered.

"What?"

Josh had heard it the first time, but he wanted to hear him speak again.

"I'm sorry," Michael repeated.

"What did he say?" Victoria asked.

"It's okay, son," Josh said rising. He turned to Victoria. "He said he was sorry."

"Sorry?" Victoria bit her lip and shook her head.

"I wanted us to be family again. I didn't expect the fire," he whispered.

"I know, darling," she replied. "Just rest now."

He sucked in a deep breath and, with effort, spoke again.

"The other." He could barely speak the words. "It was all my idea. I'm so sorry."

"I don't understand." She replied.

"We hid those things, Emmie and me."

They turned toward Emmie, who averted her eyes and nodded.

"And the tape, Mom. With yours and Mr. Tatum's voices. I found it in your closet. I…I wanted Dad to know what you did for me, that you were a good person."

Victoria turned ashen. She turned toward Josh, her lips quivering, her eyes moistened. She looked troubled and confused, but said nothing.

"Never mind, darling. Forget all about it."

She knew better. No one would ever forget.

"Will you forgive me, Mom?"

He was losing energy. He closed his eyes.

"Forgive you? I was hoping you would forgive me."

A doctor came rushing in, bent over the bed, and checked Michael, whispering questions.

"What is your name?"

"Michael Rose," the boy replied, his response weak, his words barely audible.

"Where do you live?"

He gave his address, opened his eyes again, and smiled.

"Who do you see?"

"My mother, dad, and my little sister, Emmie."

Emily giggled. She grabbed Josh's hand and kissed it.

"Thank God," Victoria said.

The doctor checked the monitors at the side of the bed.

"We'll keep the IV in and the oxygen going," the doctor said. "He's not totally out of the woods yet. He's also very tired. Why don't you folks let him rest?" He looked at Josh and Victoria. "I'd say it's up to him now."

They kissed Michael in turn, then left his bedside and sat in the waiting room.

"He'll be fine now," Josh said. "I'm sure of it."

"I hope so."

"When can we go home?" Emily asked.

"Home?" Josh laughed. Not having laughed for a long time, his reaction surprised him. He hadn't been thinking about the house at all during the past two days.

"It's probably not a very pretty sight," Victoria sighed. "But it is insured, though. And my policy will pay for housing elsewhere until the damage is repaired."

"Will I have to go to school tomorrow?" Emily asked.

"Absolutely," Victoria replied, looking at Josh.

Later, after they had brought Emily back to the motel, Josh went into Evie's room. She had been a good soldier, taking care of Emily, carpooling her to her various activities, and keeping the girl amused and content during the long hours her parents spent with Michael. Victoria had not objected. It was a time of need and she gave herself permission to be practical.

"What that boy needs now is one of Aunt Evie's delicious meals," Evie said.

"Believe me, Evie, if that would do the trick I'd consent in a minute," Josh sighed. He was exhausted by his vigil and the general tension between him and Victoria.

"I'd make him a delicious bouillabaisse and top it off with a chocolate soufflé," Evie said. She was munching on a big bag of caramelized popcorn, which she washed down with chocolate milk. Josh watched the spectacle.

"Food again, Evie?" he said, on the verge of rebuke. "What makes you think that would help?"

"It sends a powerful message of comfort, Josh. People need that at certain times of their lives, especially when they are about to lose their whole world. Michael is in mourning, Josh. Have you ever wondered why people have feasts around a mourning ritual?"

He absorbed her words without comment. It was, after all, the theme of her life.

"I'm very, very worried about him, Evie. If anything happens to him I don't know how I could handle it."

"Stop thinking such gloomy thoughts, Josh."

"I know. I still don't understand his actions."

"Yes you do, Josh. Victoria, too. "

He looked probingly at his sister, waiting for her response.

"Considering the lengths to which they went, the kids want their family back, Josh. We didn't have that option."

"The thefts, the tape. It seems…" He groped for words. "Like they were grasping at straws."

Evie snatched up a handful of popcorn from a nearby bowl and stuffed it into her mouth, washing it down with a deep swallow of chocolate milk before she spoke.

"And so they were," she said. "Never underestimate the wisdom of children."

Josh studied his sister's face through a long pause. He loved her dearly.

"I'll say this," he said. "They did get our attention."

Victoria and Josh returned to Michael's hospital room. He opened his eyes briefly when they came into the room, then closed them again and said nothing. They observed him for a while. Under the white sheets, he looked pale and wan.

"He looks awful," Victoria whispered.

"He's been through a terrible ordeal."

"I'm worried, Josh."

Josh nodded agreement.

They both kissed him on his forehead, patted his chest, then consulted the nurse in the corridor.

"We're doing the best we can," she said. Her manner and the way she said it was not very encouraging.

They went down to the hospital cafeteria. They moved through the line and brought their coffee to a table. He sensed the delicacy of the moment. For a long time neither of them spoke.

"At least he's conscious," Josh said without conviction.

"Thank God for that," Victoria sighed, sipping her coffee.

Occasionally their eyes met above the rims of their cups. Hers always turned away first. He saw no softness in them, only puzzlement.

"Sorry," Victoria mused, shaking her head. "The first thing out of his mouth was that he was sorry."

"I guess he thought that Baked Alaska had magic powers to unite us."

He had meant the words to lighten the mood. It didn't.

"Not that," she said, her nostrils flaring. "The other. About it being his idea. Alone."

Josh nodded agreement but said nothing. From time to time she would look at him as if she wished to broach an idea that was festering in her thoughts.

"Well, I don't believe it," she said finally, after a long silence. Josh braced himself, sensing a burst of anger coming.

"Are you saying that he was lying?"

"He lied before." She looked at him pointedly. "So did you."

"How could you? At this moment."

"These are children."

She shook her head and a sob escaped her. "How could they concoct such ideas…" She paused for a moment. "By themselves?"

He was tempted to recycle Evie's words about the wisdom of children. Then demurred.

"I'm as confused as you are, Victoria."

She ignored his comment.

"And that awful tape. How could he know…" She broke off abruptly. "He's eleven years old, for crying out loud. And Emily. Exposed to that. How awful." She sighed and looked off into space. "No way."

He wished he could find the words to convince her. But she had been conditioned by experience.

"Look, Victoria. Let's put that aside. Whether you believe us or not, it's not relevant."

"What is?"

"Let's…dissimulate…for his sake."

"Why not say what you mean, Josh? You want us to lie, right?"

"Why must you put it that way, Victoria?"

"Because it's the language you understand best," she shot back.

"All I'm asking is that we just play act, Victoria. Make believe we've reconciled. Show him. Make the boy feel better, recover faster. What's wrong with that?" he asked with exasperation. "Perform. You seem to be good at it."

He was instantly sorry. He watched her lip begin to tremble, but she quickly got herself under control and stood up.

"Let's go see our son."

# Chapter 19

They went back to Michael's room. His eyes were open. He seemed sad, as if coming out of the coma was an unwelcome intrusion.

"Doesn't he look wonderful?" Victoria said cheerfully, smiling broadly, determined to show her son a happy face, despite her inner feeling of despair.

"He looks great," Josh lied.

"The doctor says you'll be out of here in a few days," Victoria said. It didn't seem to faze the boy. "We'll probably have to rent a place while the house is being rehabilitated."

Michael turned and looked at her.

"All of us?"

Victoria's smile faded and she seemed momentarily confused.

"It'll just be for a few months," Josh said, obviously deflecting the question. "You'll just go on with your life like it was before."

"Before when Dad…" Michael probed.

"The first thing you have to do, young man, is get completely healthy again," Josh said, tousling the boy's hair but avoiding any direct answer to the question.

"Dad's right. That's your first priority, Michael," Victoria said smiling.

"Sure, Mom. I was only asking…you know."

"Yes, dear. I understand."

He was silent for a long time, averting his eyes from their exploring looks.

"Remember what we talked about?" Michael asked. "About being a real family again?"

"Oh yes, son," Josh said. "We're discussing that, aren't we Victoria?"

"Of course we are," Victoria replied.

Michael's eyes drifted from one parent to the other. Victoria could tell he was skeptical. For a long time none of them spoke.

"What we did…we thought it might help," Michael said, breaking the silence. The boy's voice had weakened.

"Forget that," Josh said. "What's done is done. Your mother and I are just glad you're okay."

Michael nodded and turned away, looking out the window.

"When will Emmie visit again?" he asked.

It seemed a signal for them to leave.

During the next few days, Josh and Victoria continued their vigil at Michael's side. Emily would visit after school, and at Michael's request, Evie paid a couple of visits although Victoria, obviously still fearful of her influence, did not let her visit him alone. Josh and Victoria exchanged few words outside of the hospital room. Neither had much to say to each other.

They continued to take their meals together in the hospital cafeteria. After dinner, they visited Michael again, then went back to their respective motel rooms.

On their visits to Michael's room, they put a happy face on his prospects for recovery, but continued to deflect his questions about what their ultimate future as a family might be. It soon became obvious to both of them that Michael, while out of the coma, did not seem to be recovering with the speed they had hoped for. He didn't have much of an appetite and he participated less and less in conversation. Although the nurses forced him out of bed, he would always crawl back in before the allotted time of his exercise.

They brought him books that he didn't read and cassettes for his Walkman that he didn't listen to. He was also uninterested in television. Worry was turning to alarm.

It was only when Emily would arrive late in the day that Michael seemed to perk up. She would come in and sit by his side, sometimes for more than an hour.

"When will you be better?" Emily would ask.

Michael would shrug in a noncommittal way.

"I miss you, Mikey."

"And I miss you, Emmie."

Sometimes, Josh observed, they would say very little to each other, and he could detect in them a nonverbal sibling bond not unlike what he had with Evie.

Still, Michael did not improve. Josh and Victoria consulted Michael's primary doctor who told them he was baffled by Michael's condition. The boy was weakening, had lost his appetite, and seemed depressed and dispirited. The doctor told them that it would be life threatening because he wasn't eating, a comment that left them both numb with fear.

If there was no improvement, they had jointly agreed, they would bring in a psychiatrist. Meanwhile, Michael showed no signs of fully recovering. As a precautionary measure, the doctor ordered that the IV treatment be instituted again.

One morning, he and Victoria went up to Michael's room only to find that he was worse. His little body seemed sapped of strength and his complexion had turned dead white. Even his freckles seemed to have faded. Josh was truly alarmed, although he forced himself not to show it.

When his parents came into his room, Michael opened his eyes and managed a wan smile. Josh and Victoria exchanged glances, feigning broad, open smiles. He knew she was suffering as much as he was.

"We've an announcement to make, darling," Victoria said suddenly. Josh looked at her, baffled.

Michael was suddenly alert and seemed curious and expectant.

"We've made up, Michael," Victoria chirped.

Josh was dumfounded. They hadn't discussed it. He explored her expression. Was she, as he had put it, dissimulating?

"We're not going to get divorced," Victoria continued. She turned to Josh and, startling him, put her arms around him. He drew her closer and, before she could turn away, kissed her on the lips. Victoria made no effort to move away from him.

"It was all a misunderstanding," Victoria said. "Wasn't it, Josh?"

"A total misunderstanding." He reached out and caressed Victoria's cheek. "I love your mother, Michael. More than I can say. No more nonsense in this family."

"And no more talk of divorce," Victoria said. "We were being silly and immature, weren't we Josh?"

"It was ridiculous, putting everybody through this."

They moved so that each were now on opposite sides of the bed. Each kissed one of Michael's cheeks, then brought their lips together directly in front of him.

"We want to be a loving family, don't we Victoria?" Josh said.

"How does that make you feel, sweetheart?" Victoria said.

Michael looked at them curiously, inspecting their faces, not quite certain what to make of it. Josh observed some color come back to his cheeks, and his eyes seemed to shed their sad glazed look.

"Really?" Michael asked.

"Don't look so skeptical, son," Josh said, hoping he had conveyed the message.

"It's what you wanted, isn't it darling?" Victoria asked.

"Sure, Mom. I'd love for that to happen."

"Well, it has," Victoria said, reaching across Michael and taking Josh's hand.

Josh said, "Now we've got to get you well and home...not exactly home...but the fact is that, to repeat the old cliché, home is where the heart is."

Josh squeezed Victoria's hand. He was startled when she returned the pressure.

"Mom and Dad...do you forgive me?"

"There's nothing to forgive," Victoria said.

"Nothing," Josh whispered.

"It doesn't matter, darling," Victoria said. "Just get well. That's all we ask."

The doctor came into the room.

"Well, well, what have we here?" he said. "Looks like a love fest."

"You got that right, Doc," Josh said. "Doesn't this little guy look better to you?"

"I'd say so," the doctor said. "What have you done to perk up this little fellow?"

"Secret love potion," Josh chuckled, looking at Victoria.

They left the room holding hands, but as soon as they reached the waiting room, Victoria disengaged.

"It worked wonders," Josh said.

"Yes it did. Don't think it was easy."

He tried to conceal his disappointment.

"It was an Academy Award performance," he said.

"I thought so. But at some point we'll have to tell him the truth. That won't be easy."

They went through the same act during their repeated visits to Michael's room, kissing and embracing, illustrating with fervor their supposed reconciliation. Later, Evie brought up Emily, who embraced her brother.

"Mommy and Daddy say you'll be out very soon," she told Michael.

Seeing the two children together, Josh felt some sense of foreboding. Emily, of course, knew the truth of the situation. Josh had no illusions about that. Their effort at feigning alliance outside of Michael's room was not very convincing. They continued to maintain separate rooms, and their attempts at affectionate role-playing for Emily's benefit seemed forced and insincere. Of course, when they entered Michael's room, all that changed. They became the affectionate loving couple.

"You can't stay long, darling," Victoria said. "Michael needs his rest."

"She can stay, Mom. I feel much better."

"See," Emily said. "Mikey says I can stay."

"I'd prefer he gets some rest, baby." She embraced her daughter and looked up at Evie. "Aunt Evie will take you out to the ice cream parlor."

Josh was stunned at the suggestion. Then he realized the point of the exercise. She wanted Michael to understand that she had reconciled with Evie as well. On that score, there was a modicum of truth.

"Really?" Josh asked. Evie immediately picked up the cue.

"Great idea. We'll get a delicious sundae with whipped cream and a cherry on top." She looked at Michael.

"Terrific. Wish I could." Michael said, looking at his mother. "You go on, Emmie."

His sister moved to the bed and the two stared at each other for a brief moment, then embraced. Evie and Emily went off to the ice cream parlor.

After they left, Michael addressed his parents.

"I'm a little tired, Mom and Dad. I think I'd like to sleep now."

"Would you like us to go?" Josh asked. He had his arm around Victoria and pressed her tightly to him.

"I think so, Dad," he said. His color had gone pale again, a troubling sight.

"We'll be off, then," Victoria said. "See you in the morning."

"Sure, Mom," Michael said, his voice weakening.

"We love you, son," Josh said. He turned his face to Victoria and kissed her cheek. "We'll all be together again soon. Won't we, love?"

"Yes we will, darling," Victoria said.

"Great," Michael whispered.

He closed his eyes and clasped his hands over his chest. Pale and frail, he looked like a corpse. They bent over him and kissed him, then went out of his room holding hands.

"He is getting worse," Victoria sobbed.

"You imagined it," Josh whispered, fighting his own temptation to cry. They continued to hold hands, which surprised him.

His eyes met Victoria's and held for a moment. "He doesn't believe us," Josh whispered.

"I know."

She released her hand from his and turned away without comment.

Alone in his motel room later, Josh felt a sense of heavy foreboding. They had been so certain that Michael would react positively to their announcement of reconciliation. He seemed to at first. Then something had happened that made him see through their scheme, and he had relapsed into depression.

He pondered the question. There was only one explanation. Had Emily communicated the truth to her brother in a special way, through some private frequency, beyond the comprehension of adults?

For Josh there was no role to play. For him, it was real. He wanted his wife and family back.

Near midnight, he called the hospital and the nurse on duty said that Michael was resting comfortably.

"Is he showing any improvement?" he asked her.

"He's still asleep," the nurse said. She was not the kindly gray-haired nurse that was far more sympathetic. This one was all business.

"But do you think he's improved?"

"I can't tell," the nurse said. "His vital signs are stable."

"What about his color?"

"I'm not sure that's a good indicator, Mr. Rose."

"Is he worse?"

"I just went over this with Mrs. Rose. There's really nothing more I can tell you."

She hung up abruptly.

Not long after, he heard a tiny knock at his door and jumped out of the bed to open it. It was Victoria. She wore a robe over her nightgown. When she saw him, she put a finger over her lips.

"I don't want to wake Emily. These walls are like paper."

He nodded. She sat down on a chair. Josh paced back and forth in front of her.

"I spoke to the nurse," she said.

"So did I."

"I'm very worried, Josh. I thought surely what we told him would cheer him up."

"I guess we weren't convincing," Josh said.

"I tried to appear authentic," she said.

"I was."

She ignored his remark and averted her eyes.

"Maybe there's more to it than we think," she sighed. "Something physical that they haven't diagnosed."

"Or metaphysical."

She frowned and seemed confused.

"I don't understand."

"I think I do."

"Then please explain it."

He continued to pace in front of her.

"Children know," he said. "They can't be fooled. Emily told him the truth."

"That's ridiculous," Victoria said. "I was there. She said nothing."

"She didn't have to. Don't you see? They want us back together."

"I know that. But it's not their decision," she protested.

"It was them, Victoria. Them. Can't you see that? Not me. Them."

"What are you saying, Josh? Would they go this far? They're little kids."

"You can't hide behind that fiction anymore, Victoria. We underestimate them. They're people and they have an agenda."

"They don't know what life is all about."

"They know about their life."

"We can't always make choices that only favor them."

He stopped his pacing and watched her through a long pause. He suddenly realized that there was something she wanted to say.

"You did," he said, watching her. She shook her head and briefly covered her eyes with her palms.

"I don't ever want him to go back to that school," she said angrily. "Never." She looked up at him, waiting for his comment. It was, after all, a joint decision. "Let Tatum take his gateway to success and shove it."

"You have my consent, Victoria."

"I'd sue the bastard," she said. He saw her lawyerly aggression surface briefly, then retreat. "Fact is I stupidly participated in the transaction." She sucked in a deep breath. "Besides, the evidence is gone."

"Don't let it fester, Victoria. It's over."

"It'll never be over."

"For me either," he said, hoping his implication was clear.

She studied her hands, then looked up and shook her head.

"I just wanted you to know." She averted her eyes. "When I saw our child lying there...oh my God." She forced down a sob. "I want you to know, Josh. I do believe him. I can't deny it to myself any longer. I'm sure it was the children. It has dawned on me that if you had organized this...this craziness, it would have been more logical. I just can't understand their reasoning."

"The only explanation I can find is that they wanted to create an outside menace. Force us all into an alliance."

"It doesn't make much sense. I don't understand what that was supposed to accomplish."

"I didn't then. But I do now."

She remained silent, waiting for him to continue.

"Maybe this," he said waving his arm. "You and I. Here together."

Their eyes met, but this time her glance did not abruptly turn away from him. He stopped his pacing and stood in front of her.

"I liked being that close to you again, Victoria," he whispered.

"Deprivation does that, I suppose," she answered, but the edge of sarcasm did not seem very strong.

"Rethink this, Victoria," he said.

"Not now," she mumbled. He searched her face looking for the tiniest sliver of optimism.

He reached out his hand, took hers. She did not resist. But it lay in his palm without movement. He felt his body react, inexplicably aroused.

"The body does have a mind of its own, Victoria," he told her. "Sometimes it overwhelms you."

Her hand remained in his.

"Like now," he whispered.

Bending over, he moved his face closer to hers. She did not turn away. His lips brushed hers and her mouth opened to receive his deep kiss. Her need felt as urgent as his. Reaching down, his hand brushed her inner thigh then moved upward to confirm her reaction. She raised her pelvis to meet his caress.

Lifting her, he carried her to the edge of the bed and half-standing entered her. Pressing his buttocks, she moved him forward and found his rhythm, gasping and bucking, as they reached a crescendo of mutual orgasm.

They remain conjoined for a long while, then separated and lay side by side on the bed.

"Don't misinterpret this, Josh," Victoria said.

"I'm not," he replied.

"Let's not overreact," she warned again, getting beneath the sheets. He slipped in beside her. She had turned away, and he fitted his body next to her like conforming spoons, caressing one breast.

"Brings back old times," he sighed, recalling those early days of their marriage when they could never get enough of each other.

"It does have a ring of nostalgia," she said.

He held her tightly against his naked body, but he feared breaking the spell by too much conversation.

"I love you, Victoria."

He waited for her response. None came. Soon he could tell from her deep, even breathing that she was asleep. He continued to hold her, barely moving.

It was still dark when they awoke. She arose, put on her robe, and started to leave the room.

"Where are you going?" Josh asked.

"Emily will wake up. If I'm gone she'll be frightened."

"Of course."

But before she could open the door, he was out of bed embracing her. He felt her shoulders lurch in a deep sob. She pulled away from his embrace and moved silently out the door.

Josh was shocked to see Michael. He looked worse than he had appeared yesterday morning. He motioned to the gray-haired nurse who proceeded to meet with them outside Michael's room.

"What's going on?" he asked.

"We don't understand it. The doctor was in earlier. He can't find anything wrong physically. It's as if the boy just doesn't care. He has no appetite. And all he's been doing since you left last night is sleeping. We've increased his IV intake."

"Is this life threatening?" Victoria asked.

The nurse shrugged. It was not a very encouraging response. Josh and Victoria went back into Michael's room. His eyes were open and he offered them a warm smile, but his complexion was whiter than the pillowcase and he looked exhausted.

"What is it, darling?" Victoria said after they had bent down to kiss him. Josh and Victoria were holding hands, but it did not seem to him as contrived as yesterday.

"I'll be fine, Mom," Michael said.

"The doctor tells me you're not eating," Victoria said.

"And the nurse says you've just been sleeping. Tell us what's wrong, Michael?" Josh asked.

"Nothing."

"We want to get you out of here, take you with us."

Michael turned away from them. Josh noted that his eyes were filled with tears.

"What is it, son?" Josh pleaded.

"Tell us," Victoria begged.

Michael mumbled some words that they could not hear.

"What did you say, darling?" Victoria asked. Josh put his ear close to the boy's mouth.

"You're fooling," he heard the boy say. Josh turned to Victoria.

"He says we're fooling."

Without waiting for her to comment, he turned back to Michael.

"No we're not," Josh said, clearing his throat.

"You are," Michael said, struggling to speak. "I know you are."

"I don't know what to say," he said, again turning to Victoria.

There was a long silence as Victoria and Josh looked at each other. He could see Victoria's lips trembling. Earlier, at breakfast, she had maintained an expression that denied what had happened last night. It baffled him, but he did not push it, concentrating his attention on Emily, who had offered enthusiastic reviews about her ice cream sundae experience with Evie. Victoria had seemed distant and disinterested. She was not disinterested now. Frown lines etched her forehead. He continued to watch her face, waiting for her to react.

"It's the truth," she whispered. Then she turned to Michael. "You're right, darling. We were fooling." She sat at the edge of the bed and caressed her son's face.

Josh was confused by her assertion. Tears spilled over the boy's eyes. He looked utterly devastated.

"We were fooling, Michael," Victoria repeated. "Please forgive us for that." She paused. Her nostrils dilated. "Would you believe me if I said we were not fooling now?" She reached toward Josh and took his hand. She brought it up to her lips and kissed it. Michael's gaze shifted from his mother's face to his father's. He seemed wary. "Would you, Michael?"

Wearily, he shook his head in the negative.

"It's true, my darling boy..." She was too overcome to continue.

"It's true, son," Josh said. "Please believe us."

Victoria, unable to speak, nodded her head.

"No," Michael sighed. "It's not."

"What can we do to convince you?" Josh asked.

Michael said nothing. His shoulders shook with sobs. They called the nurse.

"What's wrong?" the nurse asked.

"We're not sure."

"Maybe you should go outside for awhile. He seems very agitated. He might need a sedative."

They moved to the waiting room and sat side by side on the couch. Victoria's head rested on his shoulders.

"I hope you meant that," Josh said.

"They've manipulated us, Josh."

"Yes they have," he agreed.

She pursed her lips and nodded.

"They've got a point. It's not just about us." She was silent for a while. "I know what my parents did to me."

"And me. What our parents did to me and Evie."

"Do you think he believes us?"

"If it's the truth, he will."

He lifted her face to his and kissed her on the lips. A man had entered the room and seeing them, quickly left.

"We must tell Emily," Josh said.

"Evie is bringing her here after ballet lessons," Victoria said.

"Does she know?" Josh asked. "About us? Last night?"

"Not yet. But she was awake when I came back this morning."

When they went back into Michael's room, he was sleeping.

"I gave him a sedative and called the doctor," the gray-haired nurse said.

"What's bothering that boy?" the doctor asked when he came by. Michael was asleep.

"I'm afraid we are, Doctor," Victoria said. She explained the situation.

"All I can do is deal with physical things," the doctor said. "Which is not to say that I can discount the effect of emotions. It's just not my area. Perhaps a child psychologist might help."

They sat by the bed through most of the day. In the afternoon, the doctor came and examined him. The sedative had begun to wear off. Michael was awake.

Evie brought Emily back from her ballet lessons and she bounded into Michael's room full of high spirits and enthusiasm.

"We've got a surprise, Mikey," she giggled.

"What sort of a surprise?" Josh asked.

"I'm not telling."

She lifted herself to the edge of Michael's bed. It struck Josh as strange that she had not noticed his weakened condition.

"Wouldn't you like to know, Mikey?"

He nodded.

"You'll see."

"When?" Victoria asked. She looked at Josh and shrugged.

"Soon," Emily giggled. Then she said: "Aunt Evie took me past the house today. What a mess."

"She did?" Josh asked, surprised.

"Did you go inside?" Victoria said.

Emily nodded.

"My room and your room are fine, Mikey." She glanced at her parents. "I saw Mommy and Daddy's room. It still stinks from smoke."

There it was, Josh thought. Mommy and Daddy's room. Message received. He looked toward Michael. His eyes were locked into Emily's.

"The insurance adjusters tell me we can all be back in it in a couple of months," Victoria said. "I've called a real estate man to rent us a house for that time. Then we can all get back to normal."

Josh hadn't realized the extent of her activity. She hadn't consulted him, but then she never had. Nevertheless, he was pleased by her action.

"Isn't that great?" Josh said, directing his question to Michael.

"We'll be altogether again, Mikey," Emily said. "You and me and Mommy and Daddy."

Michael and Emily exchanged glances. They were in it together, fighting for the survival of their world. He had been dead right. It had been their conspiracy all along. Children know. When that universe falls apart, most hover helplessly like boats with unfurled sails drifting in the tide. Some, like their children, stand and fight. Now it was confirmed. However convoluted, their strategy had worked. Victoria looked at him and nodded, as if she, too, had undergone the same epiphany.

Suddenly there was a knock on the door. Emily jumped off the bed and opened it a crack.

"You can come in now," Emily cried.

Evie came in, leading two men in tuxedos. Each pushed a cart on which were a number of silver covers. They set up a table for four and an elaborate tray on Michael's bed. He sat up abruptly, stronger now, his color returned, his eyes alert.

"What's happening here?" the gray-haired nurse said, smiling broadly and winking at Evie as if she were part of it.

"Tell us, Aunt Evie," Michael said. Even his voice was stronger.

"Now you be careful, young man," the gray-haired nurse said.

"I'm hungry," Michael cried.

"Me, too," Emily said.

"Tell us," Michael demanded.

The two waiters smiled and uncovered the silver covers.

"Now Emily, repeat after me," Evie said. "That's Boueuf Bourguignon."

"Boueuf Bourguignon," Emily repeated, stumbling over the accent. Michael laughed.

"And that's lots of healthy vegetables, Choux de Bruxelles, Haricots Verts A La Provencale, Chou Fleur Blanchi."

She pointed out each dish with chubby fingers.

Emily tried repeating Evie's words, collapsing in hysterical laughter. Michael mimicked the words, making funny faces.

"And after we're having mousseline au chocolat," Evie said.

Josh looked at Victoria, who was smiling broadly, obviously reveling in the sight of her happy son.

"Let me," Victoria cried, repeating the words in a terrible accent, "mousseline au chocolat."

Josh's eyes filled with tears.

"Food is love," Evie said.

"Not quite," Josh said, embracing his wife's shoulder. "But it will do for now."

About the Author

Warren Adler has published twenty-seven volumes of fiction, which have been translated into more than twenty-five languages. Mr. Adler's novel *The War of the Roses*, a classic about divorce, was made into a hit movie starring Michael Douglas and Kathleen Turner. It has appeared somewhere in the world every week for the past fifteen years. Another book titled *Random Hearts* was made into a movie starring Harrison Ford, directed by Sidney Pollack, and released in October 1999. His earlier collection of short stories titled *The Sunset Gang*, dealing with people living in a Florida retirement community, was adapted and made into an acclaimed trilogy for PBS.

Adler's six-volume mystery series based on the fictional adventures of Fiona FitzGerald, a detective in the nation's capitol, has won a worldwide following. He is also developing a musical for which he has written the book and lyrics based on his *Sunset Gang* stories.

Mr. Adler's novels, short stories, and plays explore the complexities of human relationships and the emotional geography of individuals buffeted by the pressing and competitive challenges of the modern world.

Adler was born in Brooklyn, New York. He graduated from Brooklyn Technical High School and received a degree in English literature from New York University. After graduation he attended creative writing classes at the New School in New York.

He worked for the *New York Daily News* and was the editor of *The Queens Post*. During his Army service in the Korean War he was the Washington correspondent for *Armed Forces Press Service*. Stationed in the Pentagon, his by-line appeared in every service publication throughout the world.

Moving to Washington, D.C., after the Korean War, Adler founded an advertising and public relations firm in Washington, Warren Adler, Ltd., which he operated for eighteen years. He also owned and operated an NBC television station, three radio stations, and a publishing business. In 1974, with his wife, Sonia, then a photo journalist and their son, David, they launched *The Washington Dossier* magazine. Mrs. Adler was editor and David Adler was publisher. The magazine was sold in 1985.

During his entire business career, Adler devoted each morning to his writing, rising at 5:30 and writing for four hours before going off to run his businesses. He gave up all his business interests when his first novel, *Options*, was published in 1975. He continues to maintain that schedule working on his various writing projects on a daily basis.

The Adlers maintain their permanent residence in Jackson Hole, Wyoming, and live in Manhattan six months of the year. They have three sons and four grandchildren.